A UNIVERSITY VICE PRESIDENT FINDS HIMSELF THRUST INTO A HELLISH PANAMANIAN PRISON, AT THE MERCY OF UNKNOWN FORCES.

When a university receives a bequest of a village in Tuscany to use as a study-abroad site, Bill, the Vice President, is put in charge of negotiating the terms with the donor's angry son who thinks the village rightfully belongs to him. Bill discovers that something is very wrong with the deal and is determined to get to the bottom of it. As he begins to suspect that organized crime is involved, he is lured to Panama supposedly to sign the transfer papers. Instead he is thrown into prison and denied any contact with the outside. As hope of ever being released fades, he realizes that his cellmate's drug-dealing family is his only hope for freedom, but is the price they demand too high?

Early Praise for Tuscan Son

"*Tuscan Son* is a great read and Berne has a prescient understanding of academic politics. I thought my DC experience would prepare me for the academy, but *Tuscan Son* is just what I needed."—*Robert M Shrum, Warschaw Professor at the University of Southern California*

"*Tuscan Son* is a tour de force adventure within the modern university that is both a great read and eerily familiar. Bob Berne captures the university's inner workings and foibles with nuance and cynicism, and the novel kept me guessing throughout. This is a terrific and unique addition to the entertaining genre of the academic novel and I can't wait to find out what comes next at Olmsted University."—*John Sexton, President Emeritus, New York University*

"*Tuscan Son* is a fast paced journey through the intertwined stories of a seemingly mundane chapter in university decision-making and the worryingly plausible consequences. It is impossible to put down, with the fate of the ironic and cool-headed, honest but pragmatic university administrator at stake."—*Ellyn Toscano, Executive Director, Hawthornden Foundation*

"Intrigue follows Bill, a gutsy college administrator, across three countries—as he launches an international enterprise for Olmstead University. *Tuscan Son* comes to heart throbbing life with deception in Tuscany, survival in a corrupt Panamanian prison, and deception on the New York-based university's board of directors. Fighting for his life, Bill's instincts, cunning, and luck make it impossible to put down. "—*Candace Greene, Global Marketing Consultant*

One minute, I was a first-time visitor to Panama City, here on university business, and the next, I was dragged out of my hotel room by the national police, at least, that's who they said they were, and put in this dirty, stinking, cell. Having received only one speeding ticket in my nearly sixty-two law-abiding years, I was shocked, though admittedly, I was involved in a complex and unusual situation. Looking back, I probably should have known better.

They tied my wrists in front of me with plastic handcuffs, and we left the room. They took me through the glitzy lobby, where all eyes were on me, into a waiting police van with two additional cops inside. Needless to say, we did not stop to check-out of the downtown InterContinental.

Nausea was building up in my gut, but I reassured myself that we'd straighten all this out when we got to the police station.

TUSCAN SON

Robert Berne

Moonshine Cove Publishing, LLC

Abbeville, South Carolina U.S.A.

First Moonshine Cove Edition Jun 2022

ISBN: 9781952439339

Library of Congress LCCN: 2022909260

For Shelley

Acknowledgment

Many people helped me write this book but I alone am responsible for every word. First and foremost, Shelley, my wife of 50 years, gave me all the possible loving critical encouragement throughout the process. Our kids and their spouses, Rebecca Berne, Jacob Silberberg, Michael Berne and Rebecca Salk were an important source of support and reality throughout the process. Shelley, Rebecca Berne, Rebecca Salk, and our nephew, Craig Nadler, read and commented on numerous early drafts and collectively identified an important mid-course correction. Craig also led the development of my website.

I was very fortunate to work with a talented and thoughtful editor and writer, Dawn Raffel. She is amazing. I also benefitted from the advice of Jamie Ehrlich, Debra Englander, Erika Goldman, Cara Iason, Larry Iason, Susan Isaacs, Roger Newman, Kelly O'Connor, Michael O'Connor, Harvey Stedman and, importantly, John Sexton.

Rich Baum, Charles Bertolami, Richard Foley, Laurence Franklin, Linda Herbert, Peter Herbert, Candy Moss, Jim Salk, and David Tepper read earlier drafts and made useful suggestions.

My many unnamed colleagues at New York University deserve thanks for their dedication, commitment, creativity, friendship and inspiration.

I can answer Bea, Evan, Ida, and Leila, "Yes, grandpa wrote a book."

Finally, thanks to Gene Robinson and his colleagues at Moonshine Cove Publishing who were a pleasure to work with.

About the Author

Robert Berne was a professor, dean and vice president at NYU for 41 years until his retirement in 2017. He served as both senior vice president for health and executive vice president for health over the last 15 years of his career. Robert was born in Brooklyn, NY, raised in New Rochelle, NY, and received his B.Sc., MBA and Ph.D. from Cornell University. He has been married to his wife, Shelley, for 50 years and has two married children and four grand-children. A regular visitor to Italy, Robert spends time in central Tuscany, near where *Tuscan Son* takes place. For more details on this area see robertberne.com, Discovering the Area around Follamento. He has published numerous academic books and articles, many of which focus on equity in the financing of public schools, and *Tuscan Son* is his first work of fiction. He enjoys cycling and is a frequent and ever-trying-to-improve golfer. Robert and Shelley reside in Manhattan.

robertberne.com

TUSCAN SON

The possession of arbitrary power has always, the world over, tended irresistibly to destroy humane sensibility, magnanimity, and truth

.—Frederick Law Olmsted

Day 6

I did everything right as a university administrator so how did I end up in this Panamanian jail?

I was watching CNN in my hotel room around 10 p.m., and about to doze off, when someone knocked on the door. A minute later, two men, one my size and one twice my size, both with large handguns holstered at their sides, said in clear English that I was under arrest.

That was six days ago, and since then I have been sitting in a Panamanian jail with absolutely no contact with the outside world. No matter how many times I insist there has been a mistake, I've been refused even a single phone call. One minute, I was a first-time visitor to Panama City, here on university business, and the next, I was dragged out of my hotel room by the national police, at least, that's who they said they were, and put in this dirty, stinking, cell. Having received only one speeding ticket in my nearly sixty-two law-abiding years, I was shocked, though admittedly, I was involved in a complex and unusual situation. Looking back, I probably should have known better.

When the cops barged in, I grabbed my wallet, iPhone, keys, and American passport — which they immediately took from me — and put on my running shoes. They tied my wrists in front of me with plastic handcuffs, and we left the room. A third cop, who was watching the door in the hall, joined us as we headed to the elevator. They took me through the glitzy lobby, where all eyes were on me, into a waiting police van with two additional cops inside. Needless to say, we did not stop to check-out of the downtown InterContinental.

Nausea was building up in my gut, but I reassured myself that we'd straighten all this out when we got to the police station.

My brain could not process what was happening. I'd assumed the knock on the door was some kind of turn-down service, maybe chocolate, so I did not bother to look or ask who was there. Even in the car, I wondered if one of my colleagues at Olmsted hired these two guys to play-act, to pay me back for one of many similar, though less elaborate, stunts I had pulled off.

After driving a few blocks, I asked if we were going to the police station. The larger of the two cops who had entered my room said, "I cannot answer any questions." I thought about demanding an explanation; after all, I was a high-level administrator at a respected American university. Instead, I made an instinctive decision to be quiet.

Sitting in that van, I realized how little I knew about this country. I knew Panama had a canal, that the country was aligned with or maybe even controlled by the United States, and that the Panama Papers probably put a damper on a lot of its commerce. Essentially, I did not know the good guys from the bad guys, but maybe that did not matter. I have not found the good guys yet, six days in.

We drove for about thirty minutes, I think, because I left my watch on the night table in my room. We skipped the police station, which would have been a better destination. Instead, we approached what looked like a prison; the van went through three sets of security gates with heavily armed guards, stopping at each one, before the cops took me out. We were then buzzed through another three sets of doors and I was placed in what appeared to be an interrogation room. Only the big cop stayed with me. He had a plastic Ziploc bag with my wallet, iPhone, keys and passport next to him on the table. He cut away my plastic handcuffs, but left them in plain sight, like a warning.

I had read enough spy novels and thrillers to know that this is where the hero grabs the Ziploc bag, rips it open, snatches the keys and holds them to the cop's throat to negotiate my escape. The thought almost made me smile, and if I had smiled it would have been the last one for the past six days.

The room was neither hot nor cold, but sweat was running from my armpits down my side. The room, and maybe me, smelled like an overused, unventilated locker room. All I could think about was the old film *Midnight Express*, filled with abuse in a Turkish prison. I kept telling myself that it was just a movie, and besides, this was 2022 and nothing like that would happen now. I focused on the positive — they used the plastic handcuffs, not the metal ones that they had on their belts, and they cut them away when we arrived in the prison. I hadn't been threatened physically. Unfortunately, those were weak and incorrect signs.

For six days, I have tried to communicate any way I can with the outside world. My first attempt was in that bare interrogation room when I met my so-called intake officer, Dom Perez. He looked to be about sixty-years-old and was clean shaven, apparently unarmed, and carrying a file folder.

My wife, Franny, of course knew I was in Panama City, but in this era of cellphones, I didn't bother to tell her the name of my hotel or who I was meeting with. But my office at Olmsted has that information. Since no one has heard from me for six days, presumably someone is looking. Franny must be calling the University every hour.

That first day, Officer Perez introduced himself as a senior intake officer at La Joya Prison. He wore a formal deep blue business suit with a white shirt and tie. He was the only person I'd seen dressed like that. Everything was so new and confusing that I did not think then about his clothing. My mouth was chalk dry but I did not want to waste a favor or maybe show a sign of weakness by asking for water.

I listened to Officer Perez's canned, brief speech in his passable English. The major points were that La Joya was a federal prison and thus run in a professional manner, and that drugs and sex are forbidden and would be punished severely. He said that if I followed the rules, I would be treated well, but violating the rules would result in escalating punishment, a longer sentence, and harsher conditions. He stressed that there is limited contact with the outside world and that there may be opportunities for joining a work crew.

He paused and asked if I had any questions, which I thought was the right time to ask about my arrest. I detected the first inkling of a smile on his face. But when I asked to call the U.S. Embassy, that hint of a smile disappeared. In a tone that implied I had no clue how things work, he said, "Remind me about that after I explain a little more." His tone turned more sympathetic, but in reality, I was playing checkers and he was playing chess. I should have asked for the water.

At this point he changed his position from sitting upright in the chair opposite me to leaning over the table with a clear unspoken signal that I should lean over as well. As his head approached mine he lowered his voice to a whisper. "What I have told you so far is the official welcome information. Now let me pass along some advice from someone who has worked in Panamanian prisons for over twenty years." He paused.

"While we try to create a safe prison without inmate-on-inmate violence, this is not possible. Many of our inmates have been here for a long time with little hope of release, and the prison culture is what you would expect." My dry mouth just got even drier. "There is a hierarchy and there are two rival drug gangs. A lot of the time, the gangs peacefully divide up the prison, though each gang is always trying to expand its territory. When the gangs feud it gets dangerous and violent, even for bystanders. You may want to align with one of the gangs for protection, but keep in mind that if you are caught buying or selling drugs it will add time to your sentence."

Officer Perez lowered his voice even more, forcing me to lean in so our heads were now three inches apart. "There is also a group of inmates who have not been charged with anything, but are not getting out any time soon." The fact that this is an identifiable group made me light headed. I almost passed out. "Our criminal justice system is understaffed and under-funded and it can take a long time to present charges." I could no longer just be a good listener. I blurted out, "How long does it take and what do you think about my case? Do you know why I was arrested? How can you treat an American this way who has done nothing wrong?" "I do not know anything about your case but there are hundreds of prisoners who stay for over a year without being charged. Because you are new to the prison without any charges, my advice is to avoid getting involved with the trouble-makers. Trust no one, as everyone is out for something."

I questioned him more about outside contact. "First we need to deal with this," and he pointed to the Ziploc bag. He said that my personal property would be listed and placed in a safe room until I was released. "How much cash is in your wallet?"

I told him that since my ATM card was once swallowed by an international cash machine, I travelled with several hundred U.S. dollars and I thought I had about $800. He handed me the wallet and asked me to take out the cash and count it. I had $844 and he told me that U.S. dollars and the Panamanian Balboa were interchangeable— one U.S. dollar equals one Balboa. He said that each prisoner is entitled to a maximum of $500, to be placed in an account in the prison's comasario. I could visit once a day and draw from the account for personal items.

"Now about the outside contact. I can try to arrange it." He opened the file folder and took out a blank piece of paper, and handed it to me with a pen. "I'm not supposed to do this, but I can see how worried you are. I can try to get a short note from you to the Embassy." I felt minor relief, but he was not finished. "This could get me into trouble and I will probably lose my job if I am caught. So you need to give me $300 dollars. I have a friend who can get the note to the Embassy in a few days."

This was one of those rare moments when I was feeling modestly hopeful, but wary. Do I bargain over the price? Do I say half now, half when contact is made? What if I insult him, he gets pissed off, and he changes his mind? I decided this was no time to bargain and if he was simply robbing me he would have asked for more.

I opted for a straightforward note to the U.S. embassy with just my name, my Olmsted University contact information in New York, my wife's cell phone number and email, my email, and a statement saying I had been taken by police from my room in the Intercontinental Hotel in Panama City with no explanation. Finally, I gave them the name of "my attorney" in New York, actually a friend who is an attorney. Then I waited for what felt like more than thirty minutes. I had no real sense of time — it was probably close to 2 a.m.

When Officer Perez returned, I gave him the two pieces of paper. He put the wallet back in the bag with my passport, keys and iPhone, placed the bag on the far end of the table near the door, and left with the $300 in his pocket.

Day 7

Yesterday, after six days with no word from the outside, I decided that I better figure out something to do to pass the time. Just sitting in my cell, waiting for the next meal or, worse, the next threat from a fellow inmate, makes for an incredibly long day. I have never had so much time to do nothing but think. It does not take long to fall into a kind of dysfunctional mental state, a form of temporary insanity. After a week, I grudgingly realized that I could be staying put, at least for a while. So, when I went to the comasario I purchased a pad of paper and a couple of cheap refillable pencils.

Having spent eighteen years as a faculty member and another seventeen as a university administrator, I am used to writing. I want to be as objective as I can about what got me here. Or how I think I ended up here — at this point I am not certain. And if I never get out — my worst thought in the middle of the night —perhaps my writing will. I began to write yesterday about my arrest, but when I woke up today, I realized I have to start at the beginning.

I have to start with Olmsted.

Olmsted University today is not what it was thirty-five years ago when I first arrived as a young assistant professor. It is much better than it was then, but so are many universities. Olmsted is a medium-sized, private-non-profit, urban, research-oriented university, that is trying to compete with the very best of its peers. Students pay high tuition. How to describe the place?

It's somewhere between the traditional tweed jacket world of CP Snow's *The Masters* and the craziness and dysfunction of Richard Russo's great academic parody, *Straight Man*. As an administrator, sometimes it is anarchy, while to many faculty, it is a corporate behemoth. The faculty are entangled with virtually every aspect of society and they act like fact-finders, truth-tellers, guardians, and storytellers of that society. Olmsted is not immune to discrimination, sexual abuse and political correctness, despite our search for "the truth." As an administrator, I must deal with Olmsted's flawed university governance system.

Faculty members are by their nature an odd lot, and I include myself among them. We can be irreverent, opinionated, passionate, and quirky. The best among us love to teach, learn, and discover.

As quirky as Olmsted seems now, it is normal compared to being imprisoned in a Panamanian jail.

Day 8

My arrival at La Joya eight days ago took a turn for the worse. Shortly after Officer Perez departed, Officer Fernandez sat down opposite me. He had a large bushy mustache, common among prison personnel, which was jet black like his close-cropped hair. He was at least six feet tall, probably in his late thirties, and had a solid physique, in contrast to Perez who was frailer and older. In perfect English, Officer Fernandez said that although it was late, he wanted to give me a brief introduction to the prison. But before he started, he asked me if I had any questions.

I decided to go for broke and said, "I have no idea why I am here, and I asked Officer Perez to make contact with the U.S. Embassy."

With a puzzled look on his face, Officer Fernandez asked, "How did Officer Perez introduce himself and what did you talk about?"

"He told me he was my intake officer and he explained to me the rules in the prison. He said I could have a maximum of $500 in the comasario." I did not say anything about his sotto voce description of the drug gangs, or that I gave him $300.

Officer Fernandez pushed back his chair about six inches and glanced at the Ziploc bag on the edge of the table. "Officer Perez is not an intake officer. I am your intake officer." He then paused — here we were, close to 3 a.m., both confused and exchanging odd looks. "Mr. Perez is a volunteer. He was told to simply sit with you and offer you a drink until I arrived."

I could see my $300 disappearing into the Panamanian air, thick as it was. I was not even inside the prison yet, and I had been scammed.

Officer Fernandez continued, "Because the justice system works so slowly in Panama, people are placed in prison immediately, and then arrest papers are drawn up. If prisoners were arrested and released on bail, most would simply disappear. This is a federal prison, and while we cannot stop all the violence, we try to separate out the most violent prisoners. You will be in a two-person cell in a block for non-violent prisoners, but at certain times all prisoners are together. You will get a chance for a shower once a week and meals are served in a large dining room. I recommended that you sit near an exit and a guard." This was going to be more effective than Weight Watchers, I thought. "There are several exercise areas and you will be in the one that is less violent."

He took a breath, but I knew he was not finished. "As an American, you will be both a novelty and a target. I recommend that you find a fellow prisoner to buddy up with for the shower — one to shower, the other to stand watch. I am not trying to scare you," but he was doing a good job of it. "Do you have a lawyer?"

I thought maybe I had misheard. "A lawyer?"

"Yes."

The irony was that I had a meeting at a Panamanian law firm on my calendar for the morning after I was arrested, with an attorney related to my work with Olmsted. I was thinking that my arrest could be related to this planned meeting. I told Officer Fernandez, "I was in Panama on business. I was taken here without any explanation. I wasn't allowed to contact the U.S. Embassy and I don't have a lawyer."

"You should work now on finding a lawyer," Officer Fernandez told me. When I told him I'd prefer to go through the U.S. Embassy, he responded, "That is a good option."

Officer Fernandez seemed understanding, and he wasn't hostile or antagonistic. At the same time, his matter-of-fact tone gave me the impression that he had seen this situation many, many times before. I thought a moment and asked, "Was my arrest with no explanation unusual?" I was not sure whether I was rooting for a yes or a no answer.

"Unfortunately, no. As I said, the process in Panama is to arrest first, and then bring charges later. In fact, maybe twenty or thirty percent of the prisoners here have not been charged. The difference is that it is not usually how it works for an American — arrested, no charges, no lawyer. Perhaps you have some important people who are angry with you?"

Before coming to Panama, I had discovered some unusual and highly questionable activity as part of my job. For some reason, when I was arrested, I thought it was a stretch for those problems to be the cause of my imprisonment. Now that I am writing about it, I'm seeing it differently.

Officer Fernandez continued, "You are probably very tired and distressed, so let me go over a couple of important points and you can go to your cell for a few hours before breakfast." He reached over and took the Ziploc bag with my wallet, passport, keys and iPhone. "How much cash do you have in your wallet?"

I felt like saying, less than when I came in several hours ago but just said, "About $540 US."

"You can put all that in the comasario and you get to purchase items once a day. There is a $1,000 US limit. Your wallet, passport, keys and cellphone should be safe, but when you make outside contact I suggest that you suspend your credit cards, unless you want to cut them up now."

I decided to cut them up.

Before he went to get scissors, I asked him if I could get a note to the U.S. Embassy. He said, "I can try through the warden, but you shouldn't count on it. We are not permitted to contact outsiders on behalf of prisoners. You'll have to find another way." When I asked if he had any ideas, he said, "There are very few working phones, but you should keep asking in the prison."

This news plus my exhaustion was almost too much to bear. His next and final point was perhaps the scariest. "Because you were arrested without charges, it could take weeks for you to show up in any official computer system. If someone contacts the Embassy for you, they must say that you are in La Joya Prison." Officer Fernandez left for a minute and came back with the scissors, a piece of paper for an embassy note, and a younger colleague, who stood near the door.

I first thought that Officer Fernandez was going to give me the scissors, but he cut up the cards himself. He gave me the paper and watched as I wrote a short note, like the other note I had written a couple of hours before with so-called Officer Perez. I recounted the money and then signed a form stating that I was placing $544 in the comasario.

As I was writing the note, the younger officer walked over. "Officer Tejada is on the 'inside,'" Officer Fernandez explained. "He'll take you to your cell and check on you the first couple of days." As a bonus for Officer Tejada, who was new to this part of the prison, this was a chance to practice his English, which, Officer Tejada said, "Needs to get good."

I thanked Officer Fernandez, and Officer Tejada and I headed into the depths of the prison.

Day 9

The best time to write is in the morning, in the four hours between breakfast and lunch. I felt encouraged by some bright news: When Officer Tejada walked by the cell last night before dinner, he gave me some hope that a phone call might happen in the next few days. I couldn't stop thinking about it, and it took me a while to settle down and write.

My university administrative career was not planned. I came to Olmsted after my Ph.D. and enjoyed teaching and doing research for about a decade. My field was public finance and financial management, and I taught graduate students in Olmsted's School of Public Policy and Management.

In the 1990s, health benefit costs were increasing dramatically. Olmsted's Board directed the University to create a task force to contain them, and the President and Provost named me as chair. It was clear that without switching to managed care, the University's future was in jeopardy. Nonetheless, faculty love to debate, and the discussions in the Task Force went on and on. Finally by the end of the academic year, the committee, perhaps due to debate fatigue, voted unanimously to move to managed care.

The next academic year, the Provost asked me to go to a faculty meeting in each of Olmsted's dozen schools to present the new health plan. Most of these meetings were a little contentious—no one wanted their choices to be limited. I was able to explain how without managed care, many other aspects of the university would need to be cut back, including salaries, and that their health care should not suffer.

The questions were fairly predictable and one answer makes me smile, even here in prison. At the business school, a professor, John McWilliams, asked, "I travel quite a lot. What happens if I need medical care overseas?" I could see the Provost shaking his head, knowing I had already covered that. The questioner had a great track record at predicting recessions and thus was a popular talking head on business news television segments. I had done these meetings close to ten times and I was boring myself, so I tried to get a laugh with my answer.

"If you are travelling in Paris, and you trip and break your leg and go to the emergency room, you will be covered with the exception of a small co-pay. All overseas emergency care will be covered. But if you go to Geneva to get a face lift, you are on your own."

At that point I expected a laugh, but got dead silence instead. The dean of the school practically pushed me over to gain control of the microphone, and announced that the meeting was over.

On my way out the Provost, whom I did not know very well, approached me with a smile and congratulated me on running an effective meeting, but he had one question. "How did you know that Professor McWilliams had a face lift?"

I gulped — I had no idea.

When the dean of my own school resigned a few months later the Provost asked me to be a candidate and, after a search, he named me as dean. He congratulated me on my selection, then said, "Try to keep the face lift answers to a minimum."

Day 10

It was probably close to 3 a.m. that first night and I was scared, tired, and anxious as I began the last part of the check-in process. Officer Tejada and I went through two locked gates with loud buzzers, and entered a room that had harsh, bright lights, a table full of prison uniforms and toilet kits, and a small medical examining area. There was a large mirror that was undoubtedly two-way and four folding chairs facing it.

As soon as we entered the room, three prison staff came in from the opposite side. I had been in the prison for close to five hours but it felt much longer. My fatigue was catching up with me and I started to get nauseous again.

I was told to strip to my underwear and then I was examined by one of the three men who wore latex gloves. He did a look and feel, front and back, beneath my underwear, much more aggressive than any TSA person at an airport. He asked my height and I said, "5'7" and he fetched a bright orange uniform and a plastic garbage bag for my clothing. It went fast. At least I didn't throw up.

They asked me if I took any medication and to be honest I had completely forgotten about that, despite the fact that I was taking low dose aspirin and Lipitor for close to ten years. I told them about the two drugs and they said that I could get aspirin, but that Lipitor was not available and I would not die without it. I had neglected to bring my reading glasses. The guards told me that I would need to do without them. They asked if I smoked and I said no. I was tempted to ask whether they'd like to know if I had any food allergies and whether I was gluten free, but thought better of it.

The final task was to print out a label with a number and iron it onto both the pants and shirt of my uniform, in my case 6326877. The uniform fit fine, plus I thought I could get used to no underwear. They also gave me a toilet kit with soap, a toothbrush, and a small tube of toothpaste until I could get supplies at the comasario.

Officer Tejada came up next to me and spoke quietly in his broken but understandable English. "I know this is very tough for you, but that maybe you get out soon."

Whether his empathy was real or just standard operating procedure, I opted to believe him. "I was arrested with no explanation and it is important for me to get word to someone on the outside that I am in La Joya. Can you help?"

He said, "I understand, but I cannot contact anyone, I would lose my job. Prisoners are not allowed to make phone calls but I will try to get you to a phone. It is bad that no one knows that you are here."

Finally he told me, "Your cell is in the block where I work, and I will try to walk by on each of my shifts." I am sure I was projecting, but I really thought that he cared. I could not resist asking him one more time, "Do you know why I was arrested?"

"Things like that are not told to guards like me."

We left the room together and we were joined by another officer carrying a rough, gray blanket and pillow, as we made our way through various hallways and gates. It was such a dizzying maze that even if all the gates were left wide open, there was still no way I could find my way out — but of course, all the gates locked behind us.

The block was a four story structure with cells on the outer walls around an open interior area. Think Hyatt, but as a prison and without the glass elevators. Other than a few guards, we were the only ones moving around. We walked up two flights of stairs encased in steel mesh. When we reached cell C-B-3-15, the other guard raised his hand and we heard a loud clicking sound, and then he proceeded to open cell C-B-3-15 with a key. I guess the click released some kind of master lock on all the cells, and the key was how a single cell could be opened. The cell was maybe 8 by 6 feet and had a bunk bed on the left side, with the top bed unoccupied, two dressers on the opposite wall, and a small toilet and sink against the back wall. It was pretty dark, but some kind of low lights were on giving the cell an eerie feeling.

Officer Tejada said, "It is now 4:15 and breakfast is at 7:30." At that point, he motioned to come close. "Tomorrow you should get a carton of cigarettes from the comasario. I know someone who knows someone who may have a phone. There is no money in the prison, but cigarettes are cash."

I put my blanket and pillow on the top bed, pissed in the toilet and climbed into bed. I was still nauseous and had a huge pit in my stomach. My cellmate had rolled over when I first entered but quickly went back to sleep. I dozed a little and fell asleep at some point, and was awoken by my cellmate's toilet flush. There was a small barred window, and I could see that it was light outside.

I decided that I needed to face the day with some confidence. If I was a pathetic character, I would be more likely taken advantage of. I also realized that I was hungry, which I took to be a good sign.

After my cellmate finished peeing, he turned toward me, said "Ola," then reached out his hand and said, "Ernesto." Of course I was fully aware that he went straight from pissing to holding out his hand, but I quickly decided that it was more important to shake his hand then to suggest he use Purell.

I put out my hand and said, "Bill."

Ernesto Rivera, was about thirty-years-old, maybe 5' 10" or so and a little on the heavy side.

In some made up language, I said, *"No hablo Spanish,"* and he said, *"No hablo much English."* We both laughed and I said "Tuo English e migliori del mio Spanish." As soon as I said it I realized that I was combining high school Spanish with basic Italian, but he got it right away and said, "Okay." For the rest of the day we made ourselves understood at a basic level with Ernesto speaking English and Spanish, and me speaking some weird Italian-Spanish-English combination. I said to myself that if I could get through the day without any physical harm and with some food, it would be a success. Taking a shit would be a day two goal.

After I washed my hands and face, pissed, then washed again and brushed my teeth, the loud click went off and then a second click began to open about ten cells at a time. Ours was in the fifth or sixth group. I said, "Breakfast?"

Ernesto pointed with his head as if to say, "Follow me."

Day 11

I was hopeful that Officer Tejada is on duty today and I will hear some news after dinner about a call. Olmsted and Franny must be bombarding the Embassy. She is probably going nuts.

As I was thinking about who would rescue me, I flashed back to a conversation in Rome, just before I flew to Panama City. I had spoken to a lawyer from Olmsted's outside Italian counsel, Luigi Prevalento. He was the only person who knew what I'd uncovered. Unfortunately, I made him pledge confidentiality, and besides, he was heading to Switzerland for cancer treatment. I was pretty sure he wouldn't be able to help.

Something at dinner last night did not agree with me and I am staying in bed with constant trips puking in the filthy toilet, thus no more writing today.

Day 12

Officer Tejada stopped by last night after dinner with some modestly promising news. "I will be off the next three days, but I may be able to get to a phone when I come back. Do you have the cigarettes?" I had no idea how Officer Tejada will arrange for the call, so I will be holding my breath.

Going back to my first morning in prison, when the door of our cell opened, Ernesto motioned for me to stand next to him. An officer walked by and did a count — the first of five every day, I later learned. Once it was completed, he said, *"Vamonos,"* and we fell into line with the other prisoners in our group and walked down the two flights of stairs. We left the cell block via a locked gate and headed down a corridor before reaching a second locked gate.

I have learned from Ernesto that there are six cell blocks similar to ours, all connected to a kind of core building that houses the cafeteria, the library, a group of small meeting rooms, a tiny chapel, the comasario and a storage area for uniforms and other supplies. Also in the core building are offices for some of the prison staff and some rest rooms. Adjacent to the core building is a fairly large outdoor space with a concrete floor that serves as an exercise area. Each group of six blocks and the core building are known as zonas and I am in zona C. Apparently, the prison tries to keep each prisoner in his zona as much as possible. Meetings with attorneys and family visitors are in the meeting rooms in the zona, if only I had a lawyer.

Each zona houses either prisoners who are violent, A and B, or "non-violent," C and D. All of the prisoners are men.

The cafeteria is huge, holding hundreds of prisoners, a disorienting blur of orange jumpsuits. The tables are right out of a high school cafeteria with attached benches. There are two serving areas on opposite walls. On that first morning, I followed Ernesto, recalling the feelings I had when accompanying our two kids in some crowded big box store or during rush hour on the subway, constantly in fear that we would get separated. I had the feeling that everyone was looking at me — though now that I have been here for twelve days, I realize that had been totally in my mind. No one spoke to me and I did not initiate any conversation.

Breakfast choices consisted of burnt toast, watered-down orangeade, hard boiled eggs, and hot and cold cereal. There was a bin full of over-ripe tangerines and apples, and at the end of the food line were large tanks of coffee and pitchers of water. Like all buffets, you knew more about what you wanted after you got to the end, but I assumed — correctly — that there was only one pass. I took some toast, orangeade, warm, watery oatmeal, and a cup of water. Not knowing the cuisine and what was to come, I took a hard-boiled egg, even though I dislike them. The utensils were cheap plastic, the trays were wrinkled cardboard, and the plates and cups were paper. Hard to believe I was enjoying the food in Italy just a few days ago.

As we left the serving area, a few people seemed to recognize Ernesto, and we found a couple of seats near the door. I wondered how much of what faux-Officer Perez told me was true and if I could make it through breakfast without getting beat up. Once we were seated, a few prisoners went out of their way to say hello to Ernesto.

It took no time at all to eat everything on my tray. I followed Ernesto to the now-vacant serving area for a cup of coffee. Just after we sat down, a fight broke out in the middle of the room. It was mostly wrestling and rolling on the ground. One of the dozen prison guards hit a buzzer and all conversation stopped for a moment. Three guards went to break up the fight. As this was happening, I realized that Ernesto and the other prisoners at our table weren't paying any attention to what was going on. It scared the shit out of me, but it was over in ninety seconds and that was it. Later Ernesto told me that this kind of fight happens often, but almost always among prisoners who knew each other, with some longstanding and festering disagreement. He also told me that if this was their first incident they would be in solitary confinement for at least a week, more if they were repeat offenders.

We sat for another fifteen minutes when the guard who led us into the cafeteria held up a card that had the letter B on it, for our block, and after a quick count, we walked back through the locked gates and connecting corridor.

Once in our block, I noticed two things that I had missed earlier. First, each of the floors has a shower area. I learned that there are ten showers without stalls in each of these. Second, two opposite corners of every floor have a glass-enclosed area, where prison officers sit and watch the floors — both directly and electronically. The security system shows each cell for about five seconds, three cells at a time. With the camera moving among the cells, the two officers — one in each of the two corners — could see virtually everything. Two prison officers also walked the floors, 24-7. Ernesto said that he will explain the blind spot later.

When I got back to our cell, I had been in the prison for about twelve hours. I had made it through my first meal. Not a big deal in retrospect, but at the time I thought I deserved some kind of medal.

Day 13

After serving as dean for a couple years, I was asked to meet with the President and Provost. Needless to say, I was completely taken aback when they asked me to become a vice president. I did not see it coming, but after thinking about it, I realized I had little choice. If your two bosses ask you to do something significant and you say no, will you have their support? I doubt it. Since that time about fifteen years ago, we now have a different President and different Provost.

At Olmsted University, the President, Provost and Board chair have the greatest power and influence. Presidents often shepherd more than direct, a reality in a faculty-centric university. For the president, there are fewer levers to pull than most faculty think, but there are also more ways to move the university than most presidents admit. If your goal as president is to avoid controversy, chances are the university will slip. If you are aggressive in making changes and trying new ideas, chances are you will make a few mistakes and piss some people off, but the university has a better chance of moving ahead.

Melissa Wakefield is our first woman president. She came here four years ago, on the heels of a rapidly rising career. Early in the 1990s, she co-authored a study on how culture affects sexual harassment, which was way ahead of its time. Over a dozen years, she rose to become her university's chair of the sociology department, then dean of the college of arts and sciences, then provost. After four years as provost, she was recruited to her first college presidency at another university, down a few notches academically, just as she turned forty. After five years there, she took another presidency at a "better" university — and then five years after that, she was recruited to Olmsted. She is decent and direct, and can command a large room, but she resists change and innovation. Melissa is a "don't rock the boat" kind of president and wants everyone to like her; she thrives when things are going well, but handles adversity poorly.

Marshall Miller is Olmsted's first African American provost, the chief academic officer. After a successful career as a researcher and teacher in biology, Marshall was recruited to Olmsted as Biology Department Chair, and then became dean of our college of arts and sciences. As a respected community member who had both a strong academic career and the relative confidence of the faculty as an administrator, his successful eight-year run as dean made him a very strong choice when Melissa selected him as provost, two years ago.

Marshall is a scientist, which means he always wants more information and takes his time. But once he gives the green light for some person or program, he becomes a strong and enthusiastic supporter. It is not clear yet whether he and Melissa will form an effective two-person team. She has already killed a couple of his key initiatives and he is very recruitable elsewhere.

Their interactions are illustrated by a meeting I attended six months ago. Melissa asked Marshall to recommend which schools should be housed in a building that Olmsted had just purchased. Marshall asked me to work with him on his recommendation. Olmsted is starved for space, with every school needing more. He and I agreed that the new building was a perfect opportunity to move one of the three schools that were spread out in scattered, leased facilities. We knew that both the engineering and business schools could make a strong case for the new space, but the School of Education had the greatest need and could fit entirely within the new building, not the case for the others.

When Marshall and I presented our recommendation, Melissa asked, "If we do this, can we handle the anger from the other deans and faculty? Shouldn't we share the new space?"

Marshall and I presented all of the reasons why dividing the space would not give Olmsted the advantage that the one-school approach would, and that we should find similar solutions elsewhere for business and engineering. Melissa did not dispute the academic rationale, but kept focusing on the reactions. She ended the meeting by thanking us for the work we did and said she would let us know in a few days.

A week later Melissa wrote to Marshall and me with her decision. The building would be divided among the three schools. She asked Marshall to call the chair of Olmsted's board to let him know what we decided, which was strange as this was clearly her decision. Marshall sent me an email that said, "She is afraid of her shadow."

Charles Mannford is the chair of Olmsted's board, which has about fifty members, most of whom are alumni. Charles has been a great cheerleader for Olmsted's progress as a board member and now as chair. He is an Olmsted graduate, a successful and well-known investment advisor, and he has been a very generous donor to Olmsted. Charles is a fitness nut, has run in ten New York City marathons, and is always encouraging people around him to get or stay in shape. When Charles agreed to run for Board Chair, he disclosed that several years prior he was investigated by the SEC for securities dealings overseas, but never charged. The selection of Charles as chair was actually contested, which is unusual. Some on the board thought the SEC matter was a knock-out factor; most board members felt that he was okay as chair because the SEC was over-reaching and he was never charged.

Charles complains that our progress is slowing down under Melissa. He worries about the aging of the tenured faculty. He complains that underperforming programs and activities are rarely cut or even scaled back, and he worries that Olmsted, with 20,000 students, is already too big as an urban, private university. He is often blunt in speaking his mind, and sometimes his loud mouth turns people off.

When Marshall and I called Charles to tell him the new building would be divided between three schools, he asked, "Why?"

Marshall explained our deliberations and concluded, "Melissa understood the academic rationale for the one-school approach but she was afraid of the reactions from the other schools."

Charles, who as the chair ultimately selected Melissa and thus had a stake in her success, said only, "Not the decision I would have made," and hung up.

Day 14

The possibility of a call the day after tomorrow is a great motivator to get through what is now two weeks in prison. My commitment to write a few hours every day is making the time move less slowly, but not fast enough.

As first impressions go, I liked Ernesto. Back from breakfast that first day, he stretched out on his bed and I got up on mine. I was tempted to say a version of, "What are you in for?" but he beat me to the punch.

Ernesto's English got better as the conversation progressed, and I was able to piece together what he was saying. He claimed that he did nothing wrong, but his family was in the drug business. He worked as a limo driver, mostly for tourists from the cruise ships that go through the canal, but once in a while he had to give rides to members of his family doing their business. "I do not like doing it but no choice." About six months ago, several people died from bad drugs and the police had to do something. They raided a popular restaurant where they knew Ernesto's family hung out, and he was caught up in the sweep.

To keep the leaders out of jail, their family lawyer cut a deal. About half of the forty men who were rounded up pleaded to minor charges and Ernesto got a sentence of two years, which could be reduced for good behavior, because this was his first arrest. Had the case gone to trial, he could have gotten five to ten years, even though, he said, he was just in the restaurant at the wrong time.

I initially thought that I would be intruding on his "single room" status. But he seemed to welcome the chance to have someone to talk with. An American provided great entertainment value, and a way to improve his English. He did hilarious impersonations of American tourists who he drove in his limo.

Ernesto stopped in his story when he thought he could teach me a word or phrase in Spanish that would be useful to me. Along the way I learned that he is married and has a three-year-old daughter. They lived with his wife's family. His father-in-law owned a small grocery store, so there was always going to be food on the table. I got the impression that his wife's parents were not a big fan of their marriage and that the imprisonment did not increase his reputation in their eyes. Ernesto proudly showed me a picture of him and his wife and daughter looking happy on a beach. It was the only personal item in the cell. He said that being away from them was the hardest part of prison. I miss Franny and our kids after two weeks, so I can sympathize.

Ernesto seemed genuinely interested in my situation. I described what I did at Olmsted as the Senior Vice President for Academic Initiatives, working with the president and provost to handle the issues that they did not really want to deal with. Essentially, I was an academic troubleshooter. If I took on a problem and got it righted, then my bosses could claim most of the credit. If I worked on a problem that I could not fix or, what sometimes happened, things got worse, then my bosses could blame me. Ernesto laughed and said his Uncle Eduardo was the troubleshooter for the family and I would meet him, as he was here in prison.

I explained that I had uncovered a messy situation, and that my arrest was probably related to that, though I was not sure. He responded that in Panama I could be "uncharged" and in prison for a long time. I did not want to ask how long that could be.

Despite our short time together, I instinctively began pleading with him to help spread the word about my imprisonment, so it might reach someone in the U.S. Embassy. He gave me a long response that boiled down to the idea that he could try to help, but that any help would come with a price, that I would owe whoever helped me and there were different ways the debt could be collected. This was both a lot to get my mind around and not too surprising in retrospect. I was mulling over how to get more details when Ernesto said that we had fifteen minutes until lunch.

It seems trivial and inconsequential as I write this, two weeks after my arrival, but I needed to take a dump and I figured that this was as good a time as any. I asked if it was okay if I used the toilet and Ernesto said that the toilet was there to be used and I did not have to ask. I lowered myself off the top bunk and sat on the toilet. In most places I was used to, such as group bathrooms where urinals might be open, toilets for number 2 are mostly enclosed. I realized that I had no privacy and that I better get used to shitting in the cell, and Ernesto's chuckling signaled that he knew my predicament. He suggested that I just pretend that I was alone, and of course that only tightened my stomach muscles and made it more difficult to go. By now I thought that if I was sitting on the can, I needed to make a deposit. After about five minutes, it was a minor success, and looking back two weeks, I feel somewhat embarrassed that it was an issue at the time, but it was and speaks volumes about how I felt.

Lunch was essentially a repeat of breakfast, count, corridors and gates, and then cafeteria buffet line. The room seemed more active and noisier, but I could have been so frightened at breakfast that I hardly noticed. The choices again were slim and had I run into this food in New York I would have guessed it was the food waste after all students and teachers had left a middle school cafeteria. The main attraction was pasta with "red" sauce, presumably tomato, but I was not 100 percent sure; it included some wilted lettuce, with a bin of overripe tomatoes, mashed potatoes, and what appeared to be peanut butter and jelly sandwiches, watery orangeade, water, and coffee. I took some of the pasta, though the Italians who I was eating with earlier would not call it pasta, mashed potatoes, and a sandwich, passed on the faux-salad, and drank water. Given my near all-nighter, I was feeling exhausted and sorry for myself, but I tried to look as relaxed as I could. There were no disturbances this time. After lunch we formed two lines. Ernesto had already filled me in: One line went back to the cells, the other to the comasario. I had explained to Ernesto that I wanted to get cigarettes for a call, and now he stood next to me on the line for the comasario.

Ernesto was suspicious. He said that the guards generally divided into two groups: Either they were decent guys or they were thugs. I was not about to tell him I had already been scammed for $300. Ernesto advised me that if I had a carton of cigarettes, the cost would be a full carton. And once it was known that I had a full carton of cigarettes, I could be shaken down by the rougher inmates in our block. He suggested that I get four or five packs instead, and tell Officer Tejada, whom Ernesto said he did not know, that I had fewer cigarettes, as I did not want to be shaken down. Ernesto believed the likelihood of a call, already low, would not be diminished by having less than a carton.

The line moved pretty quickly. There were five windows with prisoners working as clerks. Each "customer" knew what he wanted; there was no window shopping. When my turn came, I said my name and asked for five packs of Marlboro lights in English. The prisoner-clerk signaled to wait. He shuffled me off to the next window, where the prisoner-clerk spoke English. He looked at the number on my uniform 6326877 and then reached for a notebook binder. As he was looking for my account he remarked, "You are new here," and that there would be a $31 USD charge to my account. I took the five packs and headed around the corridor, and when there were about twenty of us there, we began to walk back to our cell block.

In the process of getting the cigarettes, I had lost track of Ernesto. While I didn't panic, my heart rate doubled. After we entered the corridor to our cell block, a fairly large and burly prisoner put his hand on my shoulder and said in rough English that it would be a good idea for me to hand over two packs of cigarettes. My knees were weak, and the nausea returned with a vengeance. I'm not sure exactly how to explain the next word that came out of my mouth but I said, simply, "Why?" in a voice that was probably too loud for the interaction. I was waiting for his fist to connect with my face, but instead he just said "Because," also in a loud voice. The two-word exchange was loud enough that Ernesto, who was about ten prisoners ahead of me, came back and had an exchange with my new prison colleague. The colleague said that I was lucky to be friends with Ernesto, and that he would collect his cigarettes later. I now had at least a little data to support my positive view of Ernesto.

Day 15

No two days of work at Olmsted University were the same. I never complained about the complexity or difficulty of the problems that came my way; and I was involved in every part of the university. I never, ever thought the work was dangerous.

University administrations are often viewed by faculty as over-controlling. In my experience, administrators do not sit around and say, "What can we control today?" The university leadership's role is to support and enable excellent teaching and research. Let the faculty and students do their thing. I was a faculty member for close to twenty years so I know their job is not easy.

At Olmsted, there are several front-burner issues that generate attention across campus and it was one of these, the absence of global opportunities for students and faculty, that probably got me into trouble. Our neighbor, New York University, has ten study-abroad sites, and two campuses where you can earn an NYU degree, one in Abu Dhabi and one in Shanghai. The push to add global at Olmsted came from within the university in the form of a desire for students to be less USA-centric, and from outside the university where employers were demanding that graduates be effective in various settings and cultures. Olmsted was clearly behind in this arena, which would hurt us in student and faculty recruitment.

Eighteen months ago, Melissa and Marshall set up what universities often establish when faced with a major issue, a University-wide commission. The Global Education Commission was composed of faculty, students and administrators. University-wide commissions rarely are too definitive, and if ours could set out some major directions and priorities, it would be considered a success.

As expected, the commission report confirmed that Olmsted University was behind in its global initiatives. The commission understood that global operations needed to be a bottom-up, university wide activity, led by faculty and individual schools. The commission also felt strongly that all students should have access to the global programs, not just the wealthy students. Finally, the commission included a common recommendation that Olmsted form a "faculty committee for global articulation," in other words, the faculty wanted to maintain its advisory role. The tension between a *school* activity and a *university* activity permeated the entire report.

A very savvy administrator told me as I entered university administration, "No matter how thin the pancake, there are always two sides." In many cases each side is seeing things from different perspectives, for example, the university versus faculty level, and there needs to be some give and take. In the end, each side may be a little bit unhappy, which is the best you can do.

The global issues were a small part of my portfolio, but that would soon change.

Day 16

My heart was racing and my arm pits were soaked when I returned to the cell after purchasing, and, with Ernesto's help, keeping my five packs of cigarettes. I asked Ernesto if I did the right thing by not immediately giving up the two packs and he said, "Yes and no. Yes, because I am here to back you up and no because if I was not there you would be beat-up, thrown to the floor, and these guys would have taken all your cigarettes. Plus you would have been punished for fighting." Seemed like a classic no-win situation and Ernesto said it would not be my last.

Now that I have been here for more than two weeks, I realize that I can get used to almost anything. The prison has a very unpleasant smell; almost noxious, some combination of body odor, Ben Gay, and damp shoes. Obviously, there are no open windows so the time spent outside, if nothing else, lets you clear your head of the bad smell. Unfortunately the smell returns with a vengeance when we return from the yard.

Aside from his family picture, Ernesto had few personal objects, though he did have what about three quarters of the cells seem to have, a poster of the boxer Roberto Duran. Some of the cells have a few more items but not much accumulates.

Today was supposed to be Officer Tejada's first day back, and I hope to see him after dinner, when he makes his rounds. I have fallen into a pretty stable routine, wake up, breakfast, write in the morning, lunch, comasario every few days, read or talk with Ernesto sometimes working on my Spanish till an hour of exercise around 4 p.m., dinner, then more reading, talking and bed. Three times instead of going to the comasario, I went to the library where I could look at the week-old Panamanian newspapers, mainly *La Prensa* and *La Estrella de Panama,* both in Spanish, and take out one of the roughly 100 English language books. Strangely, a worn, beat-up paperback version of Doris Kearns Goodwin's *No Ordinary Times,* which chronicles Franklin and Eleanor Roosevelt before and during World War II, was there and though I had read it many years ago, I thought it better to re-read a good book than read a bad book. I signed it out and took it back to the cell. It had no due-date. It is more than 700 pages and when Ernesto saw it he smiled and said, "You will be staying a long time?" I replied, "I know the ending and I hope I will get out soon."

By now I have a rough sense of how fortunate I am to be sharing a cell with Ernesto. It turns out that he modestly understated his family's power and prestige in the prison, and it seemed as though many prisoners knew he was doing his duty to his family by serving this sentence. Thankfully, he likes playing the role of my protector. This even extends to the once a week shower where Ernesto stands by the entrance and I do the same for him. It turns out that about five of the pairs of prisoners, who shower when we do, use this buddy system. The biggest downside is that the once a week routine is about four days longer than my hygiene meter indicates, and I am contributing my share of the rank smell that permeates the prison.

Ernesto does not talk much about his drug family, though he implied that it was pretty low level and focused on the retail trade. He talks a lot about his immediate family and it is clear that he loves his wife and daughter, and that his wife was angry and upset. She wanted him to extricate himself. I am sure that if not for his wife, he would be in the center of the business. He did not say so explicitly but I think he feels that if he's doing time for the family, he should partake of some of the spoils. His wife receives a cash envelope every week, but she puts the cash in a cigar box in a closet and lives on the funds from her makeshift day care and her parents. She does not want to live on the "dirty money" but she is not about to give it back.

Ernesto took a passing interest in my situation and most afternoons I explained what I had written about during the morning. He could not quite figure out how an American could end up in a Panamanian jail with absolutely no outside contact, as he thought Americans were all-powerful and everyone was extremely well-connected. He would occasionally remind me that I could get the word out through his family, but I would be indebted to them.

I am now writing in the evening because there could be a breakthrough. Officer Tejada stopped by after dinner. "Tomorrow, no exercise and I will take you to the office to make a call. You will have five minutes and you should bring the carton of cigarettes."

I gulped and said, "I have only five packs."

Officer Tejada replied in an agitated tone, "I am taking a chance for you and we have to take care of several people. Make sure you have a full carton by 4 p.m." Before he departed he added, "You can make only one call and there will be no call-back option; this will be a private phone and the number will be blocked."

The choices for the call are two, my office land line or my wife's cell phone. One problem is that the call would be coming from a blocked Panamanian number and I had no idea what would show in New York. But both my assistant and my wife should be looking for this kind of call. I need to have a short, well-constructed message ready in case the call goes to voice mail. Finally, I hope that if I call my wife's cell phone, her mail box would not be full.

The message I plan to deliver focuses on making contact with the US Embassy in Panama. I don't want to name the law firm I was supposed to visit the day after I was arrested, Guzman and Quintero. The more I think about it, the more I convince myself that the firm, which was involved in my work in Italy, is complicit in my arrest.

Day 17

After the Global Commission distributed its recommendations campus-wide, the university leadership wrote to the university community praising the commission's work, accepting its recommendations, and moved immediately to set up the faculty committee that would advise on the next steps. Of course, anything other than this would have sparked faculty protests, a normality for Olmsted.

As universities do most of their academic programming within individual schools and departments, university-wide faculty committees are useful and common-place when an issue cuts across these academic boundaries. A key question is committee membership selection, which can be more contentious than the committee's work. Committees like this one often have fewer than twenty five-faculty members, and a couple of squeaky wheels can have an inflated effect on the direction and subsequent advice proffered by the committee. Given that Olmsted was far behind in the global arena, an underperforming group could set the university back considerably.

Olmsted University has a tradition that about a quarter to a third of the membership of university-wide committees is selected by the elected faculty members in the All University Committee (AUC), the principal governance body. In addition to the AUC selections, the provost asked each dean to name a faculty member, and nominations or self-nominations were welcome. This was a way for the provost to put a few of his trusted allies on the committee. Once the nominations were all in, the provost sat with his senior staff and preliminarily selected the membership, subject to the approval of the president.

The seven members selected by the AUC, which included the chair, were far from the worst they could have put forward. None was fervently against global expansion, none was a total "do-nothing" faculty member, and none was likely to be disruptive, a low bar to be sure. At the same time, the most respected members of the faculty did not sit on the AUC, so the deans' nominations were crucial. Each dean had her or his own intra-school politics, with vocally pro and anti-global faculty members.

The AUC faculty chair, Nancy Wright, was named chair of the global faculty committee, in part because of her AUC role, and in part because, unlike Nancy, most faculty members would pay not to be the chair. Nancy, a professor of marketing in the business school, focused her research on online business and marketing in its infancy and quite naturally developed a global dimension to her research and teaching. Nancy regularly appears on the news shows as a commentator on how online business is changing the world. She is smart, well-spoken, and hard-working; she is generally supportive of the university, which makes her all the more believable and powerful when she disagrees with a decision or policy. Her power is magnified by her close relations with the media, and though she has never used that explicitly, the implicit threat is always there.

Recently Nancy and I had a dispute over an initiative where tenured faculty members of certain departments over the age of 65 were offered a one-time payment of two years of salary in exchange for retirement. Olmsted's faculty was aging; almost no faculty retired or went elsewhere. The absence of younger faculty was a problem. At Charles's initiative, without much support from Melissa, we offered this program and Melissa asked me to manage it. While the program was totally voluntary, Nancy thought that we were badgering the older, tenured faculty. I sent a second email to faculty emphasizing the voluntary feature, but Nancy focused her dislike of the program on me. It was uncomfortable for a while but when the time period ended and fifteen faculty took the deal, the feud quieted down somewhat.

A second "big" voice on the committee was David Crist, a former real estate broker, once known as the broker to the stars, who made a lot of money branching off from one of the large real estate companies, starting his own brokerage business, and then selling it to a competitor. He is now a popular professor in the real estate program in the School of Continuing Education, and has advised the university on specific properties under consideration for purchase. His nickname is Professor Walk Away, because he almost always proclaims that you cannot get a good deal if you are not prepared to walk away.

The Dean of the College of Arts and Sciences' committee selection was Edward Frost, a gifted scholar of African American literature. His scholarship has been global since he arrived at Olmsted twenty-five years ago, and he is one of our best-known faculty members. Edward has been critical of Olmsted's hesitancy to become more global and that increases the likelihood that he will go to another university. He was a member of the global commission where he advocated for a much stronger and clearer set of recommendations for Olmsted to move boldly.

The most anti-global voice on the committee was proposed by the Dean of the Law School. Despite the law school's general embrace of global law and its complex issues, Drake Smithson felt that students already come out of law school ill-prepared, thus, adding more global content would just make matters worse. When questions were raised in class about how something would be treated in another country, he has been known to say that it is irrelevant, unimportant, and useless to an American lawyer. His colleagues roll their eyes when he pontificates about the over-emphasis on global ideas, and a recent dispute between the provost and the law dean over the law school's budget probably led to his specific nomination. From the president's and provost's perspective they needed someone from the law school and it would have been impossible to have a committee of this scope and magnitude without some negative voices.

The School of Public Health is probably the most global of all our schools and its Dean named Paula Alvarez to the committee. Paula is from Puerto Rico and came to New York when she was three. Her research and teaching focuses on maternal and child health in underdeveloped countries. She has been one of several faculty in the public health school who were outspoken about how the university's invisible stance on global issues had begun to negatively affect

47

recruitment of faculty and students. She called the commission report a bad joke and said that it could have been written in an hour and will do little good even if all its recommendations are followed.

It is after dinner, a time I normally do not write, but I am excited because I made my phone call.

I purchased another five packs of cigarettes after lunch without incident. Officer Tejada arrived a little before four and asked me for four packs of cigarettes, saying that he would be back in a minute and to have the other six packs ready. On his return he eyed the guards in the corner and after our cell row clicked, he opened our cell with a key, and he motioned for me to follow him. I felt dozens of eyes on the two of us as we headed for the administrative area in zona C.

When we arrived at the large lobby adjacent to the cafeteria, we went into an empty office. Officer Tejada asked for the remaining cigarettes and then his next move surprised me. I had not noticed but there were several rings attached to the wall and he took out metal hand cuffs and cuffed me to one of the rings. I had to sit facing the wall with my hands in front of me, which was awkward to say the least. He apologized for using the hand cuffs and said he would be gone for fewer than five minutes while he went to get the phone. The cuffs were a poignant reminder of my situation and whatever good feelings I had were dampened considerably. I was dizzy, hyperventilating and sweating quite a bit.

I decided that I would call Franny. I was fearful that if I called the U.S. Embassy directly, I would end up in some bureaucratic phone chain on hold with no real opportunity to leave a message. Thus, even if Franny did not pick up, I could be reasonably sure that she would get the voice message if her voice mailbox was not full. When officer Tejada returned he was a little agitated, but he had one of the decade-old flip phones and he said, "You can make one call." He undid the hand cuffs and left the room.

I dialed an international call using +1 for the US, then my wife's cell number. The phone took a little longer than usual but connected and rang about five times before going to voice mail. At least I got to hear our thirty-one-year-old daughter's voice: "This is Franny's phone. Please leave a message after the beep."

I had rehearsed the message in my head but once I heard the beep I nearly froze. After a few seconds which felt like several minutes, I was able to recover and said, "Franny, it's me, and I am calling from La Joya prison in Panama City. I am fine but please do everything you can do to contact the U.S. Embassy in Panama. I was arrested and taken from my hotel room seventeen days ago and I have had no outside contact and no one has explained why I was arrested. I did nothing wrong and I hope that the Embassy can get me out. I am pretty sure that this was caused by something I found in Italy. This is a borrowed phone so there is no way to call back. I love you."

I hung up, tapped on the window, and Officer Tejada came back into the small conference room. He took the phone from me, cuffed me to the wall again, and said that he would be back in a few minutes. I was already thinking about how I could have left a better message. Franny would most likely contact the university president's chief of staff, with whom I have worked for many years. I did not say to avoid contacting Guzman and Quintero, the law firm I was supposed to be meeting. But it was too late to worry about that. I give myself a B minus on the message.

As Officer Tejada took the cuffs off and we went back to the cell, he said, "Be sure to thank Ernesto for the call."

Day 18

I made yesterday's call on a Friday afternoon, September 15th, not the best time for people to spring into action. Until now, I had little reason to even know the date or what day of the week it was. Of course, right after the call a part of me thought that every guard who walked by our cell was going to unlock it and set me free, but that fantasy faded in a few hours.

Besides, I had other things to worry about, as if my worry quotient was not filled. I now know with some confidence that Ernesto is not as much of a fringe player in his family drug business as his self-description suggested.

As soon as Ernesto woke up this morning, I thanked him for whatever role he played in arranging the call. He replied, "Please do not thank me, as I have many family here in the prison and helping with the call was not that tough. I am sorry that the call cost you ten packs of cigarettes but I needed them for the guards, not for my family."

I realized afterwards that it was not the best thing to say, but I reflexively said, "Just let me know how I can return the favor."

"You will meet my uncle at breakfast."

There is no doubt that if I knew I'd be indebted to Ernesto's family, I still would have agreed immediately, but my "favor-bank" was totally out of my control. I tried to talk myself into seeing Ernesto as a friend and good person, but I now thought the worst of all these brief interactions with people in our cell block.

As we were finishing breakfast, Uncle Eduardo walked over and sat next to Ernesto, opposite me. Ernesto said that he was going for a second cup of coffee. Though I am not good at telling someone's age, I would guess that Uncle Eduardo is about fifty-five- years old, paunchy and bald with greying black hair and a jet-black moustache. He actually looked like someone's uncle. I was surprised how well he spoke English, but I learned later from Ernesto that he had a "study abroad" year in a Texas jail.

Uncle Eduardo said, "Ernesto has vouched for you and that was why the phone call was arranged."

I replied that Ernesto had been very helpful to me and that I hoped the phone call would lead to my release.

"If this one call leads to your release," Eduardo said smirking, "I want to know the number that you called."

Eduardo let me know, "Arranging a call like that is a big deal here, and there are probably hundreds of prisoners in this cafeteria who would like to make such a call. Because you are so highly thought of by Ernesto, I moved you to the top of the list and I expect that you will repay the favor. Your status as an American means that you will face much less scrutiny than members of our family. Ernesto will explain more." Just as he was finishing, it was time to line up, and he left, having never shaken my hand.

I am just back from the exercise yard with about an hour and a half to write before dinner. Ernesto's request was bad, but not maybe not nearly as bad as it could have been. At first when we got to the yard, Ernesto left me to join several other prisoners. As I often do when I am alone, I walked over to the basketball court to watch a very physical game of five on five where anything short of drawing blood or knocking someone out is not considered a foul. There were about twenty people watching and I tried to make myself as invisible as I could. After about ten minutes Ernesto came over and said, "We should walk while we talk." I asked why we could not talk in the cell and, for the first time, he said "The guards can listen in on every cell. What I am asking you to do will take place in the yard and it is easier to explain it here." I may have been projecting, but I thought Ernesto had a much more serious and business-like tone.

"My family is one of two marijuana distributors in our cell block, and prisoners trade cigarettes for grass. To protect everyone from a bust, no one prisoner has a lot of marijuana, and a single one-ounce bag

51

cost two packs of cigarettes," Ernesto said. "It is easy to get the one-ounce bags to the prisoners in the yard or in the cafeteria, but it is more difficult to move the packs of cigarettes without attracting attention."

Part of my cover was to begin smoking, and to take a pack of cigarettes out of the comasario every week or so. With this cover, my job was to collect two packs of cigarettes from the drug buyers each time we went out to the yard. I was to bring the cigarettes back to the cell and Ernesto would handle the movement of the cigarettes out of the cell. "My family wants you to be part of the drug dispensing in the cafeteria and the yard, but I insisted you begin with the cigarettes. It will be difficult to pin anything on you for having a few packs of cigarettes when you return from the yard."

I think Ernesto was trying to be the good cop to his uncle's bad cop, but for sure my opinion of him is now dramatically different. I kept telling myself that without Ernesto, I probably would not have been able to make the phone call. I wondered whether my placement in Ernesto's cell in the first place was pre-arranged. Also, I started to think about my writing, sharing the cell with Ernesto, and how I would get it out of the prison.

I decided to press Ernesto, as I had never seen him handle the cigarettes before today.

He paused briefly, "Your request for the phone call brought both of us into the family operation. The cigarettes pose little risk. I'll show you each day which prisoners to approach. Everyone exchanges cigarettes for things like sexual favors and your collections will blend in. Even though I don't want more to do with the drug business, my involvement was probably inevitable and the cigarette end is better than drug distribution. But this was not a choice for either of us."

While a voice in my head told me to not ask any more questions, my curiosity won out and I asked Ernesto, "How do you get the drugs into the prison?"

"You do not want to know. And if you are called out for the cigarette collection you should say that you are providing services in the shower."

Of all the things I had heard on this walk around the yard, this actually made me the most nervous.

"You should not ask any more questions, and you should assume that some but not all of the guards are involved."

"Is Officer Tejada in on it?" and he gave me a look that said, what do you think?

Day 19

This afternoon will be my first cigarette pick-up. I fear that while there is no legitimate reason for my incarceration, my involvement with Ernesto and Eduardo's family will create one.

A part of me wants to stop writing, as my eternal optimism is shouting that I will be out soon. But even if that is the case, writing makes the time go much faster.

The global faculty articulation committee began its work in the spring semester, moving at the usual slow and plodding academic pace. The committee met every three weeks or so, for two hours, which usually included a meal as most committees need a full stomach to do anything. The president and provost asked me to be the administration liaison, and the entire committee vigorously debated for two meetings, without me present, about whether I should attend the meetings or whether I should just periodically meet privately with the chair. After two meetings they agreed that I would attend the beginning of every meeting and then after ninety minutes the chair would ask the committee if they should go into executive session, which meant that I would leave the room. Why did this issue need to take two entire meetings?

Once this issue was resolved, the discussion got bogged down in a debate about the faculty versus the University roles. The Faculty role should dominate the university one.

I tried as best I could to show them how faculty should and could control the academics while the university ran the operations. While they grudgingly accepted that proposition, in practice they thought the university would take advantage and run roughshod over the faculty, not a totally unfounded worry. This debate consumed about five or six meetings, and meanwhile Olmsted was falling further and further behind on the global front.

Although most of the members were against me for much of the first eight meetings I attended, I made some progress with a recent example. One school at Olmsted started a program in Lisbon, only to have it close down after two years. The operation was far too expensive, students complained about the living conditions, two actually dropped out of Olmsted, and several needed to return home mid-semester because of personal issues such as addiction and anxiety. I neutralized the most vocal, "keep the university out of it," faction.

The first semester came to an end without any real recommendations.

Day 20

Now that it's Monday morning, I can fantasize about having someone get me out of here.

I was shaky but I completed my first cigarette pick-up yesterday. Prior to our walk to the yard, Ernesto suppressed his supportive side and perhaps his own nervousness made him much more officious. "Pay attention in the yard. You should take a few loose cigarettes and smoke one when we arrive. Then you should go about the pick-up and find a spot to smoke one more cigarette just before going back to the cell."

Last night over dinner, Ernesto explained the full process. "We will collect two packs from five inmates. I will do three and you do two. I will point out your marks; one is very tall and skinny and one is normal height and weight with relatively long hair." The last thing I wanted to do was approach the wrong person.

My prison jump suit had no pockets on the lower pants part but it did have a chest pocket that would hold two or three packs. Ernesto wanted me to put three packs in the pocket and hold one when we went back to the cell.

I was scared to death as we walked to the yard. It was like I had a flashing neon sign over my head that said, HERE HE IS. Ernesto and I lit up our cigarettes near the fence. I smoked without inhaling much, though the three or four coughs were probably a give-away that this was a bad act.

Ernesto put his arm around me and we turned to look at a group of about eight prisoners. He pointed out the tall one first, and then the one with long-hair. He said, "You go first." I was to walk over, make eye contact with the first mark, the mark would separate from the group and then I would say "Winston" and he would say "Marlboro" and he would give me two packs. I should then walk away from the group for three or four minutes and do it again and return to where we were now.

Ernesto would do his thing and return, and then we could walk around the yard together, smoke one more cigarette, and return to our cell.

Ernesto nodded and I headed over to the group. A couple of prisoners were surprised that I was approaching but no one did anything. I made eye contact and walked about twenty yards away. It seemed like a long time but maybe only a minute passed and my mark walked over to me. We did our Winston/Marlboro thing and he gave me the two packs, and returned to his group. I did the same thing with the long hair mark but after the exchange, he told me in broken English that he needed more drugs. I wanted to say. "Speak with Ernesto," but I did not know which prisoners knew him and which did not, nor did I know how much I was supposed to know. I simply said, "Okay," and walked away.

Ernesto loosened up a bit over dinner as we were sitting by ourselves, and he came close to apologizing for situation he had put me in. He said that he could not believe that an American would be put in here without any charges, with no outside contacts, and because I am a sitting duck he decided on his own to use the family to get me a phone call. He thought that I would contact the Embassy and get out. He did not know the call was a big enough deal to get us involved in the business. I am unsure how much of this I should believe.

In terms of my second prisoner who made the request for more drugs, Ernesto said, "You did good. If you gave him my name it would have told him that you knew more than you should. I will tell my uncle and he will take care of it. I want to keep us out of the drug side of the business."

Ernesto had lost interest in my writing, but today he started asking more questions. "I do not want to be nosy and pry into your personal life. But I hope you are not writing about the cigarettes and drugs."

I was worried that my face gave me away. I said, "To pass the time, I am documenting what I thought went on at Olmsted University that may have led to my arrest," which was the truth, but only part of the truth. "I am unsure about things and I think by writing, it could clarify my understanding."

Ernesto then asked an obvious question. "How do you expect to get these pages out of the prison?"

"When I'm released I can take them with me."

Ernesto processed this for a few moments and said, "Maybe. But I suggest you send the pages out a little at a time, just to be sure. Maybe even mix them up so that it makes less sense." It sounded as though he had been thinking about this well before the conversation started. "If you have a visitor from the U.S. Embassy, you could give him some pages and perhaps they would not be searched."

I asked, "Do you know anything about an upcoming visit?

"No."

I am writing again just before bedtime because Officer Tejada passed by and said, "I think you will be getting a visitor on Wednesday morning."

Ernesto gave me this look as though it was not news to him. "Don't get your hopes up. Your release could take a while."

I am now too focused on Wednesday to fall asleep and worried about Ernesto's role in all of this. I have a large envelope that I purchased in the comasario for my writing, and I keep it in my small dresser. But what if Ernesto is reading? I'm hiding some of the pages in the biography of the Roosevelts.

My final worry of the night was whether the visitor will be an imposter.

Day 21

The sooner I get out of here the better, for many reasons, not the least of which is my work with Ernesto. I pride myself on my honesty and I am worried about how easily I began to do the pick-ups. I tell myself I have no other options, but is that true?

My second day involved a pick up from the same two prisoners, plus a third, and the long-haired one again asked about additional drugs. I said I heard him, and he was annoyed. My third mark was a short fire-plug of a guy who looked like he lifted weights every minute he could.

I spent a little time this morning developing a plan for the manuscript pages and best not to describe that too much here. Assuming it seems safe, I will try to get almost all of them out on Wednesday.

While summers tend to be a little quieter, many of the university rhythms for the leadership run over twelve months. Faculty believe that administrators spend all summer at our second homes, but it is the only time to get serious work done. During the summer, a phone call to the Olmsted University development office, which is the code word for the fundraising office, was likely the starting point for my current predicament. The head of development, Laura Goodbloom, runs a highly controlled operation, under the theory that the university will raise more money if there is no freelancing, and there is some merit to her approach. Laura reports to Melissa but their relationship is frosty, perhaps because Melissa feels that Laura is too close to Charles.

This particular call was from an attorney in Italy. He told the junior development person who answered the phone that he represented the estate of a recently deceased alumnus who had made a significant gift in his will. He went on to say that the gift was so large and complex that a high ranking member of the Olmsted leadership team needed to travel to Tuscany to meet with him before details could be revealed. Even though he was speaking to a development person, he concluded the call by saying that the university should not send someone from that office, but instead a member of the university leadership who can actually make a decision. Naturally, this last request pissed off Laura. She thought that Melissa should send her to Italy after additional vetting. I am sure she was already picking out restaurants.

Laura told Melissa to ignore the attorney's request and send her to Tuscany. Melissa did not like it when senior staff boxed her in, and when it occurred, her entire aura changed, negatively. Meanwhile, when the issue came up at a meeting of the President's senior staff, the University's General Counsel, Cathy Creedmore, said that the right thing to do was to send *her*. While that was probably reasonable advice in most circumstances, Cathy was generally a pain in the neck, who, instead of figuring out how to get things done, was constantly putting up roadblocks. Everyone thought she should be fired, but unfortunately Melissa was not the firing type. Instead, Cathy stayed on at great cost to the university's progress.

At that point in the conversation, and I am not sure why, I piped up that Franny and I were taking two weeks of vacation in late July, early August and we were going to visit Tuscany. If schedules meshed, we could meet with the attorney. My colleagues laughed openly, all except Laura and Cathy, both of whom were angling for the assignment. But Melissa was taking my suggestion seriously. She asked Laura to reach out to the attorney to say that we would be back to him shortly. Then she asked Laura, "What do we know about the potential donor?" Laura answered without making eye contact, "We do not have anyone in Tuscany on our radar screen."

Melissa responded, "Maybe we should have."

A couple of hours before the next senior staff meeting, Melissa asked me to stop by her office to talk about Italy. I was not going to lobby for myself, especially because Franny was not too keen on giving up even a day of vacation to do university business. I said, "You know, a cold call like this often turns out to be nothing. Or maybe it involves some artwork." Melissa then asked. "What do you think of Cathy?" and I said what I had said several times, "She is a great liability and we can do better." When I left the President's office I had no clue what she was going to do, and probably she had even less of a clue.

At the next meeting Melissa listed "Call from the attorney in Italy" as the last agenda item. The major items were the summer review of the budget and the expiring appointments of two deans. As the meeting was about to end, Melissa said, "I want Bill to meet with the attorney in Italy for several reasons. He's going to be there anyway, it's unlikely to be a consequential meeting, and if it is something, there will be subsequent meetings."

Both Laura and Cathy said, almost simultaneously, "Sending Bill will be a mistake and we are willing to go together so that both the legal and development issues can be advanced at the meeting." This was an interesting ploy as they were not known to work well together, but the common enemy — me — made them allies.

Melissa said that they were both making more out of this than was warranted, and reminded everyone that the attorney had specifically requested not to send a development person. She angered Laura and Cathy further by asking them to each prepare a memo for me describing key points for the meeting. They were really pissed off. As we were leaving, both Laura and Cathy said I was out of line and not to expect a memo from either of them any time soon.

When I told Franny that Melissa had taken me up on my offer, she said that we should stay in an area that she could explore while I went to the meeting. I emailed the attorney, Lorenzo Luccamezzo, and explained that I was the Vice President for Academic Initiatives and that President Wakefield had asked me to meet with him in response to his call.

I received a reply within half hour in perfect English. "I suggest that you meet with me in my office in the town of San Giovanni D'Asso on Tuesday, July 26th at 10 a.m." After looking on a map to locate San Giovanni D'Asso, I let him know that this time and place would work well, and I asked if there was anything I needed to review before the meeting. He said, "No need to review anything in advance. I am looking forward to meeting you. My office is on Via XX Settembre, number 30, in the middle of town."

Franny and I were flying to Rome on Friday, July 22, landing on Saturday morning the 23rd. We had planned to spend two nights in Rome, then rent a car and drive north through Tuscany spending about a week there, visit Florence for a few days and end the trip in Venice. With the meeting in San Giovanni D'Asso on the 26th, we decided to stay four nights in the town of Montisi, which is about five miles away, and use that as a base to visit San Gimignano, Siena, Montalcino, Montepulciano, San Quirico, Pienza, Buonconvento and some other hill towns. We booked a room at a small hotel, La Locanda di Montisi, and with the meeting about a month away, I did not think about it much. I hoped the three hours or so for the meeting would not make a big dent in our vacation.

Day 22

About 10:30 a.m., Officer Lopez came to the cell to escort me to one of the conference rooms. As almost nothing since my arrest went very well, I worried that this was too good to be true. I brought with me the folder with the thirty out-of-order pages to give to the visitor if I thought it was a good idea. As it was my only copy, I did not want to make a mistake, and I was hoping I would see a way to get the pages out without being inspected. But, frankly, getting *me* out was a lot more important.

As he was opening the conference room door, Officer Lopez said that he would be waiting outside and that I had twenty minutes. Seated in the conference room was a thirtyish man who introduced himself as Archibald Lindsay III, a U.S. Embassy employee working for the Embassy Counselor. He was over six feet tall, had the build of someone who was on a crew team, clean-shaven with short hair. I almost asked him what prep school he attended. He said to call him Archie, and that he had joined the State Department right after law school, and this was his third assignment. He hoped that he would become a career ambassador. Then, seeing that I had no real interest in his oral resume, he said that the Embassy had just learned that I was in La Joya on Monday and he got here as fast as he could.

Archie then went through an apology based on the hard-to-believe scenario that until I left the voice message, the Embassy could not find me. He said, "The Embassy received countless calls from Franny and many from Olmsted explaining with increasing alarm that you were missing. A junior Embassy staff person followed the well-used protocol and checked with the Embassy's police and hospital contacts and there was no record of you anywhere. The staff person checked with Guzman and Quintero and all they knew was that you did not show up for your meeting three weeks ago. In a few of the more recent inquiries, the police checked the prison records and the Embassy was told that you were not in the system. Because there are cases where there is no foul play, no police or hospital records, and the person in question does not want his employer or family to know his location, the Embassy did not pursue it further. "I thought that it was strange that you are in La Joya with no listing in the prison data base, but that must have been the case."

He then asked, "What happened?"

I had made up my mind ahead of time that before I said anything, I would ask to see his ID. It was an awkward starting moment but Archie took out a card from his wallet that looked official to me. He seemed only a little put off.

I decided that it made no sense to rehash all the reasons why I thought I ended up here. Much of it probably could be traced back to what happened in Italy with Lorenzo Luccamezzo, but I hoped that Archie could get me out without all of that history. I explained that I was scheduled to meet with attorneys at the Panamanian law firm of Guzman and Quintero on university business when the police came to my room and arrested me with no explanation. "I still have no explanation."

Apologetically, Archie again said, "Your imprisonment was not known to the Embassy until Monday, and we moved as quickly as possible."

"I'm not blaming the Embassy but I'm scared and anxious and hope you can find a way to get me out very soon."

Archie's face and body language gave away his answer. He seemed to slump about six inches in his chair, and said, "The Panamanian criminal justice system is complex and uncertain. The Embassy will support fully your release, but the work to get you out needs to be done by a Panamanian attorney. Your case is not typical but it is not unheard of to be placed in prison in Panama with no explanation. Though it takes time, assuming you really did nothing wrong, an attorney with the support of the Embassy should be able to get you released, just not immediately."

A part of me thought he might say something like, "This was all a big mistake, I will have you out by tomorrow," but the "just not immediately" was more aligned with my sense that good news was a precious commodity.

"Something strange happened shortly after the Embassy was notified about your imprisonment. We received a call from Guzman and Quintero, offering to represent you. As the instruction for this kind of call specifies, the Embassy staff person who answered the call did not acknowledge that you were in prison, but the caller did not ask for any verification. It seemed like he already knew.

"When I asked around the Embassy, several people knew of Guzman and Quintero but no one had any direct experience. I discovered that they were listed in the Panama Papers related to tax evasion, though they were small-time compared to some of the other law firms."

I was now used to unexpected connections. Could Guzman and Quintero be connected to Ernesto's family? Did Guzman and Quintero have some other contact in the prison who let them know that I made an outside call? Did Guzman and Quintero contact the university when I did not show up for the meeting? If that was the case, why could no one find me earlier? It seemed like way too much of a coincidence for them to wait for three weeks and then call the Embassy, just after the Embassy found out I was in prison.

Archie said, "Unless you want to use Guzman and Quintero, my primary role is to get you connected to a local attorney. I recommend you use Hector Roberto Mendoza, a sole practitioner who knows the ins and outs of the criminal justice system as well as anyone. He is a street fighter, not a legal theorist, but I think that is what you need right now. Hector handled some tricky cases for the Embassy and has always found a way to get to the right place. One example was a tourist who had his identity stolen. The thieves ran up thousands of dollars on multiple credit cards and even took out a loan, but Hector was able to untangle it with no major financial loss to the tourist, who actually spent a few nights in jail."

I thought for a moment and realized that though the case was only marginally related to mine, I had little choice so I asked Archie to contact Hector Mendoza.

Archie said, "I have already contacted him and I expect him to visit you on Friday or Saturday. The university will cover your legal fees." He looked at his watch and said we had five minutes left. "I do not have much experience with La Joya, but you should keep to yourself. Be careful about falling in with the wrong people."

Too late for that I'm afraid.

He had me sign a standard privacy form, which would allow the Embassy to disclose information to people whom the Embassy thought could help me. He asked, "Is there anything I can do for you?" I felt like saying you can wake me up from this bad dream.

"Please call Franny and let her know I'm okay, and that we are working on my release. Also can you please ask Hector if he can bring me a pair of "250" reading glasses? But I have a bigger favor to ask. I am wondering if you can take about thirty handwritten pages out of the prison to keep for me at the Embassy."

I could see the wheels turning in Archie's head, and felt for sure he wanted to say no. I pre-empted his thinking by asking if his briefcase was searched on the way in. He said, "The briefcase was searched but very superficially."

Archie asked if these were my only copies and I said yes, that I would not hold him accountable if the briefcase was examined and the papers taken away. I explained, "I have shuffled the order of the pages and I doubt they will make sense to anyone."

Archie agreed that he would take the pages, but volunteered that he would give them up pretty quickly if any questions were raised. I moved the folder across the table with the signed privacy form and he put them in his briefcase.

Day 23

As soon as I finished my meeting with Archie I began to think through what I would tell Ernesto. I wanted to find out what he knew about the meeting, which would give me some clue about his connection to Guzman and Quintero. But I could not ask him straight out.

Ernesto waited until we were seated in the cafeteria before he asked me what had happened.

"Archie said the Embassy was not able to locate me until Monday, when the university called. He told me that I needed to hire a local attorney."

"Which firm did he recommend?" which was a total give-away.

I decided that I would give him the attorney's name, but not tell him that Guzman and Quintero had contacted the Embassy. My answer to "which firm" was "Hector Roberto Mendoza. He has a one man-practice."

Ernesto thought for a minute and said, "Okay."

Franny and I had a good two days in Rome, walking and eating and doing the Vatican tour. A couple of years earlier we'd booked a private tour which included about five minutes with just the guide and the two of us in the Sistine Chapel. I am not a religious or very spiritual person, but those five minutes were as powerful as anything I had ever felt. On this trip, the Sistine Chapel was packed with people standing shoulder to shoulder, but it was still spectacular.

We rented a Fiat 500 and headed north on the Autostrada. In about two and half hours we were in Montisi. We settled into the hotel, proceeded to Montalcino for a glass of wine, went another fifteen minutes to San Angelo en Colle and ate a great dinner at Il Leccio. I thought the Tuscan countryside might be the most beautiful place in the world.

After breakfast on Tuesday, I left Franny and drove to San Giovanni D'Asso, a small town with a two block main street, a castle at the southern end and a bar and a beautiful "green" garden, Bosco Della Ragnaia, at the northern end. I found the address the lawyer had given me and was surprised there was no sign. The unlocked door led to stairs that went up to three sitting rooms.

Avv Luccamezzo came out of the far room and greeted me with, "Mr. Vice President, *piacere,*" I said, *"piacere, buongiorno,"* and we shook hands and I said, "Bill," and he said "Lorenzo." He was about my height, 5'7", but probably weighed about 240 pounds, more than a hundred pounds more than me. He resembled a mushroom with small legs and a huge torso, dressed in a fancy Italian suit with a Ferragamo tie. He was partially bald with jet black hair, and he was probably close to sixty years old. In clearly understandable English, he asked if I wanted coffee, and I said yes. He poured two espresso cups out of a metal thermal pitcher.

As is the custom, we began with some small talk, with him asking me what I did at Olmsted. Then he asked, "How familiar are you with Italy?"

"Franny and I vacationed here five times and we love Tuscany more than any other place. We are even taking some Italian lessons at home but our progress is slow. Are you from this part of Tuscany?"

"My father was a lawyer here and I followed him into his practice. We have too many laws here in Italy and I advise my clients on which ones need to be followed and which ones can be finessed, skirted or ignored. It can be like a game show at times."

I laughed. "Just like my work at the University."

"My father passed away ten years ago. Between you and me, increasingly I am getting my clients' teenage kids out of trouble. I live about five kilometers to the south of here, in Follamentto D'Asso, where my main law office is located."

Small talk done, he launched into business. "A unique situation prompted my call. Roberto Follamento, my client, passed away at age eighty-five two months ago. He was a very wealthy man, the wealth a result of multiple generations of smart and successful investments in real estate and various Italian companies. Roberto's wife died a decade ago and he has one son, Angelo, who is fifty-five."

I could not help but note to myself that his last name was the same name as the town where Lorenzo worked and lived.

Lorenzo continued, "Roberto was an Olmsted University graduate, class of 1953. His parents had wanted him educated in the States, and bought him an apartment in New York, which his estate still owns, even though he returned to Italy right after he graduated. Roberto was surprised that Olmsted never reached out to him, and I am not going to start working with fundraising people at this stage. As you will see, Roberto was a grateful alumnus.

"The bequest to Olmsted consists of a significant amount of money and real estate, but acceptance of the gift comes with a set of restrictions that are not negotiable." Lorenzo paused to let this sink in. I was waiting to see why this was not too good to be true. "If Olmsted does not accept the gift, other institutions are listed in the will and will be approached sequentially. How will you make your decision?"

I would have loved to know the nature of the gift but thought it was not appropriate to ask.

"Of course it's not up to me. The key people will be the Board Chair and maybe several other board members, the President, Provost, and General Counsel." I purposely omitted the Director of Development. "If there is an academic component, then there will be faculty involvement. These steps may take some time but I am familiar with only a couple of significant gifts that the university walked away from, in one case where we would have been required to start a high school."

There was an elephant in the room and I did not want to ignore it, so I asked, "Is his son supportive of the bequest?"

Lorenzo changed from easy-going and relaxed to tense and almost indignant. "Angelo is getting a very substantial amount from the estate. Unfortunately, he hired his own attorney from Florence to investigate whether the will is valid, even though he signed it. I really believe that

69

once he works through some of his grief and realizes how wealthy he will be, he will calm down and drop the legal action. If Olmsted gives him a continuing role, things could change for the better."

"Well, life can be complicated." I did not say that Angelo's counter claim would reduce the university's interest. I was sure Lorenzo knew this.

I was about to ask Lorenzo what he thought the next steps would be when he volunteered that he could explain more, but would like to do so over dinner tonight with our wives. Franny and I had planned to go to Conte Matto, a family-run restaurant in Trequanda, but we could do that another time and I made an executive decision and accepted. He said that we should meet that night at Osteria Buona Fortuna in Follamento D'Asso.

Day 24

This morning at around 9:30 I was taken to a conference room by Officer Lopez. It was sooner than I expected and I had just organized another thirty pages of out of order text including several sensitive pages that I had stashed away in the library book and had not given to Archie. I had developed an alpha-numeric code-like system for the pages so I could get them back in the correct order someday. When I entered the conference room, a man with a closely cropped beard and short hair stood up and introduced himself as Hector Roberto Mendoza. He was wearing a blue work shirt and tie, a sports jacket, and jeans. In excellent English, he said, "You can call me Hector in private but it is best to use Mr. Mendoza in public. I understand that this is a horrible situation, especially for an American, but if you I hire me I will work relentlessly to get you released."

"You should think of yourself as my attorney."

"Thanks. I made some inquiries but I prefer that you tell me what you think I should know before I report on what I found."

I wanted in the worst way to believe that Hector was independent. If he was connected to the Follamento family, Lorenzo, Guzman and Quintero, or Ernesto's family, then I was in trouble. Thus again, I was in a position of doling out enough information to try to get released but not so much until I could at least make an educated guess that Hector was not part of the problem.

I opted to go with the bare bones version. "I am a New York-based Olmsted University Vice President in Panama on university business with a meeting scheduled for Wednesday, August 30th, when on the 29th the Panamanian police arrested me with no explanation. Through some connections that I made in prison; I was finally able to make a phone call on my seventeenth day here. I left a voice message for my wife, who called the university and they contacted the U.S. Embassy.

Archie visited me two days ago. I have tried to find out why I am here with no success. My wife and the University called many times prior to Monday but they did not know I was in La Joya and the Embassy claimed that they could not find me on any prison lists."

Hector asked, "Who were you supposed to meet with on the 30ᵗʰ?"

"A law firm."

"The one who called the Embassy on Monday?"

"Yes."

His next questions were probing. "Were you surprised that Guzman and Quintero did not find out where you were sooner, but they called the Embassy right after the university did? Could someone at the university have orchestrated your imprisonment?"

His second question caught me off guard. "I don't think so."

"You don't sound confident in your answer."

"Until now, I didn't think for a moment that someone at the University would be involved, but I know that nothing is impossible."

Hector thought for a moment and then said, "Do you think that Guzman and Quintero were involved in your arrest?"

"They could be."

"What is the reason that they could want you in prison?"

"I was involved in university business in Italy where I discovered some unusual and potentially illegal activities. I thought my meeting with Guzman and Quintero might actually help me out of a tight situation, but I was wrong. Could a law firm like Guzman and Quintero arrange for my arrest, without any wrong-doing?"

"Yes, in Panama, they can, and whoever did it probably knew that you would be in prison for a while before anyone came to your aid. All of this is consistent with what I found, or more correctly what I did not find. I went to both the federal and local police and prison administrations. You are not on file with the police and the local prison had no record of you. On my first attempt with the federal prison administration, they also said they had no record of your imprisonment, but when I told them I was visiting you at La Joya on Friday, they said they would check again, and then said that you were on a 'detainee' list, not a prisoner list. As I had never heard of a detainee list I asked for an explanation, and the only thing they said was that there was a reason to detain you with no cause for arrest at this time. I asked who was responsible for your detainment, and the administrator said it was a judge, based on the testimony of Guzman and Quintero. I found this out yesterday, and I wanted to meet with you before I went any further. Guzman and Quintero is a powerful and politically connected law firm, and while their stature has been reduced based on their appearance in the Panama Papers, they are still a force to be reckoned with."

I had a good enough feeling about Hector to push. "Have you ever worked with Guzman and Quintero before?"

Hector smiled. "They are in a different world from me, mine being much lower on the food chain. They would never work with someone like me, a solo lawyer, who moves around the courthouse and the jails. But I have a friend from law school who used to work there, and I may start with him when I get back to the office. The good news is that you are not connected with anything illegal in any of the databases. The bad news is that you are in prison; getting you out may take some time. Please, whatever you do, stay out of trouble. I have had many clients who served more time for what they did in prison than for their original mistake." The chronic pit in my stomach got much larger.

I asked, "Do you know that the university is covering your fees?"

"Archie had told me that, and I will email the university general counsel."

I looked at Hector's briefcase and asked," Can you do me one more favor?"

He smiled and asked, "Do you want me to bring out some of your written material? Archie asked me to tell you that the process worked fine for him. All he had to do was open the briefcase to show that there was nothing besides paper in there. I think that the same will apply to me."

I slipped the folder with the mixed-up, hand-written pages across the table and Hector put them in his briefcase and said he would give them to Archie. He also handed me a pair of reading glasses. I could not ask for more. Of course if Hector bothered to read the pages he would learn a little more about my situation in Italy but that was a risk worth taking.

Hector and I shook hands and he said, "I will be back by Thursday."

There were no cigarette pick-ups in the yard—Ernesto said there was a conflict and we should wait for word from his uncle. This gave him a chance to ask about the meeting with Hector as we walked together outside. He asked, "Do you think your lawyer will get you out soon?"

"I like Mr. Mendoza and I think that he knows his way around the legal system."

Ernesto straight out asked, "Did he mention Guzman and Quintero?"

"I mentioned the firm when Mendoza asked me who I came to Panama to see. I have an entirely different feeling knowing that someone with local knowledge is working to get me out. No contact would have been made without your help and so thank you again." No doubt now that Ernesto was connected somehow to Guzman and Quintero.

At dinner his uncle came over and suggested that I get coffee and sit somewhere else. When I joined Ernesto on the line to return to the cell, he looked ashen.

Day 25

Ernesto said nothing from the time we returned to the cell last night after dinner until we reached the cafeteria for breakfast. The cafeteria had a different feel; instead of a din of conversations with frequent loud shouting and laughter, it was much quieter, almost like at a banquet just after a speaker has started to go to the microphone. We went through the food line quickly and sat at our usual seat.

He said, "I feel that I need to warn you that another family is challenging ours. They have plotted the takeover for months, lining up prisoners, guards and even a few assistant wardens, plus they have help on the outside. Several of the guards who were loyal to my family were transferred to other prisons or other cell blocks, and this occurred gradually so that my family did not realize that it was both orchestrated and systematic. Our rivals waited until they had a strong position and then told my uncle that our time was up. My family will not give up without a fight. We could end up with a sharing arrangement, but as of now, the new gang is not willing to negotiate. At dinner last night my uncle told me to resume the pick-ups. We need to be extra careful."

The timing of all of this could not have been worse. But there was no way I could say to Ernesto that I needed a sabbatical from the cigarette pick-up, precisely at a time when the family franchise was being threatened.

I left the meeting with Lorenzo feeling that there was some chance that the bequest could amount to something, but I realized that with the claims of the son, the University could turn it down. The increased scrutiny facing all universities makes us weigh the downside of opportunities much more than the upside. When I met Franny around noon, and she asked how it went, I said it was possible but not certain that it would turn into a significant gift, and that we had a dinner date with the attorney and his wife in the town of Follamento D'Asso that evening. Franny rolled her eyes, but we both agreed that we'd drive to Follamento an hour early and look around the town.

We spent to afternoon driving a loop from Montisi to Pienza to Monticchiello where we had a late lunch at La Porta, and then to San Quirico before returning to Montisi. Pienza is one of the most charming towns in all of central Tuscany, and we always get some of the local pecorino cheese. Franny is an artist and teacher, and she brings details to life that I would easily miss. San Quirico, a lesser-known town but pretty nonetheless has a garden which often serves as a venue for exhibits of outdoor sculpture. On this trip there were about a dozen large terracotta sculptures by the artist, Sbarluzzi, from Pienza, and the stop dampened some of her annoyance that we were using vacation time on what she thought would not amount to anything. She knows that I am a workaholic and rightly feels that vacation time is precious.

Follamento is on the west side of the road from San Giovanni D'Asso to Torrenieri and it has entrances at both the northern and southern ends of town. We drove by the northern entrance and turned right into the southern entrance. The town itself is on a loop from the main road with one-way streets on either side of a piazza, which is surrounded by a residential area

The low sun gave the piazza an incredible glow in the late-day light. It was shaped like an oval with pointed ends where the two one-way roads met. About ten buildings lined each side with retail on the ground floor and what appeared to be commercial or residential on the top two or three floors; no building was higher than four floors. The center was marked by a large well with an iron arch that looked imposing. The piazza was empty except for the three seating areas for the osteria, pizzeria, and bar that jutted out into the unoccupied space. It was about 7:15 p.m. — too early for anyone to be eating dinner.

Along the east side, the first three shops were the cheese store, hardware store, and butcher. The next four were the Town offices, Osteria Buona Fortuna, where we were going to eat, an art gallery with an eclectic collection of oils, water colors and sculptural ceramics, and a wine shop, at Piazza Follamento, 20, above which there appeared to be one unit, the law office of Avv Luccamezzo and Son. Franny looked at the art work in the gallery and commented that many of the paintings were quite good but over 10,000 euros, pretty expensive compared to what we expected. The last two shops on the east side were a shoe store and shoe repair, and finally the local office of the Carabinieri, the Italian federal police. The evening light and the town's charm and beauty led me to take about 30 photos on my iPhone. As it turned out, these were good to have.

Turning north across from the Carabinieri offices we walked past the bike shop, a one-chair barber shop, and a travel agency, advertising trips to Australia, Africa, and Peru. Next we passed a small bakery-homemade pasta store, a bar-coffee shop, and a bank with an ATM. Finally, we passed the post office, a pizzeria and the alimentary that doubled as the place to buy not only touristy olive oil, cheese and pasta, but also staples such as milk, eggs, and some fresh fruit.

We entered the restaurant at eight. My mindset was to enjoy the dinner and get as many details as possible, then switch into full vacation gear.

Day 26

Yesterday's hour in the yard was bad, but it could have been worse. I recognized a few of the guards, but there were several new ones. I was surprised to find our group of marks in the same spot. Ernesto said we should get it out of the way first thing. I did my two and Ernesto did his three. Ernesto said that rather than walk with him, I should hang out near the basketball court and keep to myself.

I watched the pick-up game for about twenty minutes, though it seemed like two hours, and then from across the yard, I heard raised voices. I recognized Ernesto's uncle in the center of a crowd of about thirty inmates, face-to-face with a much larger and younger prisoner. Everything in the yard stopped and all eyes were on the dispute. After about a minute the shouting escalated to shoving and then a full out brawl. Ernesto moved to the middle of the raucous crowd and was fighting for about thirty seconds when the whistles blew, an alarm sounded, and twenty extra guards came into the yard, swinging their night sticks liberally. The fight lasted only three or four minutes but there were lots of bloodied prisoners lined up against the fence when order was restored. The guards marched them out of the yard first, after which the rest of us went back to our cells in dead silence.

Ernesto has not returned. This morning, I ate breakfast by myself for the first time. There were three times the usual number of guards and no conversations took place.

In the osteria, I introduced Franny, and Lorenzo introduced his wife, Nicoletta. She was, like Lorenzo, on the stout side, looked at least ten years younger and was very pretty. Though Franny and I were wearing casual vacation clothing, Nicoletta and Lorenzo were dressed up; he was wearing a sportier suit and tie than the one he had on earlier and she had on a dark dress with a sweater. The maître d welcomed us with warm hugs. He asked if we wanted to sit outside and Lorenzo said that he preferred an inside, private table so we sat in the back corner.

Lorenzo asked, "Have you had a chance to look around?"

"We arrived about an hour ago. The town is beautiful. Franny and I wondered why we never stopped here even though we passed by maybe a half dozen times."

"I was born and raised right here in Follamento, and Nicoletta is from the nearby town of Asciano. We met as teenagers and have been married for 35 years. We have two kids, a boy and a girl, in their late twenties and early thirties."

I smiled and said, "We have also been married for thirty-five years and our son and daughter are close in age to your kids."

The maître d brought over a glass of prosecco for each of us and then told us, actually speaking to Lorenzo, what they had for dinner. Similar to several other restaurants in the area, either there was no menu, or Lorenzo and Nicoletta were such regular customers that no menu was required. Lorenzo insisted on ordering the house antipasto for all of us, and then each of us ordered a pasta and main dish which turned out to be a ton of food. The maître d asked Lorenzo, "Would you like the usual house red?"

He answered emphatically, "No, no, no, please bring us a nice Brunello."

We continued light conversation over dinner which included an animated discussion of the similarities between our President and certain European politicians. It was a draw on who was more outrageous and ill-suited to lead a country. After we ordered coffee and desert, Lorenzo finally said, "I would like to tell you more about the possible gift to Olmsted.

Lorenzo sat back as though he was about to reveal the keys to the kingdom. I glanced over at Franny and I could tell she saw the drum roll in Lorenzo's eyes. "Roberto owns, owned that is, the entire town of Follamento as did his father and grandfather. His grandfather acquired the town in the 1930s, by initially buying some of the property, but during the war a lot of the town was abandoned and thus he was able to acquire the entire town by about 1947." Lorenzo took a moment for this to sink in. He appeared to expect a response from me.

I obliged and said, "In my experience it seems unusual for a single person or family to own an entire town."

"This is also rare in Italy but not unheard of."

"What about the businesses in the town? Do they lease the space from the family?"

"All of the businesses with a couple of exceptions are owned by the Follamento family. The exceptions are the bank, the Post Office, and the Carabinieri, and in all three cases they lease the space from the family."

"While the real estate ownership seems unusual to me, the ownership of all the businesses is something I have never heard of."

"It is rare, but, again, this is not the only case in Italy." After a deep breath, he said, "Roberto's will states that Olmsted University, or others in line if Olmsted declines, will be given all the real estate and ownership of the businesses. Olmsted will be required to continue to run the town as it had been in the past in perpetuity, but now in addition, it will become a study-abroad site. Every student who comes to Follamento for a semester or more will be required to work in one of the businesses or for the town itself, for twenty hours a week, paid at the New York minimum wage, which is above the going rate in Italy."

This was nothing I had imagined and I immediately thought of the cost of maintaining the real estate and running the businesses. There was a considerable risk that the university would be unlikely to accept without some financial backstop. Also, I thought that the "in perpetuity" aspect would be tough to accept, and I believed that the work requirement would disturb some students and faculty. I decided to ask what I thought was a logical though impertinent question, "Is there any financial support for the maintenance of the buildings and the running of the various businesses?" As soon as the words left my mouth, I realized that I had probably gone too far on the first date. I quickly added, "I hope that question is not out of line, but it will be asked of me as soon as I return to New York."

Lorenzo again took his time answering, probably trying to give me the impression he was thinking about the next university in line if Olmsted refused the gift. But he was just playing with me. "That is the right question to ask. The gift will include a 100 million euro endowment, the income from which can be used for exactly the purposes that you stated, plus financial aid for needy students. The university can invest the endowment subject to the approval of two trustees, me, and a representative named by the university. I hope we can reach an agreement in a matter of months."

I thought that was ambitious but opted to simply nod yes.

This was an enormous idea to take in and at the time I was unsure if Olmsted would be able to accept the gift, especially because of the timidity of the president, combined with the Olmsted faculty, who were just beginning to consider global initiatives. At one level, the gift represented an audacious opportunity, while at the same time the risk was large. But I was not the decision maker, and I thought I knew enough and had gone far enough to bring the idea back to the university's leadership.

I said to Lorenzo, "This is an unbelievable opportunity for Olmsted. I or a colleague will be back in touch very soon." I probably said grazie about twenty times. We finished the meal with the traditional grappa and I was grateful that Lorenzo suggested that we walk around the piazza for a few minutes before Franny and I drove back to Montisi.

Day 27

The fight in the yard took place two days ago, yet there is still no sign of Ernesto or his uncle. Last evening, Officer Tejada stopped by the cell to let me know that he thought he might be transferred to another part of the prison. He passed the cell on most evenings, but we did not speak and his presence was more of a vague insurance policy, welcome nonetheless. Last night he said, "I will get no warning so you should not be surprised if you do not see me."

I knew that I was not supposed to speak of Ernesto, so I looked over at his empty bed and then turned back to officer Tejada and asked, "When?"

He just shrugged his shoulders and rolled his eyes.

Franny and I were blown away after the dinner with Nicoletta and Lorenzo. The scale of the potential gift was orders of magnitude more than anything I had envisioned. Franny said, "I have to revise my feeling that you were wasting your, or should I say our, time. I thought the gift would be a collection of antique books or furniture or gaudy art work. You know better than I do that Olmsted's leadership is so timid they could turn it down. But if they accept, do you think that you will be in the lead instead of letting someone else take credit?"

My mind was racing about the possibilities. Though it was after eleven when we returned to Montisi, Franny understood that I needed to email New York before we went to bed. We planned to visit Siena the next day and then visit Greve in Chianti before going to Florence and Venice.

I wrote to Melissa and cc'd the provost, general counsel and head of development. I explained that the donor's lawyer was smart and even-handed, as best as I could tell from the two encounters, a clear example of incorrect first impressions. I presented the nature of the gift and the restrictions, and the potential problem of the son, Angelo. I said that I could get on a speaker phone if the group wanted to talk before I returned in August, and that I was going to send Lorenzo a thank you email and copy Melissa. I concluded that I thought the gift was extremely intriguing, and though it had issues, I believed it was worth a serious examination. I attached about a dozen of the photos from my cellphone.

When Franny and I awoke, there was an email from Melissa, who agreed that it was an unusual and a "difference-making," one of her favorite terms, kind of gift. She noted that many things needed to come together, but that it was definitely worth further investigations and serious conversations. At least for now, she preferred that I stay on lead and she even went so far as to write a thank you note to Lorenzo indicating that I would be the lead person. This surprised me, and pleased Franny, but likely angered Cathy and Laura. In concluding the email to the group, Melissa said she was about to go on a trip and indicated that a face to face conversation should take place between her and me and the provost, general counsel, and director of development later in August. She also copied Charles Mannford, the chair of the Olmsted board.

After I wrote an email thanking Lorenzo, I felt that Franny and I were free and clear for the vacation. But as we were walking around Siena deciding where to have lunch, my phone rang and it was Charles Mannford. He is somewhat impetuous, so this was not the first time he had called about a matter that I thought should be discussed between him and the president. "I am not happy that Melissa is not moving more forcefully," he said. "I want to use my private plane to organize a trip for me, you and Melissa in mid-August, so we can meet Lorenzo and the son, and see the town for ourselves."

It is extremely dangerous for anyone in a position like mine to get between the board chair and the president, and it is important to say the same thing to both people. "I'm fine with a trip, but be aware that Italy slows down in August, and we may not be able to meet with both Lorenzo and Angelo in that timeframe. I recommend that you write to

Melissa and suggest that either she or I write to Lorenzo and ask when we can come over to continue the conversation."

He did not like this idea as he thought that he could decide such things and Melissa's plodding style was getting to him, but he said that he would call her. His tone and forcefulness were off the charts, even for him.

Just after Franny and I had lunch, the phone rang again, and predictably it was Melissa. "**Charles is meddling and he should leave it to us to figure out the timing of the next visit. While Charles may rank this as priority number one, I, as president, have a lot going on and am very busy,**" another of her favorite refrains." Charles was so enthusiastic, I wonder if he can be objective."

At this point Franny was rolling her eyes and becoming modestly agitated as she foresaw a trip through Italy with me on the cell phone every few hours refereeing between Melissa and Charles.

I tried telling Melissa that if she did as Charles suggested and asked Lorenzo about a visit, then by the time some mutually agreeable dates were identified it would be September or October anyway. But Melissa could not stop herself from describing Charles's actions as over-reaching, not realizing that he thought her passivity and kick-the-can-down-the-road style needed prodding. When she sensed my annoyance, she asked a straight-out question, "Do you think the board chair should be on the initial visit?"

No matter how I tried to bob and weave, she seemed to want me to take a side. I responded as best I could. "There is certainly a gray area where you are likely to think Charles should not be involved and he thinks that he should. As you know he is at times impatient with our sometimes sclerotic decision making and in this case, as board chair, he sees fundraising as one of his key priorities. The upshot is that it is better for Charles to be aggressive on this gift compared to academic issues such as curriculum, faculty hiring, and assessment of faculty. Besides, my take on the situation in Italy is that stature and titles matter, making the visit by the board chair a sign of importance to Lorenzo and Roberto's son, Angelo. I suggest you pick your battles and this is not one to fight." I decided that Charles's view that Melissa was a status quo person, not an innovator or an entrepreneur, was not the message that I needed to deliver.

Her response was, "I guess so." I was pleased to get that answer, as it meant that the call was closer to being over. With Franny waiting to get going, I decided that I would take yes for an answer. Finally, with my non-response, she said, "When you return, please make an outline of the bases we need to touch to move this ahead, and in a couple of days I will write to Lorenzo with a copy to you asking when we can arrange a next visit."

While I was pleased to get to this place, it could have happened with less phone time. Franny was ready to throw my cellphone off the top of the tower in Siena's beautiful fan-shaped piazza. Sometimes my colleagues care much more about who is in charge and involved than the substance of the matter. If Melissa and Charles had a better one-on-one relationship, we would have enjoyed more of Italy.

Day 28

Today is my four-week anniversary, but no cake.

After I finished writing yesterday, I went to lunch with the same eerie quiet, no Ernesto, and no uncle. On the way back to the cell the guards let us know that there would be no exercise time.

I was lying on my top bunk, basically dozing, when a guard whom I did not know, Officer Ruiz, woke me. All he said was, "Come with me." My heart rate doubled. I thought that perhaps Hector had secured my release. I asked the guard if I should bring anything and he shook his head no. Hope springs eternal. It was also possible that I was somehow implicated in the gang dispute, but thinking about that made me weak-kneed and dizzy.

He handcuffed me and we walked to what appeared to be an interrogation room. There was a table with one chair on one side and two on the other, a chair in the corner, and a two way mirror on the wall. Officer Ruiz pointed to the single chair, and he sat on the chair in the corner. As soon as I was seated, a fortyish-man came in wearing a suit and tie, and sat opposite me. He introduced himself as Mr. Nieves from the Panamanian Prison Authority.

Mr. Nieves looked down at a piece of paper in a folder, looked up at me, and waited about twenty seconds before he spoke. "I am here investigating drug dealing and I want to ask you some questions." Door number 2!

He pulled out a grainy black and white photo that showed me standing by my marks in the yard. "What were you doing?" He cleverly left me uncertain of exactly how much he knew. To buy some time, I asked if I could take a closer look. The folder in front of him was not thick, so there was some chance that the picture was all he had. I decided to take it one step at a time and answered, "It looks like I am standing with other prisoners in the yard."

He slowly took the picture back. "How do you know those men?" he asked. I answered truthfully, "Almost everyone I spoke with was someone who was known to my cellmate, Ernesto." Because they know that Ernesto is my cellmate and we ate together, I decided that mentioning him was not giving anything away. But that did give him a follow-up question. At this point I would have loved to get some water but I did not want to ask.

"What do you know about Ernesto?"

"I know a little about his family. He drove a limo."

"Do you know what business his family is in?"

"Ernesto told me that he was in a restaurant with family members when there were many arrests and he was put in jail even though he did nothing wrong."

"Do you know what his family does?"

"Ernesto said that he is a limo driver and not in the family business."

Mr. Nieves smiled and said, "You should stay clean and not get involved."

I decided to take a chance and asked, "Do you know anything about why I am in prison?"

He looked in the folder and he said, "The printout says your charges are pending." This was the first time I had learned anything "official" about my situation. At least they did not have me in on trumped-up charges, at least not yet, so I suppose that was the good news. Nieves was not getting up so I asked, "Do you know when Ernesto is coming back to the cell?"

"That depends on how my investigation goes." He signaled to Officer Ruiz that I could leave and he said again, "Stay out of this."

The rest of our time in Italy was very enjoyable. We visited Siena and Greve before going to Florence. Siena is full of history and it has one of the most beautiful piazzas in the world. Greve is in Chianti and it also has a small charming piazza and we ate fabulous dinners in both places. Florence and Venice are classic Italian cities, both of which we have been to a couple of times so the visit is more leisurely and fun when you do not have to check off all of the must-see sites. On this trip, I was able to appreciate how in-synch Franny and I are, a love of travelling near the top of the list. Our kids make us both proud on many levels.

When we returned to New York, Melissa called the meeting. Marshall, Laura, and Cathy were there. Cathy had gotten over not going to Italy but not Laura, who seemed to think that I was horning in on her fund-raising portfolio. "I understand why you feel this way," I said, "but that is not my intent. Melissa is probably reacting to Lorenzo's aversion to meet with development people." She was not buying and was probably worried that she had no advance knowledge of the donor.

I described Lorenzo, then Roberto Follamento and the potential gift. I spoke a little about the size and architecture of the town, and the family's ownership of the real estate and business, the student work requirement, the 100 million euro endowment and the presence of the son, Angelo. I showed about a dozen photos of the town which looked almost unreal in the evening light. Both Cathy and Laura, after getting briefed by Melissa, had done some research. Roberto was not a very public person; he owned a minority interest in a British soccer team, had a well-known palazzo in Siena and a villa near Lake Como, both of which presumably would go to Angelo, some other interests in commercial real estate in Milan and a few other places in northern Italy, and he was on a number of corporate boards, including several banks. He appeared in photos of many social events. Neither Cathy nor Laura found anything that would spark a controversy. There were a couple of human interest stories over the years about Follamento D'Asso, but they read like they were written by a PR person. beautiful town, happy workers, generations stayed in town and so on. It sounded almost too good to be true.

Marshall immediately raised the faculty issues, which is his role. "I wonder whether this will be seen as forcing the faculty global committee's hand. The work requirement is odd, and maybe off-putting." In talking about it with Franny during our trip, she came up with the idea that it could be integrated with an Italian language requirement, which Marshall liked and he continued. "I am sure that if we decide to have a study abroad program in Italy, there is zero probability that, absent the gift, we would select Follamento. This is not a knock out factor, only we are unlikely to have a second site in Italy so we need to be sure that it will accomplish what we want it to. And finally, though this is not academic, I am a little surprised and uncertain about an individual and subsequently a university owning a town and its businesses, and employing virtually all of its residents."

Melissa said, "I think another visit is the next step, and Charles offered to fly a small group over on his private plane. I also would like Ed McDonald, the chief financial officer, to be at the next meeting, but in the meantime Bill should bring him up to date." She paused and though no one spoke, everyone was anxious to know who she thought should be on the next visit. She restated that she thought that I should remain on point, which endeared me no end to my colleagues.

When everyone else left, she asked me, "Do you think that the gift will happen?"

"It may, but the obvious wild cards are our faculty and the son. In terms of the faculty, they may see it as a great opportunity to do something that ordinarily would take years to build, or they may say, who wants to be in the countryside when the great cities of Milan, Bologna, Florence, Venice and Rome are more appropriate and this is simply philanthropic opportunism. I think that the timing of our solicitation of faculty input will affect their opinion. Presumably, the later we bring them in, the more negative they are likely to be."

Melissa seemed surprised by this, and asked, "Do you think that one or more faculty members should be with us on the next visit?"

"I am leaning to yes, in part because of the timing issue and also because Follamento is much more impressive in person."

Melissa said, "My instincts are that it's too soon for faculty input, and I am focused on the risk of the entire endeavor and how many things could go wrong." I could see that her thinking was evolving even as she was speaking. "On the other hand, the last thing I want to do is give the faculty a reason to think we're doing this without them." As I was leaving, she said to herself but loud enough so I could hear, "Why don't donors give their money for what we want to do?"

Day 29

Wednesday morning, around 9:30, Ernesto, a shadow of himself, returned to the cell. He had several bandages on his hands and head, a black eye, a missing tooth, and he seemed about 4 inches shorter. He got in his bunk and in a stream of consciousness in his improving English, he recounted the last few days. I was on the edge of the top bunk so that I could lean forward occasionally to make eye contact.

"After the guards broke up the fight, I went to the clinic with about twenty other inmates and stayed there, handcuffed to a chair. The four medics moved back and forth, first just stopping all the bleeding and cleaning the wounds, taking x-rays where they thought something was broken, but none for me, bandaging the wounds, and sparingly giving out painkiller. By Sunday afternoon I was in solitary confinement, and between then and now I was out of the cell only three times, twice for questioning and once for a "hearing" that added six months to my sentence. This six month addition sucks and is worse than any of my wounds.

"The two sides have a deal for sharing, but we will not know for sure until lunch when I speak to my uncle, who is in worse shape than I am."

"How do you know about the sharing arrangement if you were in solitary the whole time?"

He sat up in bed, which looked like it was difficult, and motioned for me to get him a pencil and paper. Ernesto wrote "Nieves." He is on the family payroll, and when he "questioned" Ernesto, he signaled that a deal was close. Nieves also said that I seemed more frightened than anyone he's ever spoken with. "He was worried you were going to faint or have a heart attack." This was the only time Ernesto managed a semblance of a smile.

It took Ernesto almost an hour to give me that account; it exhausted him and he took about an hour nap before lunch. The hour was not long enough to get into my writing so I read more about the Roosevelts, learning about FDR's incredible ability to be vague with even his closest advisors, probably good advice for me as well. On the way to lunch in his weakened state, Ernesto asked, "Are you due to see your lawyer soon?"

"Hector said he would try to be back tomorrow."

Despite the return of most of the wounded warriors, there were few voices audible in the cafeteria. The uncle came by looking worse than Ernesto. I was given the signal to take a walk and I moved to an empty table. From where I sat, I could see the conversation was unusually animated. His uncle left after only five minutes and Ernesto signaled for me to return. "A sharing arrangement is being discussed outside the prison. I think it will be a done deal within a week. We are not to do any pickups until we get the go-ahead." *Could I be out by then?* "My uncle and I argued about your role. I want to protect you, but my uncle thinks having an American on our family's side will be good if things began to go off of the rails. He was angry and left the table when I pushed back."

I thanked him and he said that I should not thank him yet.

After our Thursday meeting on the bequest, I met with Ed McDonald, the Olmsted CFO. Edward is a typical numbers person who, like many in his position, seems to be bored with just doing the financial work, and as a result offers an opinion on everything from academics to politics to architecture, clearly showing everyone that he should stick to finance. University CFOs can be enablers and problem solvers, or they can be of the 'just say no' variety, and Ed was much more of the latter. Ed is on a short leash. Last year he missed Olmsted's budget forecast; his budgeted surplus turned out to be a deficit. Also, his brother-in-law's firm sold office supplies to Olmsted and Ed failed to report it on his conflict of interest filing. His claim that he did not know about the contract was not believable. Charles was ready to fire him but Melissa made a big deal about giving him another chance.

I briefed Ed on the details of the gift including the town and its businesses, endowment, and the restrictions set by the bequest, and I let him know about the son. As soon as I presented the overview, he said that his initial concern was that the gift should pay for itself and not require funding from Olmsted. He asked about restrictions on the endowment and I let him know we would have only one of two trustees, which made him appropriately nervous. I reiterated that the earnings on the endowment would be restricted to spending to maintain the village and cover short falls from the businesses, and for financial aid. Ed, who was short on creativity, said, "This is more than a study-abroad site. We need expertise and funds to run the businesses and maintain the real estate and infrastructure." I thought that he would be a nay-sayer at Monday's meeting.

The weekend gave me a chance to relax a little, until about 5 p.m. on Saturday when an angry Melissa telephoned. She'd received a call from Charles. "I am seething and I need to vent with someone," she said. Lucky me. The issue was the perennial one, what is the purview of the chair versus the president? Melissa became president under the previous board chair, who was a master at setting direction without getting into the weeds. The beauty of that approach is that when an individual matter did rise to a high level of importance, Melissa was eager to seek the chair's advice, knowing he would offer to help, but not meddle. By being too eager to show that he is smarter than anyone else, Charles fostered avoidance strategies by Melissa and the senior leadership. It was the classic case of more is less.

According to Melissa, Charles asked us to meet Monday at his office in downtown Manhattan, and said, "I want to move quickly."

She pushed back, "I suggest that the leadership group meet on Monday and then we meet with you later in the week."

There was really no question who was going to win this argument. They set the meeting for Monday morning in Charles's office.

Melissa was so angry that she was stammering and shouting with me on the phone, which was not her usual style. "I'm so glad I put you on point as Laura is too close to Charles and would be calling him every hour." And here I'd thought my selection was based on my expertise and judgment.

After she did her download, I suggested that she and I and anyone else who she wanted to involve should meet either early Monday morning or the next day, Sunday.

Melissa had a pretty strong aversion to having meetings on the weekend and even more aversion to getting up early, but as she calmed down, she recognized how a meeting on Sunday could be helpful. She and I agreed to meet Sunday evening in her university apartment, and I was to invite Marshall, Laura, Cathy, and Ed, and also tell them about the Monday morning meeting in Charles's office. To save the five minutes all of them except Marshall would have spent bemoaning a Sunday evening meeting, I emailed everyone, and by the time I went to bed, everyone replied they would attend.

Melissa's apartment reflected that she changed jobs regularly. It felt as though everything was rented from 'Furnishings R US' without any personal touch. The exception was a poster-sized photo of Melissa. hand raised, mouth open speaking in a venue with thousands of people in the audience.

It was clear that she thought we should take the gift seriously. Hearing no objections, I said, "Our first priority is to find out as much as we can about the gift, and simultaneously develop a pathway to assess whether it is right for us at this time. We should move expeditiously, but in Italy things always go slower than here, so there should be sufficient time to find out what we need to know. There will be a long list of complex academic, legal, and financial issues. The largest question, an existential one, is should a university be doing this — owning a town, running the businesses, and employing almost all of the townspeople in conjunction with a study- abroad program in a place we did not select? This question needs careful scrutiny, and ultimately it will be up to Melissa to recommend an action to Charles and the board."

Cathy said, "We should engage a U.S. law firm with a real presence in Italy," and that sounded right to everyone.

I continued, "Angelo poses a significant risk and while the issues regarding him are not solely legal, it probably makes sense to include him on the legal list for now. Marshall outlined some of the key academic issues at the last meeting and I agree that the on-going faculty assessment of Olmsted's global profile is a serious complicating factor. Clearly, the financial risk is significant. Given Lorenzo's comments on development staff, Laura's role is not clear at this point."

This introduction gave everyone the opportunity to fine tune the issues I presented and it seemed that Marshall, while worrying about the faculty reactions, turned from a skeptic to neutral or even a mild enthusiast, with Ed and Cathy concerned about how much work the assessment would entail, pushing their needles more to the negative. Laura was angry, but this was more than mitigated by the fact that if we got the gift, a monetized value would go into her fundraising totals. Other issues raised included facilities, where the kids of our faculty and staff in town would go to school, housing the students, and the remoteness of the town, but the conversation always seemed to flow back to the faculty.

At about 9:45 p.m., Melissa said, "This has been productive and I hope that the meeting with Charles tomorrow will focus on more immediate next steps. Given the scope and complexity, I want one person to be on point and that person should continue to be Bill for now."

Day 30

I did not know how worried I should be. Stuff happens, so Hector's failure to show up should not be such a big deal. Every time someone walked by the cell I measure the cadence of their steps and figure out if they will or will not stop. Perhaps I put too much faith in Hector and assumed that when he said, "Thursday," he meant Thursday. Now that it is after dinner and I'm sure he won't show up, I will try to write.

Ernesto could not shower yet because of his wounds but he did accompany me, which was in his self-interest as our cell is small and I was quite gamey. He was stiff, sore and in pain.

At lunch, Ernesto's uncle still appeared to be pissed-off, and shooed me away for about 15 minutes for another animated conversation. Ernesto reported that my situation came up briefly but the main topic of conversation was the ongoing negotiations. "Both sides are close to a deal, but we are not there yet." He seemed to know a lot of details and spoke more assertively than usual, which again caused me to doubt his self-proclaimed peripheral role.

As we lined up to return to our cells, the assistant warden announced that time in the yard would be reinstated on Sunday, but instead of each block going out all together for an hour, half of the block would be going out for 30 minutes. This would complicate business.

On Monday morning, we drove to Charles's office on lower Broadway in one of the University's vans. We went up to his offices which had a fantastic view of New York harbor, and waited for a few minutes in the main conference room. The room was old-school classy, lots of cherry wood, large comfortable chairs and prints by known artists, Miro and Kandinsky the ones I recognized. I could tell that Melissa was nervous and still angry.

Charles arrived right at 10 a.m. and everyone took their coffee and sat down. The table was arranged with two seats at the head and Melissa sat next to Charles; normally Charles sits alone at the head but maybe he was sensitive to her feelings, which was unusual for him. Of course he did not say, "Okay Melissa, why don't you begin," and instead he directly launched into his opening monologue: "This potential gift is very complex with many moving parts, but I see no mileage in going slowly. We should visit in the next few weeks. My plane holds seven people comfortably, so please select the six who will attend."

I thought Melissa would argue for a delay, but she must have read Charles as not being moveable on this point so she opened with the question, "Should faculty be included?"

Charles immediately shot back, "Why?"

She not so gently reminded him, "The faculty are working on a global approach for Olmsted and we could be seen as short-circuiting their role."

Charles is the last person to want to encourage faculty unrest so he backed off quickly, but added, "I am okay with faculty on the trip as long as they adhere to our schedule. Pending Lorenzo's schedule, the trip should take place in August."

Charles then got into the details. "We should confirm with Lorenzo that it's okay to meet with Angelo. If Angelo's expectation is that he was going to inherit the town and the businesses, he could be a real impediment. If I put myself in Angelo's position, he is likely very angry. He could use the complex Italian courts to slow us down, so some offer to Angelo on our part may be desirable, even if only symbolic."

Melissa asked that I write to Lorenzo to try to get some specific dates, and Charles asked, "What about Laura's involvement?"

I'm sure this drove Melissa crazy as she viewed Laura as Charles's mole. She said, "The gift was in the will without any development work. Bill is the right one to be on point with Laura on the team. Lorenzo expressed antipathy to development people and we should take that into account."

Charles did not push the matter further and an obvious side look at Laura by Charles signaled that they likely had spoken before the meeting. Charles said, "There are enough of us involved that if anyone has a vacation planned, the trip should not take precedence, as long Melissa and I can make it."

Melissa had calmed down a little but was reignited by Charles' comments about Laura. That was probably on her mind in the van when she said, "The six remaining seats on Charles' plane should be Bill and me, Marshall and Cathy, and two faculty members."

Not surprisingly that left Laura and Ed off the list and Ed chimed in, "I could fly over on a commercial flight if I can be useful."

"There will be plenty of time for that."

I said, "I will email Lorenzo this afternoon and hopefully we will know something by this time tomorrow."

Melissa said, "Bill should work with Marshall to decide the right faculty to invite."

After some modest turbulence, we had landed in a good place.

We went back to campus and after lunch I began to write the email to Lorenzo when my assistant, Stephanie, poked her head into my office and said that an Angelo Follamento was here to see me, and then asked if she should schedule an appointment. I was monumentally taken aback but recovered and said that she should show him in.

"*Buongiorno, buongiorno, buongiorno.* I apologize for showing up unannounced. Lorenzo told me that you had met with him in Follamento and that you wanted to meet me as well." He did not say that he had other business in New York and gave me the impression that he made the trip to New York specifically to meet with me. Angelo, though middle-aged, appeared to be at least ten years younger, clean shaven and good looking. He was wearing a dark gray suit that looked like it was made on his person, at a cost of my clothes budget for about five years. His hair was black with flicks of gray, and he carried himself with the kind of confidence that very few people can convey. I felt like asking him where he parked his Ferrari, but didn't. He surprised me by pointing to a poster-size photo I had in my office of Mike Piazza hitting a homerun, and asked, "Are you a Mike Piazza fan?" My look conveyed my surprise that he would know Piazza and he said, "I follow Italian-American athletes and Piazza is one of my favorites." He was clearly smooth and his English was excellent.

I asked him if he wanted anything and I had Stephanie bring him a black coffee. I could see his face momentarily frown and it must have been the American coffee.

He said, "Should we talk about the weather, politics, and the economy, and then get to the point of my visit, or get right to the point?"

"Let's get right to the point." I thought at the time that he might have a sense of humor.

"Do you know the details of the will?"

"I know the broad outlines of the generous gift from the meeting with Lorenzo."

"I witnessed the signing of my father's last will. I am well taken care of financially and in terms of various properties in both Italy and here in New York, where we have an apartment, but the town and the businesses are what I want to talk about. For the past twenty or so years I have been running the town in terms of the real estate, municipal services, and businesses.

"I expected my father to live longer and I was working on a different arrangement when he died. Though nothing was committed to writing, I wanted my father to structure the will so that while Olmsted, or another university if not Olmsted, would own the town and businesses, I would continue my role."

"Was Lorenzo involved in these discussions?"

"He was aware of them, but I am confident he had advised against it. He worked for my father, not for me."

"There are two main reasons for my request. First, it will take some time for Olmsted to get up to speed on the ins and outs of the local customs and practices, and I can transfer this information as I am doing my job. Second, I feel that it would be seen in the town as a giant slap in my face, and given that I am well-liked and respected, the job for

Olmsted would be much more difficult than it needs to be." Not quite a threat but almost. He concluded, "I think that Lorenzo or another attorney could write an airtight agreement that would do what I am requesting. The Italian courts are much more efficient when all sides agree on an issue," a not so vague threat this time.

Clearly, I had neither the authority nor expertise to get into a negotiation with Angelo. "I will speak to the University leadership and let them know that you visited and proposed a specific arrangement." He asked if my wife and I wanted to join him for dinner. Fortunately we had other plans, but I would have made something up if we hadn't. I thought that this was mostly about pride and appearances, both of which are important in Italy, and that he could have asked for much more.

Day 31

When I was taken from my hotel room there was no way that I would have imagined spending a month in a Panamanian prison. Among all the horrible things, my own hygiene is at an all-time low and even after a shower I feel dirty.

I was increasingly questioning my own decisions. I pride myself on acting with integrity and maybe I agreed to the cigarette pick-ups too easily. I was focused on accessing a phone. I thought for a moment about relaying information through Hector to Cathy about what I found in Italy, but I was worried that it would lead to Follamento's closure which I desperately wanted to avoid.

Again I am writing at night as Hector was here, with less than perfect news. I was ushered from my cell to a conference room mid-morning. Hector apologized sincerely for not showing up yesterday, and said that going forward I should treat his schedule as a goal rather than a fixed date. He said that he had spoken with Franny, who is relentless about my release, and she and the kids were extremely worried.

Right away I could tell from his quietness and limited eye contact that the news was not good. He started by saying what we both knew, "Some pretty important people must want you in jail." Then he gave away the punch-line, "It will take more time and effort to get you out. Every time I was able to reach a point where I thought that I could learn something useful, I hit a dead end. No one knew why you are here or how to get you out. My source at Guzman and Quintero was surprised by how little he could learn. When he tried to use a little cash to encourage some people to talk, they uniformly refused. That is a sign of the power of the people behind your arrest. As an attorney, I have limited ability to penetrate the walls that I encountered. I would like your permission to hire a private investigator, one who could open some doors that I cannot. I regularly work with someone who is very good."

I was feeling paranoid and asked, "Can the private investigator be trusted?" What he said made me feel more paranoid.

"That is a good question, but he is a reliable childhood friend who is unlikely to be part of the problem. His services are not cheap."

"How much?"

"$5,000 to $10,000 to start."

I was feeling as though I had no choice so I said yes and Hector said, "He does not need an advance based on my word. You can pay when you get out." The best news of the conversation was that Hector did not say, *if I get out.*

"How are you doing and are you staying out of trouble?"

I did not feel I should explain the details of the deal with Ernesto and just said, "The month here is taking a physical and psychological toll on me, but I am hanging in there."

"I will aim for a visit next Friday. I apologize for not making more progress."

It was a long walk back to my cell.

After Angelo left my office, I thought I was dreaming, even though I knew that his surprise visit was audacious and very real. As I processed what he said, I realized that it was a direct threat, give him authority over the town or he would use the courts to fight us.

Given the implications, I put aside the email I was writing to Lorenzo and walked over to Melissa's office. She was doubly annoyed, first because Angelo had now confirmed that he was a person to be reckoned with, and second because Charles was right that he would not go along quietly. She asked, "What do you think?"

"I have an open mind about finding a role for him that will address his pride, and maybe go further if we think it is in the University's long-term interests."

Melissa suggested that I brief Cathy and then Cathy and I should call Charles. She delegated the call to avoid having to hear Charles gloat.

I went to Cathy's office and predictably, she said, "This gift may not be worth it."

We then called Charles, and you could feel the "I told you so" coming over the speaker phone even though he never uttered those words. He concluded with what I was thinking, "He could have asked for much more."

Before I left Cathy's office she asked me whether I thought that she should be in touch with Lorenzo. This was a good question and I suggested that she raise it in our next senior staff meeting with Melissa.

Cathy said, "I am looking at two U.S. firms, each with a presence in Italy. Getting someone on board ASAP is important. This would all be a little easier without Angelo." She did not know how right she was.

I finally got the email off to Lorenzo around six New York time, midnight in Italy. I wrote, "The President and the Chair and possibly three others in the leadership group, including me, and maybe two faculty members would like to visit during August if that is feasible from your perspective. I understand that you may not be available but the President and Chair are both very excited about the bequest and want to meet you and see Follamento for themselves relatively soon." I gave him all my coordinates including office and cell phone and then forwarded the email to Charles, Melissa, and my colleagues.

About half an hour later, my cell rang as I was walking into our apartment and it was Lorenzo. I noted that he was up late. "I am very excited about your response," he said, "and while I am normally at my beach house during August, I will come back to Follamento after Ferragosto, and we should plan on a visit Wednesday to Friday, August 17th to 19th."

I wondered whether he knew about Angelo's visit and whether I should mention it. If he knew, then he would know that I chose not to mention it and if he did not know, I would be giving him a lot of information. I made the judgment on the spot to tell him.

But as I was about to speak, he said, "One more thing, how did the meeting go with Angelo?" Now my question was how much to reveal. I had no real sense of their relationship, and whether Angelo and

Lorenzo were or would be become allies with the University as the common enemy. That could kill the entire project or worse, make it miserable once we accepted the gift. I decided to level with Lorenzo, even though I had just told Cathy not to call him.

"Angelo surprised me by showing up unannounced."

Lorenzo said, "Angelo loves the element of surprise."

"He got right to the heart of the matter, that he was working on his father to change the will, and that while he was a witness to the existing will, he could tie up the estate in court if he does not have a more significant role akin to his current role, in a sense mayor and CEO of Follamento."

Lorenzo let out a long sigh and said, "I tried to talk Angelo out of his position but he would have none of it. We should not change the legal parameters even to avoid a court battle. I want Olmsted to consider a role that would permit him some authority for appearances, but with university oversight. I will give it some thought before the visit in August." I wondered how much of this was orchestrated by Angelo and Lorenzo together.

I wrote to Charles and Melissa about the dates that Lorenzo had suggested and asked them to let me know if I could confirm. I wrote separately to Melissa, Charles and Cathy to document the Angelo visit and his threat to bring us to court, as well as Lorenzo's response.

Getting the gift to the finish line was not going to be simple. This was reinforced the next day when I met with Marshall and asked about the two faculty members to accompany us on the trip. Picking the faculty should have been seen by him as a way to increase his own influence but he asked me to call the AUC faculty chair, Nancy Wright. "I know you have some history with her but she is appropriate person."

Confidentially, I spoke with Nancy and gave her the parameters of the potential gift and the dates for the trip. I sensed some coolness. I said that I would like her to recommend who should go. Of course, I knew even before I called that it would be her and one other. She asked, "How will this gift affect my faculty committee's work on recommending a global approach for Olmsted?"

"This is a legitimate concern, but the gift was unsolicited and unexpected, and the donor could go to the next university on the list."

She reluctantly agreed after considerable push-back that included rattling off the natural questions about why this remote place, the questionable academic content, even though nothing had been designed, what about Florence, Rome or even Venice, and the imposition of the work requirement.

"All these issues need to be raised but despite your critical questions, it is a unique opportunity if we can get all the pieces, including the academic ones, to fit together."

She calmed down a little and said, "As AUC faculty chair and chair of the global committee I will be one faculty member, and I will get back to you on the second recommendation. How much can I share with the committee at this point?"

There is a saying at Olmsted University that confidential means you only tell only one person at a time. I understood her dilemma that if we got too far out in front with the gift, especially with her in the know, she could be criticized by the committee for holding back information. But I also worried that the nature of the gift could spread, get covered with sketchy details by the media, and that would kill it. "Please use your judgment and perhaps you can line up the second person, and then let the committee know confidentially that it is only a potential gift, with faculty involvement at the outset, and ask that they not discuss it outside of the committee until the negotiations are further along."

As I hung up I thought I should contact the director of public affairs for Olmsted so he could get a head-start in case anything went public.

Day 32

This morning I was escorted to a conference room to meet with Hector, who was just here yesterday. I saw a new emotion from him, a mix of genuine concern and anger. Yesterday he had a visit from Mr. Nieves, the man who had recently questioned me about my role in the drug business. According to Hector, Mr. Nieves had several purposes for the meeting, but the headline was to convince Hector that he should stop trying to get me out of prison. Mr. Nieves would not reveal his precise role or for whom he was speaking, but Hector gleaned from the conversation that he was part investigator, part consultant to the prison system, and also somehow representing powerful people, code for criminal families connected to drugs. Hector knew characters like him and nothing about them was good.

My head was spinning. Did Panama have only a dozen citizens and they all knew each other? Were Ernesto and his family even more powerful than I thought? How much had I disrupted in Italy? As I calmed down I realized that if Hector was indeed a double agent of some kind, then he would know everything anyway, so why not continue to believe that he was independent and working for me and tell him what was going on? While that logic seemed sound, I was not sure I was thinking straight and smiled inside when I simultaneously thought about calling a time-out and crying, just a little. I wish Franny could give me advice. I do not know why I continue to be surprised by all of this.

I regained my bearings and decided to tell Hector about my connections in the prison. "My cellmate, Ernesto, claims he is a bit player in a drug family and got swept up in a broad arrest and needed to take the fall for some of the real criminals. Ernesto and his uncle, who appears to be a leader of the family, are connected to some of the prison guards, and it was Ernesto who arranged for my call to Franny which led to Archie's visit and hiring you." I stopped to see Hector's reaction.

"Is that it?" he asked.

"No. As the price for my phone call, Ernesto and I are now picking up cigarettes in the yard which are payments for drugs. There is a turf war between Ernesto's family and one other family which led to a brawl in the yard about a week ago. Around that time Nieves interviewed me as well."

I had hoped that Hector would say something like, this is all no surprise and it is manageable, but instead he said, "You cannot make this stuff up." That was my line.

As I was explaining this, for the first time I could begin to see the pieces fitting together. Hector saw it too. He boiled it down and said, "It is likely that the people who wanted you in prison had the power to arrange for your arrest and the connections to work with Ernesto's family to both insure that it is not easy to get you out but also to give you some kind of hope of release and protection while in prison."

I did not want to go into details on the root cause of my predicament, that is Follamento and the discoveries I had made, but I am sure that the people who wanted me in prison are working through Guzman and Quintero. I told Hector, "Guzman and Quintero are connected to the Olmsted work I was doing in Italy and they are likely playing a significant role in my imprisonment."

Hector did not respond immediately. He finally said, "When I got the call from Archie, I thought it would be a minor matter that could be rectified easily and quickly. Maybe it was mistaken identity, maybe some foreign bank regulatory issue that could be resolved, maybe identity theft and fraud. I now know it is something more. I understand there is a part of the story in Italy that I probably do not need to know, at least for now. Maybe someone wanted you out of the way for a while, and no matter what I do, you will not get out until those who put you here want you to get out. In that case maybe you should not spend money on me and the private investigator's fees and just ride it out."

I could not tell if Hector wanted out so I asked him straight out, "Do you want out?"

"No, I never walk away from a case and there is no guarantee that my 'until they are ready' scenario is correct. Besides, if nothing else, my work may speed along the process."

All of this was both clarifying and depressing. "Do you think Guzman and Quintero can keep me imprisoned this long?"

"Yes, longer if they need to."

I pressed Hector on how I should interact with Ernesto and his family.

"You need to keep trying to read Ernesto to get as much information as you can. The Nieves visit seems to me to tie together Ernesto's family and Guzman and Quintero and is unlikely coincidental. Using you as a runner was perhaps not part of the initial plan. The family realized that they had a good thing, but the result could be a lengthier jail term. If you get caught, then Guzman and Quintero would not necessarily care if you were in prison longer than necessary and the new charges would lessen the chances that Guzman and Quintero's role will be known."

The guard signaled that our time was up. Hector left me with the universal sage advice, "Stay out of trouble."

Over those summer weeks before the return visit to Italy, I organized our team and began our due diligence. I knew that Cathy would likely delegate as much of the legal work as she could to the about-to-be-hired American-Italian law firm. **I was sure Nancy would come through with another faculty member, and Stephanie, my assistant, was amazing and will do unobtrusive research on the internet before the visit.**

Also, I looped in the Olmsted Director of Public Affairs, Gabe Houseman. Gabe was a veteran public affairs person who was part reporter, part storyteller, and part salesman, actually just what was needed to present the University in its best light and to handle crises as they occur, which is often. He was surprised that Melissa was okay with

Charles taking the lead as his judgment was not terrific, but he saw that she had little choice. He asked why I had omitted Laura and any development folks and I explained Lorenzo's request. He was especially probing about Cathy and was worried that the Angelo issue would cause her to recommend that we turn down the gift regardless of the actual plusses and minuses. But he saved his most probing questions for my interactions with Nancy and my history with her, and he worried out loud whether the evolution of the gift ahead of the faculty report will cause the faculty to walk away.

His initial recommendation was to have more faculty members on the initial visit. I explained why I thought that was impractical but together it led us to come up with the idea of a larger faculty visit in September, perhaps arranged around some aspect of the committee's work, to see if both the full scope of the gift and the fact that they will have the lead role in setting the academic parameters could negate the process issue of putting the cart before the horse. I said that I would raise this with Marshall.

The day I met with Gabe, Nancy emailed and we agreed to meet the next morning. I wrote that I would gladly come to her office, which sent her into a rant about the oppressive corporate university, the meaning of which was that she did not want her colleagues to see that she and I were meeting. When we met the next morning in my office, Nancy said, "It's crazy to even consider the gift with the faculty committee in the midst of its work. And why would we send students to the Tuscan countryside to work in a small village when there is so much more in Rome, Florence or Venice?" This interchange highlighted some of the different points of view for faculty and academic leadership. Leadership cannot permit the perfect to drive out the good. Only a small number of donors will make significant gifts without imposing personal preferences. Admittedly, this gift was an extreme example, but every gift has elements of this that often faculty assume can be manipulated or avoided.

"We are dealing with an estate that has little room for change in the basic parameters," I said, "but within that, the entire design of the student and faculty experience is in our control. Rome, Florence and Venice were easily reachable for academic work and cultural experiences, and the unique character of a less urban experience could be a positive given that the students are spending much of their time in New York." She also did not like the work requirement. "It can be incorporated within the Italian language component of the program. The overall cost of spending a semester in Follamento will be less than in an Italian city, and that savings could be passed along to students."

She chuckled. "Or the University can make a larger profit. Do you think that faculty members will agree to live in Follamento?"

"Rather than make a case, let's talk again after we visit."

That back and forth calmed her down a little and permitted us to segue into the question of the second faculty member. She was troubled by having to pick just one. Of course she could pick two and not go herself, but that was not an option.

"You should pick someone who is open-minded about global and will have some credibility with the committee."

"Who do you think will be good?"

I hoped that she would ask that and had an answer ready. "Paula Alvarez, David Christ, and Edward Frost come to mind."

"Can I get back to you in a few days?"

It seemed to me that our disagreement over the faculty retirement issues continued to be on her mind, but maybe that was in my head.

Day 33

There was a lot of tension this Sunday morning as the uncertainty about whether there would be time in the yard was on everyone's minds. At breakfast Ernesto said, "I think it will take a few more days to finalize the sharing arrangements and it is good to forego pick-ups for the first few days, just so that everyone can sense that peace is restored. Feuds like this are bad for business." From my perspective they were bad for a lot of reasons.

Since yesterday's conversation with Ernesto, I have been more sensitive to his words and body language, now that it is likely that he was part of the plan to keep me here. I had taken him at his word, in part as a survival technique. Now he was more cautious and it showed. Just before I started writing he asked, "Did Hector deliver some bad news yesterday? Wasn't it an unscheduled visit?"

"Why do you think so?"

"You are acting differently."

"Hector is making progress unraveling my situation, but it's going slower than we anticipated." I thought that by revealing to Ernesto that Nieves had visited Hector, Ernesto might know that I suspect him so I chose to leave that out for now.

"It is important that the thirty minutes in the yard does not lead to any violence or trouble." I was past thinking that Ernesto was an innocent bystander or on the periphery. I decided to keep my enemies close.

While the Follamento gift was a small part of my workload, Franny noticed that it was taking more and more time. The workload escalated even more when the possibility of the gift became public knowledge.

After Nancy and I spoke, she was overtaken with a terrible fear that she would be seen as an accomplice to the University's actions if the gift became public, because she knew about the gift so far in advance and would have been on the maiden voyage to Follamento. Without letting me or anyone in our leadership group know, the day after we spoke she organized a conference call among the committee members to fill them in on the gift and the visit.

The committee's reaction was as expected, though probably a few degrees more negative than I would have predicted. She told me in a call that words such as "ridiculous, un-academic, crazy, counter-productive, and dispiriting" had been used and the general theme was that the "corporate" leadership was really after the money and not in the least interested in the faculty's ongoing consideration of the best global approach for Olmsted.

I said in response, "Turning down the gift is an option but I think it would be irresponsible on our part to say no without any investigation."

She was not so sure about that. According to Nancy, "During the conference call, the negativity and accusations of the corporate university were so loud that the committee had a serious discussion about boycotting the upcoming trip. The committee concluded that the mere consideration of the gift confirmed their suspicions that its work will not be taken seriously. When it was obvious that the committee was divided on the idea of the boycott, several members declared themselves unwilling to travel with the leadership group, but all three names you suggested, Professors Alvarez, Christ, and Frost, said that it made sense to assess the gift with objectivity before a decision could be made." It was at this point that Nancy told the committee that if the gift survived the initial visit, she would lobby hard for a larger faculty visit early in the upcoming semester. Her position made her very uncomfortable.

Nancy's phone call to me came right after the student newspaper, the *Olmsted Oracle*, ran a story on its website that announced the gift. Nancy knew that the leak probably came from a disenchanted committee member and wanted me to know that she had asked for confidentiality.

The article got some things right and some wrong, typical of the student newspaper when it is based on hearsay without the availability of a university press release. What was right was that it involved a study-abroad site in Tuscany that would be open to undergraduates, but what was wrong was that it was a done deal. The good news was that Nancy never revealed the donor's or the town's names, and thus it was speculative and, without the actual facts, so damage with Lorenzo probably would be minor. Without a name for the donor or town there was less of a chance that it would be picked up by the mainstream media. The more positive result was that the student newspaper ran a short editorial suggesting that if the gift could jump start Olmsted's lagging global program, it would be a good thing. I called Lorenzo immediately and let him know that the process of selecting faculty for the visit had led to an article by the student newspaper that revealed some features of the gift, but that no names were known or used. I gave him the link and also the link to the editorial.

As soon as the article came out I met with Gabe to go over our response. He was angry that he did not have a chance to present the issue in the first place, and after blowing off some steam he, too, realized that without details about the gift, that the damage was small. Gabe asked me, "Can I contact the newspaper leadership to let them know that the gift was not yet reviewed and that such an assessment would need to precede any decision on whether to accept the gift?"

I agreed, and he had a good meeting with the students, who changed the language on the website.

The article did generate a call from the chair of the Italian department, Angela LoPresti. I essentially repeated what was correct in the article and indicated that if our initial trip in August gave us a green light, then we and the faculty committee would organize a subsequent faculty visit and she would be included. She was clearly excited as Italian was a small, though fairly distinguished, department, and said, "I trust that everyone there will need to take Italian."

"That is my expectation as well."

She probed about the location and I told her that I would let the faculty know more by early September.

Angela joined most of the groups that railed about the corporate university but one-on-one was fair and open-minded. Her scholarship on women's roles in modern Italian literature was well-respected in the U.S. and in Italy. She concluded by saying, "Italy has so many great cities. I am looking forward to finding out which one it is." I doubted that Follamento was on her short list.

Meanwhile, more quickly than I thought, Cathy selected a firm to represent us in Italy. Pressman and Richardson was a medium-sized multinational firm with offices in New York, London, Shanghai, and Rome. The firm had done some work for the University involving bequests and had four lawyers based in Rome. A partner, Luigi Prevalento, had a second home in Siena, about forty kilometers from Follamento, and he had walked through the town a few times, but had not known its history and ownership. The firm immediately began its background research.

At his request, I met with Ed McDonald, the University CFO. He was still put off by being excluded from the August trip, and that fed into his normal worries that this would become a gift that keeps on taking. He visualized a run-down town needing maintenance, more than the income from the endowment, and the several hundred citizens of Follamento who were employees and counted on their jobs for their livelihood, and presto you have a money-losing study-abroad program. I was unsure whether his recent miss on the budget forecast fed into his negativity.

"That will not happen."

He wasn't even mildly reassured. I am not sure I was either, and he reminded me that we had taken other gifts that cost us well in excess of the required funding and often involves a donor's pet project, one that the University would not have done without the gift. We continue to fund an Institute for the Study of Network Television, which is dedicated to a disappearing industry. The conditions of the gift led to the hiring of four tenured faculty, when one would be sufficient today.

The jokes about ISNT never end. But despite not being aligned with the University's priorities, these gifts sometimes added to prestige and endowment totals and we did not say no. His worry was not without merit. "You will have full access to develop a financial forecast. You should partner with Drew MacCaffey to assess the infrastructure and its condition." MacCaffey is our vice president for real estate.

Every time I saw Laura, she treated me as if the absence of development involvement in the Follamento gift was my idea. "All donors need to be serviced," she said, "and my office is best equipped to do this."

"If a servicing role emerges you will be the first to know but right now servicing Lorenzo means acceding to his wish to have no development people near him."

Laura was neither convinced nor feeling any better after she spoke with me. I wonder to this day whether she might have spotted things that I initially missed.

Meanwhile, Nancy was almost totally paralyzed by the cross-currents and personalities that would argue for or against each of the three faculty members she was considering for the trip. David Crist, the real estate expert, was lobbying the hardest to be included. He thought that everything was a real estate deal and he wasn't too far off on this one. Edward Frost was probably the most cosmopolitan of the three and though his expertise was not closely tied to Italy, he was a long-term advocate for rapidly ramping up Olmsted's global portfolio. Paula Alvarez was the most outspoken of the three and an ardent supporter of increasing Olmsted's global programs. But it was her outspokenness that scared Nancy and she feared that Paula's view would drown out her own. Every time Nancy called me, she went on a tirade about the three faculty members and then asked for more time to choose one.

Day 34

Yesterday's half-hour in the yard felt like three hours. Very little was said and very few people did anything other than eye the opposing family members. Ernesto said afterward, "Both sides want a deal but we still have a lot of the business. We will bide our time."

I was pleased that there was tension because that could delay the restarting of my "minor" role. Ernesto thought that if the yard dynamics could calm down over the next two to three days then by Wednesday or Thursday, deliveries could begin. I hoped that it would take longer.

Ernesto started to ask me more questions about my past in his own Columbo-like way. "Do people from your university come to Panama often? What kind of business do they do?" These questions seemed strange and may have had a purpose, but when you spend this much time with another person you naturally get curious. Up until now I was too nervous to ask him similar questions but despite my new view of him, he was friendly and was taking care of me in a way.

In the yard yesterday, I asked Ernesto, "What do most Panamanians think of Americans and the United States?"

"It is two-sided. The overriding feeling is one of oppressor, given its actions in Panama and the delay in turning over the Canal. But many middle and upper class Panamanians benefit greatly from America and this reduces the overall negative feelings. Both rich and poor Panamanians have American friends so that the bad feelings are more towards the country, not personal."

After many conversations, Nancy finally chose the second faculty member in the utmost academic way; she traded favors. As she was about to make her choice and probably go with Edward, she learned that her nephew had applied to the Master's program in Public Health and was on a wait list for September. I would have loved to be a fly on the wall as Nancy and Paula made their deal, Paula goes on the trip and the nephew gets into the MPH program. Nancy told me that Edward and David, though disappointed, were assured that they would be prime candidates for the second trip.

About two weeks before the visit, the details were shaping up. Charles said, "We'll fly over to Florence during the day of August 15th and spend the night in Florence. We then drive to Follamento late morning on the 16th and the visit will be August 17th, 18th and 19th. On the 20th we will drive up to Florence and fly to New York around 11 a.m."

I felt good about the full group of seven -- Charles, Melissa, Marshall, Cathy, and me, plus Nancy and Paula. In suggesting a format for the meeting, I asked Melissa and Charles, "Do you want separate meetings with Lorenzo or Angelo at any time on the trip? What do you think about having the two faculty members present at all the meetings?"

They both asked, "What do you think?"

"As this is a fact-finding trip, not a time to negotiate, we would gain a lot of credibility by having the faculty members at all the meetings. Holding any separate meetings will arouse suspicion."

Melissa readily agreed while Charles gave all the reasons why it could create problems before agreeing.

Charles asked me to come down to his office about ten days before the trip to talk through the Angelo issues. Actually, once I got to his office, I realized that "talking through" was more "listening to" and Charles listed the many ways that Angelo could screw up the gift. He concluded by saying, "As much as Angelo is a potential thorn in our side, I'm reluctant to give him much." Charles is an enormously successful investment advisor, and is smart and knows it. Often an idea is not good unless it is his own. My normal approach in this spot would have been to say that because in Italy, appearances are paramount, we could give Angelo a position that appears to be high level, but which is not all that critical in reality. But with Charles, if I laid that it out, the danger was that it would be my idea, not his. As silly as this sounds, I needed to get Charles to suggest my plan, without me saying it.

I started by asking, "Is there a way for us to have our cake and eat it too?" hoping that my idea was so obvious that he would come up with it.

He said almost dismissively, "Giving a little will be an invitation to give more and it will be a constant struggle to rein him in."

"Maybe we give what seems to him to be a lot but is actually not much to us."

At this point he asked, "What exactly does he do? I thought he knew but maybe not.

"I have only the outlines, but I think he is the equivalent of the CEO of the town businesses, and given that his father owned the town, he is also the equivalent of the mayor or city manager for municipal services."

Then you could see that the light went on. Charles asked, "What if he keeps those roles, and he reports to a trio, Melissa or Marshall, you, and Lorenzo?"

"As long as we can be clear that all of the academic activities are excluded from his purview, then this is a plan we can work with." I smiled on the inside though I feared I might become Angelo's babysitter.

The results of Stephanie's internet research were coming in dribs and drabs, with surprisingly little new and consequential, or so I thought at the time. Follamento had a wine festival the first full weekend in November. Also, Roberto Follamento was active in various causes such as cancer research, local theaters, and Etruscan archeological sites, and in general he steered clear of Italian politics. He gave smallish to medium-sized gifts to many organizations rather than focusing on a few with larger gifts, and as a result the internet was full of organizations that honored him with a dinner or a faux award of some sort.

Stephanie also discovered that Roberto had a significant art collection, mostly contemporary work, and we learned later that it all went to Angelo. Occasionally Roberto was on the internet in a photo with a gallery owner. I asked Stephanie to keep digging.

Day 35

I have been thinking about Franny and our kids constantly these past five weeks. Five weeks! I should have taken a few photos of them out of my wallet but who knew? If someone had told me immediately after I was picked up at the hotel that I would be held in prison for five weeks, I would never have believed it. This time in prison makes everything that happened with Olmsted so trivial.

When I was taken from the cell this morning, I thought for sure it was good news. Unfortunately my five week anniversary present was more bad news. Hector was not looking happy. "My reliable, effective, savvy private investigator showed up in my office first thing this morning and told me that he is off the case. He found someone at Guzman and Quintero who agreed to meet with him in a local bar, and when he arrived three men greeted him and told him that his well-being was in jeopardy if he kept asking questions about you. More important, he was told that there is nothing that he or I can do until it is decided by others that you can get out. They concluded by saying that another person poking around might not end the day in one piece."

Hector was extremely apologetic but I told him repeatedly that it was not his fault. Inside I was angry but saw no mileage in expressing it. "I thought my guy would not be intimidated by such threats. Maybe it was even more ominous than he described. At least it confirmed that Guzman and Quintero are pulling the strings, and now we can treat Ernesto as their representative. Don't let him know anything."

"If Ernesto asks about our meeting I will say that you were here because Franny was insisting on coming to visit and you wanted my permission to dissuade her," I said.

"Actually, that is not far from the truth. Franny keeps pressing me to visit and I have explained that her presence would add another opportunity for your enemies to get to you. She is always polite but she gets more riled up with each call. I almost expect her to show up uninvited. She asks a lot of good questions, most of which I cannot answer. Unless you say otherwise, I will continue to say no. I will try and return Friday, and I will speak with Archie between now and then. All of the pages you gave me are safe in the Embassy."

"Had I known you were coming today I would have brought more, including those I have hidden."

When I returned to the cell, Ernesto asked if I got any good news. I almost laughed but stayed with the story of Franny wanting to visit. Ernesto seemed to buy that and then he told me that at lunch he had learned that the commerce in the yard would be back on Thursday.

I emailed Lorenzo and asked him, "Should I email Angelo that we are looking forward to the visit?

Lorenzo responded, "A call is better than an email; it is less likely to be misunderstood and is more personal. Let me know how it goes."

When I called Angelo, he said, "I hope you remember the conversation we had in New York."

"I conveyed your thoughts to Olmsted's leadership, but this initial visit is predominantly fact-finding. The details of your issues will be addressed if this visit leads to a green light."

"Do you really think that the University would turn down such a gift?"

It was a bit of a trick question and I needed to answer carefully. "While the gift is extremely generous and exciting, it needs to meet a range of academic and financial criteria, and we must feel confident that it will not lead to unexpected costs or other controversial issues. The Olmsted team will be impressed with Follamento. You will enjoy meeting the group and vice versa."

He ended by saying, "I hope things work out."

I reported back to Lorenzo, probably after Angelo had already done so. Lorenzo said, "I hope you will find a way to deal with Angelo," but he did not offer any possible solutions.

A week before the trip I sent the itineraries and meeting schedule to Melissa and Charles. Charles called and said, "I'm concerned that Melissa and I will not be having a top-level introductory meeting with Lorenzo."

I explained again, "Having such a meeting will send a bad signal to the faculty and reinforce their biases about being excluded." He reluctantly backed off and okayed the schedule.

About four days before the trip, I sent it to the entire team and Nancy actually wrote back and asked, "Are there other meetings that are not on the itinerary?" I said, "No," and she said, "Good, I feel better."

Stephanie was now coordinating her internet search with the legal team and the lawyers in Rome. Without my asking, the legal team included Angelo in the search, and the only issue that came up was that about a year ago he was in the local papers for causing a scene in a restaurant in Montalcino when he showed up without a reservation, was not seated as the restaurant was full, and the local police had to be called. All in all, it was quite amazing that with Roberto's and Angelo's wealth, they managed to keep negative postings to one small matter.

On the morning of the 15th, we took a car service out to Teterboro airport and the university contingent got a glimpse at how the one tenth of the one percenters live. Sit in a waiting room for five minutes while security folks glance at the passports, get on the plane and go. Once we took off, Charles spoke briefly about his private plane, then about the trip. This was the first and only time that I saw him wearing jeans. I zoned out on all of the details on the jet, except that it was bigger, could fly farther, and was more expensive, than planes owned by other board members. He was very positive about Follamento, and a few times I cringed as he came close to giving the impression that accepting the gift was a no-brainer. But he generally walked back from that and asked us all to keep a sharp lookout for things that could make us say no. He concluded by saying, "No matter what we find, the next few days should be enjoyable, even though Tuscany is in the midst of a Europe-wide heat wave." .

Day 36

I owed Ernesto for the call, but at this point haven't I paid him back? I am worried that my luck is running out. I know that Franny's advice would have been not to do his bidding in the first place. Am I still the credible administrator at Olmsted or the shady prisoner in La Joya? Where do I put this on my resume?

My dread prompted me to push Ernesto a little at breakfast "I learned on Monday that I may be getting out soon, so can I sit out when business resumes?" I thought it could not hurt to ask but I was wrong, very wrong.

Ernesto freaked out and if he could have he would have pummeled me. He was totally silent as we went back to the cell and then he paced around, speaking at times quietly, and then shouting, "You do not understand what I have done for you! Your request is a betrayal and disloyal." Finally after Ernesto burnt off some steam, I went into faux-apology mode. "I should not have asked. Tomorrow I will do as you direct." That calmed him down a little but the damage was done.

We landed in Florence about 11 p.m. and went straight to the hotel. The group had bonded on the plane and that continued over breakfast where Melissa diplomatically said, "This is a unique and important potential gift for Olmsted but we should not accept if it is not right for us."

Charles was more pro-gift. "This gift's potential is transformative, and we can mitigate most of the negatives."

I could see that his comments made Nancy and Paula uneasy, and Paula asked Charles, "Have you made up your mind?"

I held my breath.

"Though it can be a transformative gift, I would not accept it if in the end there are significant negatives that cannot be compensated by the positives."

At least he didn't say that his mind was made up. Faculty often approach decisions such as this with specific knock-out factors that cannot be overcome by any positives. In this case a legitimate knock-out factor would be the absence of faculty control of the academics.

After breakfast we drove the ninety minutes or so to Follamento. The Hotel Buona Notte was modest but comfortable, and after we ate a light lunch, everyone had the afternoon free to deal with the sweltering heat and jet lag, and leisurely wander around. By late afternoon, the entire delegation was at a table in the piazza outside the Osteria Buona Fortuna sharing wine and cheese.

At dinner, Melissa went around the room and asked about first impressions. In different ways, everyone said they thought that students and faculty could flourish here. They saw from our van ride that Florence was within easy reach, as is Rome, Bologna, Venice and even Milan at a five hour drive.

The next morning, the Olmsted folks arrived in the hotel conference room right at 10:30 for our meeting with Lorenzo. He strolled in at 10:40 a.m., on-time in Italy, wearing a perfectly fitting gray suit with a vivid lavender tie and white shirt. He turned up the charm factor to the max. "I know that this will be a complex and difficult decision for Olmsted, and I want to provide as much information as I possibly can," he said. "Roberto Follamento was an unusual man who made a unique gift." Just then, Angelo walked into the conference room and took a seat along the wall, with everyone else at the table. Lorenzo looked non-plussed only for a second, regained his cool, and said, "Ladies and gentleman, I want you to meet Angelo Follamento, Roberto's son." He played it beautifully, as though this was the plan all along.

"The motivation for Roberto's gift was his tremendous gratitude to Olmsted where he received a wonderful and enlightening education many years ago." Lorenzo continued. "Roberto sensed that while the residents of Follamento benefit enormously from the operation of the town and its businesses, a gift to a university could spread its effect to students and faculty over generations. Roberto hoped that Angelo would play a continuing role." This struck the right balance of acknowledging Angelo without dictating precisely how he was to be treated.

"Italian demographics, economics, and politics can be depressing at times. Young people tend to leave small towns like Follamento to study and work, and rarely return, setting up a vicious cycle of decline. Follamento is an exception with many young people returning after university, and the collective town spirit and the burgeoning tourist industry have kept the standard of living relatively high. Roberto knew that if an institution like Olmsted owned and oversaw Follamento, the operation would require support, and the 100-million euro endowment is designed to address that issue. Roberto desired Follamento to continue forever."

"As you get to know Follamento over the next few days, you should feel at home. Everyone in town knows the purpose of the visit and they have been asked to answer all questions fully and honestly." I wondered how much they had been prepped.

After coffee and cookies, just as we were moving into a different conference room for our planned meeting with Angelo, Cathy pulled me aside and asked, "What do you think about the 'in perpetuity' aspect of the gift?"

"Many gifts are thought to be forever but if you are getting at the issue of what happens if things change and we need to alter the arrangements, I agree that we may need a mechanism for that."

Day 37

At breakfast today, Ernesto said, "I will check out the yard this afternoon and give you the go-ahead if the new deal is on." His tone was cold and business-like, and I could not tell whether this was his anger at me versus his general anxiety.

Right after breakfast I was taken to the administrative area, and I thought it was Hector visiting a day early but it was Archie and Charles, the Olmsted board chair. Charles said, "You look and smell awful. You lost some weight and I assume there is a soap shortage."

Until that point, while I knew I smelled, so does everyone else, and I did not think about my appearance. "I'm surprised to see you." A surprise visit from Franny would have been wonderful, but I got a visit from Charles as a consolation prize.

Charles skipped asking me how I was doing. "I'm in Panama City on business to see clients and attorneys. I am concerned that your six weeks in this Panamanian prison will be bad for Olmsted."

Charles asked me point-blank, "Why are you in prison?" I was not going to level with Charles for fear that my suspicions about the reason could hurt me. I had discovered a problem in Follamento that I'd been sure I could solve by myself. Every move turned out wrong. But unloading all that information right now to Charles is not what I wanted to do.

"Some people with clout in Panama want me in jail, and I don't know why."

Before Charles could respond, Archie intervened. "On my recommendation, we've hired Hector Mendoza, and he is doing everything he can to get Bill released."

Charles said, "You were scheduled to meet with Guzman and Quintero. I know a couple of lawyers there and I met with them on my way here. They said they are doing what they can to gain your release."

Pure BS. My suspicions increased substantially. It was unlike Charles to accept such a response and not push them harder. Could Charles be complicit in some way? I thought back to Hector's question about whether someone at the University was involved.

Charles turned to Archie. "What exactly is the Embassy doing?"

Archie looked uncomfortable. "I filed a formal protest, but it has not been answered. As I explained, Hector is our best hope."

That was news to me.

"It doesn't appear that you and your colleagues are doing everything you can," Charles said.

Archie assured him, "We are doing everything we can."

"Then why isn't he out?"

Archie did not answer.

The guard signaled that the time was up. I asked Charles, "Please call Franny when you get back to New York and let my colleagues know I'm okay."

Charles did not ask if there was anything else he could do for me, nor did he convey that he cared. He said only that things were going well in Follamento without me. I wondered why he did not sign the Follamento papers I came here to sign.

I expected Angelo to work the room before our meeting with him. Instead, he moved to the new conference room by himself and sat at the head of the table.

Once we were all seated, Angelo was about to speak when Charles broke in and said, "We are pleased to meet with you. Your relationship with Olmsted will be very important if we accept the gift." It was a decent non-specific opening.

"Olmsted will completely ruin my life by accepting the terms of the gift," he answered angrily. "Before my father's unexpected death I was working on a different idea that would have placed me in a more central role." Everyone could sense that Angelo knew he was shooting at the wrong target, but the right target was dead. He ended by asking, "How would you feel if your father did this to you?"

There was a long silence that I felt I had to break. "Can you summarize what you would have changed in the will?"

Before Angelo began his answer, I got a super critical look from Charles that signaled I should have shut up.

Angelo said, "I am pleased that you asked that question. For more than twenty-five years, my father entrusted the operation of Follamento to me and maybe once or twice a year I would review the status of the town and its businesses with him. Everyone knew I was in charge. I handled the ancient buildings, the infrastructure, and the businesses, but really what I did was engage with the residents and ensure that they are living a good and productive life. I established a citizens' council that meets every two months and is attended by roughly 150 people who raise issues and offer new ideas. There is a core group of about twenty people who advised me more regularly and while there are no elections except my unopposed contest for mayor every two years, people feel that their voices can be heard. The academic program can be introduced without changing my role."

When Angelo finished, we all knew the ball was in Charles's court and he did not disappoint. "It was good that Bill asked the question." I smiled, as he continued. "We all appreciate your detailed answer. We are still very early in our fact finding but at this stage I hope there is a creative way to address your heartfelt concerns. In our preparation for this meeting, I talked about a role for you that recognized the importance of your leadership." I smiled again. "At the same time, it's important that you understand that we have not seen any of the formal legal language and we are here for these three days to determine if there is a match to be made among the Follamento family, the town of Follamento and Olmsted."

Lorenzo entered the room. He had a file folder in his hands that he placed on the table as he sat down.

Angelo said, "Thank you, Charles, for the thoughtful answer and while the visit has just started, I am encouraged."

I was pleased that the temperature was reduced significantly and Angelo hadn't formally threatened legal action, though everyone in the room knew that this was his nuclear option.

Melissa spoke for the first time. "I agree with Charles that we are at the earliest of stages but it is clear how much expertise you have and if the University accepts the gift, we will be better off if we can take advantage of that."

When it was apparent that no one else was going to speak, Lorenzo said, "I am pleased this issue has been raised so openly and early in the visit." Coincidentally, or maybe not, he said, "I have here copies of the part of the will that pertains to Olmsted," and he passed the folder down the table to Charles.

Several in the Olmsted delegation asked Angelo and Lorenzo questions such has the population of Follamento (about 650), the schools (Follamento has schools through grade 8 and then the students go to Siena for high school), the legal status of the town (a legal commune, with elections for Angelo as the mayor every two years), where people work (about 120 residents work in Follamento while another 160 adults work in the surrounding area), and health care options (two physicians and a dentist in town and a hospital in Siena).

After the questions and answers the Olmsted group went to lunch at the hotel before our tour. Both Angelo and Lorenzo led us in a leisurely three-hour walk around town.

All of the locals were primed to see us and it was obvious that they had been prepped. In every shop one or more people spoke serviceable English. Everyone explained how well they were doing (no one was doing badly) and how their businesses were changing due to increased tourism and online sales. We sampled the gelato at the alimentary and we then walked on the outside streets, ending at the osteria for a glass of wine. The key piece of new knowledge for me was that there were about 250 apartments in the various buildings in town, and that about sixty were vacant, which could house students, faculty and staff.

As we broke for dinner, Charles gave each of us a copy of the will.

Day 38

When we arrived in the yard today, I spotted Mr. Nieves. I assumed that Ernesto observed or even knew ahead of time about this, yet he went ahead with his pick-ups. I did not want to appear to be watching him, but I was.

After he completed his three marks, I expected him to walk over to me to let me know it was my turn. Instead, he walked in the other direction and some fifteen seconds later the whistles blew and the guards announced that we were to head back to our cells. As I was headed to the line, two marks sought me out and gave me the cigarettes. At the doorway, Mr. Nieves was picking people out to stay back in the yard, and I could see Ernesto and his three marks in that group. I had about twenty seconds to decide whether to drop the cigarettes, which someone could spot, or hold on to them. I held them and was as scared as I have ever been. I got to the head of the line where Mr. Nieves made eye contact, but did not select me.

I got back to our cell shaken. Ernesto returned after about an hour, and signaled that he would explain over dinner. In the cafeteria he said, "The round-up was organized by the guards themselves, as a way to let both families know that the business can resume only with their permission. You should have known it was okay when you saw Nieves." I told Ernesto about the two marks who gave me the cigarettes and he said that was a bonus.

In my meeting with Hector this morning, there was a sliver of good news, although it didn't take much now to qualify as good news. Despite the threats and intimidation, Hector continued to use his sources to try to find out what it would take to get me out. All the signs still pointed to Guzman and Quintero. Given their involvement with Ernesto's family, Hector thought that they needed to be careful. Actual participation in the drug business could be bad for their international business, which probably generated most of their income. Also, Archie had a colleague, probably a spy, who represented the U.S. Commerce Department and was a link to the Panamanian business community. He had helped Guzman and Quintero with several regulatory issues in the United States, and Archie had asked this Embassy person to inquire. Initially, Guzman and Quintero claimed no knowledge of my case, but when Archie's colleague pressed, he was told that there might be some movement soon.

"Can you do me a favor?" I asked. "Please contact my assistant, Stephanie, and ask her to see if she can find anything from the SEC investigation of Charles several years back. I'd like to know whether Guzman and Quintero or any other Panamanian Law firms were involved." Maybe I was grasping at straws, but his visit was gnawing at me.

In the hour before dinner, I assumed that everyone, like me, read the ten pages of the English version of Roberto's will pertaining to Olmsted. As Lorenzo had explained, all of the land, other assets such as bank accounts, minor liabilities, and buildings that were incorporated as Follamento would go to Olmsted in the form of a stock transfer of all the shares of Follamento Corporation. Though I thought it was insignificant at the time, Follamento Corporation is incorporated in Panama. The will indicated that the Panamanian law firm that handles the corporate structure of Follamento is Guzman and Quintero in Panama City. The Corporation, the town, and Olmsted have to abide by both Italian and U.S. laws. The 100 million euros, an asset of the estate, not the town, will go to Olmsted as an endowment to be held in the Bank of Italia, NY, where it currently resided, with the investment strategy of the endowment to be approved by two people, one appointed by Olmsted and one appointed by Lorenzo or his successor. Five percent of the endowment is to be used for the upkeep and improvement of Follamento, to support the businesses and town operations, and for financial aid for Olmsted students. There is a second endowment of 50 million euros, set up as an insurance fund, to handle any claims against the Follamento Corporation.

In perpetuity Follamento is to continue to operate as a Tuscan town and Olmsted is to establish a study-abroad site. All students must work in the town offices or businesses at least twenty hours per week and they will be paid minimum wage at New York rates. All students not fluent in Italian will take Italian as one of his or her courses. Olmsted will be given full authority over Follamento Corporation, and will nominate one person to serve as mayor every two years and presumably run unopposed. It was not clear what would happen if someone else is nominated. A paragraph in the will stated that Angelo's role would be specified by Olmsted, but that his expertise and knowledge would be a great benefit.

All of these conditions were spelled out in language that included ample description of the grandness of this bequest and the broad benefits to Olmsted. Roberto described the importance of Olmsted's adherence to the will, including its feature of in perpetuity. In the rare circumstance of a need to change Follamento's broad structure or operations, or both, the same two-person committee that specified the investment strategies would need to approve the change, unanimously. Roberto stated that no changes should be required for many decades.

I was unsure why Angelo signed this, though it is impossible to know what his options were at the time. I assume that the non-Olmsted part of the estate, most of which went to him and was described by Lorenzo as substantial, was an effective incentive.

At the reception before dinner, Cathy made a bee-line to Charles. He must have known this was going to happen and cut her off, saying, "We can all meet back at the hotel after dinner." Cathy was not satisfied and kept at Charles until he said, "You are not doing your cause any good," and she backed off.

On the way to the dinner table Charles sought me out. He said, "Roberto was pretty clever to use Panama as a way to try to avoid Italian taxes. I wished I could have met him." Charles' familiarity with Panama did not resonate with me at the time.

Dinner was surprisingly convivial. Marshall initiated a table-wide conversation where everyone brainstormed about what it would be like to be a student for a semester at Follamento. The conversation felt like it was a snowball, gaining momentum, with each person trying to outdo the previous one. By the end of this part of the conversation, half the students would meet his or her soulmate, and the other half would discover Italian art, European history, or religion. I figured that Marshall was a go. The only minor downer was Angelo, who made a short speech in which he told us to check our conceptions of American efficiency at the door. As I expected, Lorenzo and Charles each tried to prove that he was worldlier than the other. Lorenzo was understated and Charles was overstated, so it was fun to watch. Eventually Cathy warmed up and everyone had a chance to say how wonderful a study-abroad site could be.

As we were breaking after the desert, coffee and grappa, Charles asked that we meet briefly at the hotel. Once we gathered, he was smart to turn to Cathy first, who said, "This is unworkable. I foresee dozens of issues being deadlocked with the two-person committee. Italian or European laws can change which will affect the academic program."

Charles asked for an example and Cathy said, "Part time work could be restricted to no more than twelve hours a week, making us out of compliance with the will."

Charles rolled his eyes and said, "The committee of two, the duo, could adjust."

"What if they do not?"

"We must be in compliance with Italian laws so they would have no choice."

"What if an insurgent candidate ran for mayor?"

"We can worry about that if it happens. To me, the deal we strike with Angelo is the key, as the University may not want the gift if it would involve years of litigation. If we can strike a deal with Angelo, it must include a clause that he cannot sue."

Finally, Cathy asked Charles, "Why Panama?"

"Panama can be a tax haven and I assume Roberto did his homework and saved Italian taxes. Once we gain control, we can reincorporate in either Italy of the United States, assuming there is not a huge tax bill."

Cathy did not look convinced.

Day 39

Just as I was getting ready to sit down to write this morning, I was told I had a visitor and escorted into a conference room where Hector was waiting. I could tell right away that it was not good news.

"The Embassy person called me late last night and said that he needed to talk. I met him in a downtown hotel, and he explained that he was being sent to Brazil the next day. He was not too forthcoming even though I pressed him to see if the sudden assignment was related to his inquiries with Guzman and Quintero. After some prodding he said, 'It can't be entirely ruled out. I do not know how long I will be gone but I know that contacting Guzman and Quintero while I am away is out of the question."

'This means I will get out when they want me to get out."

"That's an exaggeration. But I did not want you to go through the week with false hope."

"False hope is better than no hope."

"I will be back on Friday. I have another angle but it's better if I do not tell you until I know more."

Today's pick-up in the yard was like it was before the family sharing plan started, except for my interaction with Mr. Nieves. After I did the three pick-ups, he walked up to me and shook his head disapprovingly.

When we got back to our cell, Ernesto said, "To everyone in the yard, it looked like you were feeding information to Nieves. Your safety could be in jeopardy."

"He approached me."

"That does not matter. I will check in with my uncle in case there is some kind of target on your back. The next time Nieves approaches, walk away."

I don't think the family sharing plan is going as expected.

135

Late this morning Ernesto was escorted from the cell and returned just before lunch in a better mood. He volunteered that his wife and daughter visited and it made him very happy. They were with the family attorney, which Ernesto thought was strange.

"It is funny how seeing them was great, but now I miss them more. I wish they had come alone."

When I asked why, he said that it was just a feeling. Or was it a message?

On the second full day of our visit to Follamento, I woke up with a queasy feeling. Perhaps it was just another case of when something is too good to be true, it is not true. Then, just as suddenly as it came, it disappeared over breakfast with the delegation as I finished my cappuccino. I had not thought again about that feeling until I was writing today, but it was a premonition, for sure.

The plan was to tour three notable Tuscan towns within forty kilometers of Follamento, Montalcino, Pienza, and Siena, each beautiful, different and charming. Lorenzo was our guide. After a walk-round Montalcino, we had lunch at Trattoria Latte di Luna in Pienza where we sat at a large table and ate some of the terrific local pasta, called pici, with wild boar sauce. We drank Vino Nobile, the red wine from Montepulciano, which with my unrefined wine palette I thought was equal to Brunello. We then drove back toward Follamento and up the SS2 to Siena through amazing landscapes which took us about an hour and fifteen minutes. Siena is much larger than either Pienza or Montalcino and is charming, with its retail shops of all kinds and the breath-taking, fan-shaped Piazza Del Campo. After we visited the grand Duomo which was a respite from the heat, Lorenzo herded us back to the van in plenty of time for the dinner that Charles was hosting at the Osteria Buona Fortuna.

The dinner was very convivial. After Charles made introductory comments. Melissa followed, "If Olmsted accepts the gift, then Follamento will be a centerpiece for our global initiatives."

Marshall added, "The total immersion into a functioning community will give students and faculty a perspective they would not have in a large city such as Florence and we are in fact close enough to access Florence's rich culture."

Nancy said, "Being here for a few days is the only way to accurately get a sense of Follamento's amazing potential as a study-abroad site."

Paula added, "Nancy's point highlights the importance of a faculty visit in early September."

I was almost afraid that the comments were too effusive. But Lorenzo was beaming and even some of Angelo's edge appeared to come off.

On the last full day in Follamento, we had lunch in the pizzeria and while it did not mean anything to me at the time, I saw an unusually large number of large pizza boxes being taken out.

Charles suggested that we gather in the hotel meeting room at 4:30 p.m. He began by passing out index cards and said, "Each of you should put a number on the card from one to ten that represents your initial personal assessment, not an institutional one, based solely on the visit, knowing we have incomplete information, with one being a definite no and ten being a definite yes. I recognize that a decision is premature, but I want a sense of the people in the group, without names on the cards." Across the table I could see Nancy begin to object to such a crude approach, but she did not say anything. I put down a nine, which would have been a ten except for Angelo. Charles collected the cards and reported the results, a seven, two eights, three nines and one ten. He said, "I am pleased that regardless of what we do as a university, seven people with very different perspectives thought so highly of the possible gift, which means we really need to make sure we are not overlooking anything."

The full Olmsted Board would meet next in early September and Charles thought that Melissa and Marshall should present the possible gift. I was pleased that Charles, though in the lead on the visit, understood that this needed to come from Melissa as President. Marshall, to his credit, asked Charles if Nancy and Paula could attend the Board meeting. As soon as the words were out of his mouth, he realized that he should have asked the question privately, but it was out and to Charles's credit he said of course with no hesitation. Everyone agreed that Cathy should begin discussions with Lorenzo using the outside law firm and that Ed should gain a solid understanding of the finances. Charles could not resist saying that we need to double check Ed's budget estimates. Drew MacCaffey, Olmsted's real estate person, needed to come over and assess the infrastructure with Ed. Nancy and Paula reiterated that a faculty visit in September was essential and everyone agreed. I pointed out that the Italian department should be represented on that visit even though they did not have a person on the faculty global committee and no one objected. Marshall asked, maybe rhetorically, "While the AUC has no formal role, perhaps the leader of the student government and a leader of the administrator's group should also be on the September faculty trip."

At that point Charles said, "I don't want to put a damper on such a productive and positive discussion, but we must address the Angelo issues."

"We need to create an arrangement for Angelo where he can continue to be involved with the non-academic part of Follamento."

Melissa said, "Bill should continue to be on point and maybe he can talk with Angelo this evening."

"I will arrange to sit next to Angelo and will explore his feelings about the 'town manager' role with the condition that there would be accountability to the University."

Nancy then said, "We need to keep all this confidential until we can brief the faculty committee. I am much more positive than I was before the visit, but faculty care deeply about controlling the global agenda for Olmsted and they are capable of saying no simply because it is a university-driven action."

Paula said, "I agree 100 percent with Nancy." We then broke to get ready for the community dinner. On the way out, Nancy said to me privately, "This is more exciting than sparring with you over retirement policies."

Day 40

Ernesto's uncle shoos me away at almost every meal. I continue to ricochet back and forth between thinking that my situation is totally controlled by Guzman and Quintero through Ernesto and the family to a more benign scenario in which Ernesto and the family are taking advantage of an American who needed a favor. Ernesto keeps shaking his head about his family's visit. At one point he wondered out loud whether he should move out of Panama City with his family, though he said that was not really an option.

Before we went to dinner, which would involve the whole Follamento community, Charles pulled me aside and gave me one of his glib pieces of advice. "Keep Angelo interested and happy and don't give him any specifics."

There were about thirty long tables, each seating about twenty people, and our delegation was split up and spread among them. I do not know how the restaurant did it but they served about 600 people efficiently with an antipasto, a pasta dish, fried chicken with grilled vegetables, and a chocolate mousse for desert. The wines were a local Montalcino red and a San Gimignano white, and we ended with grappa and espresso. The English spoken by the folks at our table was impressive, though there were stretches when I got only the gist.

The townspeople knew why we were here and many came up to me during the evening and said that they hoped that Olmsted will accept the gift. It was clearly programmed, but nice nonetheless. Angelo called out everyone in the delegation, thanked us for taking the time to learn about Follamento, and said, "I think that the three days could not have gone better."

After coffee I asked Angelo, "Would you like to take a walk?" Though it was late, it felt like it was still around eighty degrees.

He asked, "Do you think that Olmsted will accept the gift?"

"There is a lot of work yet to do, but the odds are increasing. We want to keep you in an important role."

"Will Olmsted change the legal structure in the will?"

"That is a question for the future, but I do not think it's required for Olmsted to reach an agreement with you."

He quickly realized that he was getting ahead of himself and said, "If we agree to my role I am sure we can structure a separate agreement. Besides, the University will not be as tough as my father." We both laughed and he gave me a hug before we parted.

Charles was waiting for me in the hotel lobby. "How did it go?"

"Angelo was anxious about his role and I told him that I thought we could work something out. He said working for the University will not be as tough as working for his father."

Charles shifted gears and asked, "How will the faculty react to the gift?"

"We need to let Nancy and Paula be our emissaries and salespeople. We should emphasize that faculty input is essential and we are seeking their input early in the process."

Charles said, "No way."

"That is exactly what can kill it, if the faculty thought the Board has made up its mind."

"It's your job, with Melissa and Marshall to get to yes." Then he hesitated and said with a smirk, "If we want to accept it."

Everyone on the plane home was exhausted and only a little business was done. I asked Marshall, "Are you okay with me taking the lead?"

"I'm more than okay and it will be good if the gift is accepted, but we should not spend any capital to get the faculty approvals. I cannot believe the subservient role that Charles made Melissa play."

I spent the most time with Nancy and Paula. They were clearly anxious about the faculty reaction. That led them to plan a conference call with the committee right after we returned, even though it was late August.

Cathy was agitated, in part because Charles had told her to move quickly and in part because she felt we had little bargaining room. She asked, "What is your take on Angelo?"

"I think he could be a town-manager with significant oversight by the University."

"I don't like or trust Angelo, and the agreement must be crafted carefully. Charles became even more positive after he read the will and I wonder if he's being influenced by something we don't see."

I spent time with Melissa. She said, "Charles showed a side of him that I had not seen," then corrected herself by saying, "It was a side I have seen but never this overbearing."

"Do you think Charles will overrule you if you have good reasons for saying no?"

"I hope not."

Just before we landed at Teterboro, within earshot of Melissa, Charles said, "Bill, please keep me up-to-date on our progress on the due diligence." I caught Melissa rolling her eyes.

Charles went off in his car and we all went back to Manhattan in a university van.

Day 41

Forty-one days with filth, fear and uncertainty and no real hope of release is getting to me. This morning I woke up thinking that I'm not doing enough to gain my release. I'm beholden to Ernesto, I'm dirty and smelly, and I cannot believe someone else from Olmsted or my family is not visiting. I know Hector told Franny not to visit but she often does not listen to that kind of advice. I would not mind her or one or both of our kids spending some time assessing Hector, who is my only option. As I run through different scenarios in my mind I easily work myself into total despair. Maybe I should be more aggressive the next time Hector visits. Of course if I piss him off, I lose whatever lifeline I may have.

Yesterday's pick up was routine, which is scary in and of itself. The two old marks were easy, but the third wanted to engage. He was about twenty-five, of medium height, had short cropped hair and beard, and had many tattoos. He spoke reasonable English and wondered how an American could not get himself out of here. He said that he was a nurse and was caught stealing prescription drugs from the clinic where he worked and got six months as part of a plea bargain. He was working mornings in the infirmary and he only had a month to go. I thought of asking him about the risk of doing drugs with only one month to go, but I didn't want to prolong the conversation.

Before dinner yesterday, Ernesto said, "I have heard nothing about your release. I am pushing back on my uncle's demands to get you involved on the drug side of the business. I am not sure if I can resist much longer." All of this fed into my depression and my resolve to be pushier with Hector.

The biggest pre-Labor Day event on Follamento was the conference call with the faculty global committee. Nancy and Paula made it clear this was an unsolicited gift, they were treated as equals on the trip, and there were many strong academic dimensions which they explained in some depth over 30 minutes. Nancy and Paula then asked for questions and comments, and the first to speak was Drake Smithson, the Law School faculty member on the committee who was probably the most anti-global.

True to form, Drake began with, "This is a no-brainer. The University has not thought through its global agenda and thus this is the proverbial cart before the horse. Why go through all the work of setting a thoughtful approach when a gift like this ignores the faculty directions? Why would we go to the Tuscan countryside, when all the great cities of Italy, not to mention Europe, are available?" Earlier Paula noted that Florence was only ninety minutes away and Drake turned this around and said, "If Follamento is that close to Florence, why not base our program in Florence and visit Follamento, not the other way around? I would never permit my child to spend a semester in a place like Follamento."

Edward Frost spoke next. "I agree that Drake will not send his child anywhere because Olmsted has no global program. This gift is too early from the strictly process point of view, but given the unique features that Nancy and Paula described, especially immersion in a functioning Italian village, with an academic program totally designed by Olmsted faculty, near to Rome, Florence and even Venice, with an endowment that could make this affordable for all Olmsted students, I agree it is a no-brainer, but a no-brainer yes, not no."

Almost everyone on the call spoke after Drake and Ed, most with probing comments, the positive outweighing the negative by about two to one. At the end of the two hours, Nancy was savvy and said, "I do not want us to come to a conclusion on this call. A delegation of faculty with a student and administrator will be going to Follamento on September 6th. We'll have our next meeting on the 15th and I hope we can draw a preliminary conclusion on September 22nd."

Drake asked, "What's the rush?"

"If Olmsted delays, the lawyer for the estate may offer it to another university." I was surprised by this, and while it was somewhat true, we had no pressing sense from Lorenzo that he was going elsewhere that quickly.

After the conference call, Nancy called me back. "I know I overstepped in my comments of Lorenzo moving on but I do not want this debate to waste an entire semester."

"How will you select the three or four faculty from the committee for the trip? We will have a few who are not on the committee."

"I will get back to you. Should Drake be invited?"

"Yes, because he will likely be more positive after seeing it."

"I worry that he will influence others negatively but it may be worth the risk."

I cleared September 7th and 8th for the visit of faculty and 5th and 6th in Follamento for Ed, Cathy and Drew to pursue the financial, legal and infrastructure items. I got pushback on going over Labor Day from Franny but it was mild and subsided quickly. She knew that it was important for my work and maybe part of my legacy, but long weekends are usually ours.

Follamento had a bookkeeper/accountant, and an outside accounting firm in Florence, and they both worked closely with Angelo. Lorenzo volunteered to make them available. Cathy was annoyed that she had to spend time on this, but Ed and Drew were pleased to be going.

I spoke with Melissa and Marshall, separately, about the faculty visit and they delegated the choices of who to go totally to me. Surprisingly, Melissa voiced displeasure at the faculty involvement, even though she knew it was the right thing to do. She seemed a little off but maybe it was the travel.

I contacted the student government leader and the administrative council leader and they both spoke to me at length about the potential gift and how to select someone. In the end they named themselves for the trip, the prerogatives of leadership.

I thought six was the right number of faculty and I asked Nancy for four names. I told her that I would name two, including the head of the Italian Department, Angela LoPresti. Virtually everyone on the committee lobbied Nancy to be included and she was not happy to choose four out of fifteen. For continuity she decided that Paula should go a second time. The other three, were Drake, Edward, and Ellen Bowman, an anthropology professor. That left one for me to choose. David Crist, the real estate professor, sent me a long email making the case for his inclusion. After checking with Nancy, I invited him.

Before we left for Follamento, we needed to craft an announcement. The article on the student newspaper website over the summer did not garner much attention. But once the faculty trip occurred, word would be out. After hearing from Melissa and Charles, I thought we should make an announcement just after the trip, even though we wouldn't have made a decision yet.

When I spoke with Gabe and gave him the full contours of the gift and the evaluation process we were using, he agreed to contact Melissa and Marshall for quotes, but not to put any faculty on the spot. On the Saturday morning of Labor Day weekend, the day we were flying to Italy, I arranged a conference call with Lorenzo and Gabe. Lorenzo loved the idea and agreed to send Gabe quotes from him and Angelo. Even though he was in favor of the release, Charles did not want to be mentioned or quoted. Gabe agreed to send me a draft in Italy in a few days.

Just as I was heading to the airport, Cathy called. "We need to slow down."

"We will have plenty of time to talk on the trip."

Day 42

Hector came this morning. He started by saying, "We need to try a different approach. Convincing Guzman and Quintero to let you go is fruitless. I have a different angle though it is risky."

"I am willing to take some risk."

"Even though Guzman and Quintero put you in jail, they are not the only ones who can arrange your release," Hector said. "It is possible that with the right incentives, Ernesto's family can get you out."

"Ernesto's uncle is pressing to get me deeper into the business."

"That is all the more reason to use the family to get you released. Can you come up with ten to twenty thousand dollars?"

The question sent me into a brief spiral, harkening back to the three hundred dollars I gave to Officer Perez on day one, and I had this sinking feeling that Hector was setting me up. I just lost it and started to sob.

Hector was surprised and wanted to know what was wrong.

"What if you are just holding me up for the money and you are actually working for the family?"

I thought he would say screw you and walk out but he smiled and said, "You are under a lot of pressure. Is there a savvy person back in New York who can come to Panama? This person will see what I am doing and verify that I am not working for the other side. Also this person can disburse the money when the pieces are in place for your release." I was embarrassed that I had not thought of this and immediately I knew that Al would be the exact person.

Albert Johns had been the head of public security for Olmsted for a decade, and stepped down about two years ago. He was a former New York City police officer, rising to the rank of captain before he took the job at Olmsted. He had great contacts in the law enforcement community and he treated students as he would want his own kids treated.

On the spot, I asked Hector, "Please contact Al in New York. Franny will have his contact information and she can arrange the money. Please let Al know that I will pay all of his expenses plus a daily fee. Also, ask Al to contact David Goodman, the current head of security at Olmsted."

Hector agreed to contact Franny and try to come back Thursday or Friday. "By the way, I have not heard back from Stephanie on the question you asked regarding Panamanian law firms."

I flew to Rome the night of the Sunday, September 3rd and drove to Follamento. Edward and Drew were impressed with their initial look at the town and Cathy was annoyed that she had to come back so soon. She relaxed some after a terrific meal and red wine at Osteria Buona Fortuna. The Italian law partner, Luigi Prevalento, from Pressman and Richardson, Olmsted's outside law firm with an office in Rome, was scheduled to arrive that evening and the outside accounting firm partner was driving down from Florence the next day. Lorenzo would start the day tomorrow with Cathy and Luigi, and Angelo would meet with Ed and Drew. I thought it best to join Cathy and Lorenzo for a few minutes in the morning and then spend the day with Angelo, Ed and Drew and the financial folks.

Lorenzo was his most charming self, and it appeared that the legal group was working well together, even with Cathy in the mix. I joined Ed, Drew, Angelo and Stefano Contrato, the accounting partner from Florence, and Sabrina Marchetti, the Follamento bookkeeper and accountant. Stefano was about fifty and had worked on the Follamento account for a dozen years. Sabrina, who was about forty, was from Follamento, and received her undergraduate degree in fine arts and a Master's degree in business in Bologna. She wanted to be a painter but the senior bookkeeper/accountant position was too good to pass up.

Sabrina explained that while Follamento was owned by Roberto's estate, it was a formal town in Italy, in the commune of Montalcino,

Province of Siena and region of Tuscany. The revenues were similar to any Italian town with inflows from various levels of government and from taxes and fees, even though it had a single taxpayer, Roberto. Every month, Sabrina would send a revenue and expenditure report to Stefano and Angelo, and he would prepare an annual report at the end of each December. Both Sabrina and Stefano said that the town had about 350,000 euros in the bank as a reserve, and over the course of the year ran on a break even basis. The revenues and expenditures were about 6 million euros a year for the past three years. Stefano brought the last five years' annual reports to give to Ed and Drew.

Because all of the property was owned by Roberto, he was responsible for one hundred percent of the upkeep and maintenance, plus larger projects such as renovations. The Italian and Tuscan equivalent of "landmark" laws forbid the construction of any new buildings so modernization had to occur through architecturally sensitive renovations. Angelo approved all projects depending on financing and urgency.

The other large category of expenses related to the small businesses. While each shop manager tried to stay profitable, it was not possible. But in the aggregate, the shops did about 30 million euros of business a year and either broke even in total or ran a very small profit. Each shop manager kept a spreadsheet of daily revenues and expenditures, and Sabrina and her assistant reviewed them monthly.

The upshot of all of this was that Ed had a significant amount of financial documentation that he could review. Even by the end of the first day, I saw the relief on his face as he knew that with the 100 million euro endowment and the 50 million euro insurance fund, it could work financially.

Ed's day-end demeanor stood in stark contrast to Cathy's. When I met with her Tuesday evening over a glass of wine before dinner, she was fixated on several things. "After today I realize that there is no obvious way to extricate ourselves from Follamento if we want to. Also, I am very concerned about the two-person committee, which can easily result in organizational paralysis. In terms of Angelo, I do not know how we can create a role for him without usurping University decision making authority. Finally, I do not know how we can run the academic and non-academic sides of Follamento and stay within the confines of Italian law. Angelo and Lorenzo know so much about so many things and we know so little. This worries me." All these points were important, but all were, in my judgment, solvable, except the last and it was a prescient comment.

Day 43

Just when I thought my life was in total turmoil, things got worse. After Ernesto's heated talk with his uncle at breakfast, he summoned me back to the table and said, "This afternoon you need to tell your three marks that business will be suspended starting tomorrow. Do not tell them anything else. There will be a raid in the yard in the coming days. Our family will know about it and the other family will not. Things could get nasty."

In Follamento, I felt that the finances were on track. That left the legal issues so I decided to spend day two with Cathy, Lorenzo, Angelo, and Luigi.

It turned out to be the right move. Luigi gave us an opinion that with Lorenzo's and his advice on which laws to follow, Olmsted could stay within the confines of Italian and EU laws and adhere to U.S. laws. This made Cathy anxious. In Italy no one follows most of the laws. I thought that Cathy's head would fall off from shaking it so much.

We spent most of the rest of the day on Cathy's three other questions. In each case Cathy raised the issue and Lorenzo and Angelo said that the current provisions were all we needed to take care of it, with the exception of the issue of Olmsted's withdrawal from Follamento.

On the issue of the two person committee, Lorenzo said repeatedly, "The University's and our objectives largely align and it is important for both sides in any dispute to work out a compromise." Cathy tried to poke holes in this through examples and Lorenzo explained how it would work.

Cathy raised the issue of Angelo's role, and procedurally I thought that should have been done more privately. I was lucky to be present because I outlined a framework for Angelo's role, a kind of town manager reporting to the University, and Angelo and Lorenzo thought that was workable. Angelo said that he hoped he would report to me, and that did not do my cause any good with Cathy.

There was agreement by everyone that a pathway for Olmsted to extricate itself from Follamento was not in the will. Roberto Follamento thought that "in perpetuity" did not require an extrication provision and Lorenzo was not eager to accommodate our concern. Cathy said that there were all sorts of draconian but low odds events that could lead to Olmsted's withdrawal such as Italy ceasing to be a democracy or war breaking out or a severe world financial crisis. Lorenzo grudgingly accepted those scenarios as possible but very unlikely." Luigi stepped in and said that he would work with Cathy to come up with language for Lorenzo to review.

I had some time before the dinner with the administrators, faculty and the student, so I went back to the hotel to check emails.

The most important was a draft of a short press release from Gabe:

Olmsted University is pleased to announce that we are evaluating a bequest from an alumnus that involves property in Europe and an endowment that will support a study abroad site for students. The late donor's representatives are providing the University with extensive information and we will seek advice from the deans and the faculty global committee on whether this is right for Olmsted. We will consult more broadly with students and administrators and ultimately the University's leadership will make a recommendation to the Board who will make the final decision on whether to accept the gift. Additional information on the donor and the gift will be made available once the University completes its assessment and a decision is made by the Board.

In Gabe's email, he warned that this press release would create an avalanche of questions but he and I thought we could hold firm. I sent the draft press release to Melissa and Marshall, and after I heard from them I would share it with Cathy.

The van transporting the rest of the Olmsted contingent to Follamento from the Rome airport arrived in time for dinner at the hotel. During cocktails I checked in briefly with Ed and Drew and both were pleased with the progress they made. I asked both of them, "How do you know if the Follamento folks are giving us full and truthful information?"

Ed replied, "Neither of us saw anything amiss. There were extensive worksheets that would have taken weeks to fabricate. I'm going to be very careful."

I touched base with all six of the visiting faculty and the administrative and student representatives during dinner the next night. With the exception of Drake, who seemed to have his mind made up, all were either neutral or positive. Several commented that no paper or power-point presentation in New York compares with a two day visit. Even Drake conceded, "It appears to be more interesting than I thought it would be." Both the student and administrative representatives were effusive in their support.

I planned to stay in Follamento another day to meet with Angelo and Lorenzo and then fly home on Sunday from Rome. I was relieved that the visit had gone as well as it had. I was starting to blend acceptance of the gift with my own success, which while invigorating, could have affected my objectivity.

Day 44

This morning in the yard, I noticed some interactions occurring with the other family, while Ernesto and I cooled our heels. On Ernesto's instruction I told the original two marks that I would let them know when we would resume. They nodded and I disengaged. My third mark did not accept my explanation and followed me to ask questions. I told him, "I do not know why I was told to stop the pick-ups." I changed the ... "Do you know about the infections in the infirmary?"

... he said, "The rumor is true and two prisoners are at a local hospital but I think they will recover."

"Are you worried about your safety?"

"I'm taking appropriate precautions. But yes, I'm worried." Then he walked away.

On the plane home from Follamento, I resisted purchasing the internet and I had close to fifty messages when I landed. None needed an immediate answer, except that Charles, Melissa and even Marshall sent me multiple messages about my take on the visit. I wrote a quick, largely positive email to all of them during the ride to our apartment. Marshall thought that the press release was okay and he made a few small changes, but Melissa wanted to meet about it first thing the next day.

... t her request, I gave Melissa a detailed download on the trip and ... she wondered out loud, "Do we need any press release at all this ...int?"

"If there are no leaks, then we do not need a press release, but that ...s very unlikely. The web piece by the student newspaper over the summer was not good."

"Okay, work with Gabe and get it out."

Gabe and I got the release to the near final draft and though it was evening in Italy I sent it to Lorenzo. He wrote back with his okay. Cathy and Charles also signed off on it. An hour before we were to hit send, I sent it to Nancy who appreciated the heads up and offered no changes.

The two meetings of the faculty global committee were very contentious. At the first meeting on September 15th where I was present, before Nancy could even welcome the group, several faculty members voiced annoyance because they were being besieged by questions from colleagues as a result of the press release. Nancy said, "We should say the University is considering the gift," she said "asking our committee for advice, but that no more details can be revealed at this stage." Several faculty said that was ridiculous and we should be able to more details.

Nancy then asked for my opinion. "We need to wait as this is sensitive for the townspeople and donor's family. What we say next will be different depending on whether we accept the gift." The Committee liked that I made acceptance uncertain.

Nancy then asked Paula to summarize her observations. She did an excellent job of describing the town, its population, and the way she saw it being used as a unique study-abroad site. Though Angela, Chair of the Italian Department, was not on the committee, it was smart that Nancy invited her and she spoke with passion and eloquence on the academic value that Follamento would bring to Olmsted.

At that point Drake interrupted and asked why we were considering the details of the gift when the process issues should come first. "The influence of the committee will be greatly diminished if Olmsted accepts this gift, and in the long run, while the gift may be tantaliz now, the overall loss of the committee's ability to shape the glob agenda will be a net negative for years to come."

Nancy was taken aback, but regrouped quickly and said that she was fine discussing process before the substance.

Drew had lined up two other committee members who spoke against accepting the gift. George McDonald, an economist in the

College of Arts and Sciences, said, "Saying yes to this gift will completely kill all future faculty influence."

Stacey Weathers, a poetry scholar in the English Department, said, "I am against wasting time on learning more about this when it will relegate the committee to a minor or non-existent role if we go ahead."

I could see a few other faculty members nodding in agreement but no one spoke up. Edward, David, Paula and even Angela all argued that with full faculty control of the academic component, it would be detrimental to students to turn down this gift on process grounds.

It took nearly ninety minutes for the discussion to wind down and Nancy called for a non-binding straw poll, asking the committee members to signal yes or no whether we should move ahead to consider the substance of the gift before taking a final vote at the next meeting. Of the twenty members present, only four voted no, fifteen yes, and Nancy said that was strong enough to move ahead with the discussion.

Drake slammed down his folder and as he was leaving said, "The committee is irrelevant, no actually it is an administrative pawn of the corporate university."

Nancy said that the committee should come on the 22nd prepared to speak about the substance and take a vote, then asked if anyone had something to add in the last few minutes.

"The gift seems promising, but how do we know what we do not know?" Edward said.

"We will do our best but I am positive we will not know everything."

If not anything else, I was certainly right about that.

Day 45

Hector visited briefly this morning. Archie confided in Hector that he had a hunch that something was off with Charles and he did not appreciate the condescending treatment. Archie said Charles was evasive when he asked about his contacts with Guzman and Quintero. Hector said, "I am not talking to Archie about the plan to use the family.

"Al will arrive in Panama City Sunday afternoon. I will bring him to visit you on Monday morning. He wanted to know if he can bring you anything."

"He could bring Franny but I guess that is out of the question." I caught a faint smile from Hector. "Just a couple of paperback presidential biographies as I finished the book on the Roosevelts and some really strong soap will help. You will like Al."

Hector's news on the family issues was mixed. Through his contacts he was able to speak to someone high up in the family, but that person asked for time. His contact had not heard of the law firm, and he needed a few days to get back to Hector. "Looking at it optimistically, I could have received a flat 'no' so we should not give up on the idea," he said. I had lots of questions about how it might work if the family agreed to help but Hector said, "No questions now, as it is too soon."

I confirmed with Hector, "Ernesto has not mentioned anything. But there is greater urgency because of the decaying sharing arrangement." He understood. I gave him the last of my written pages including the ones I had stashed away, so at least part of my story will get out, even if I do not.

"I have been giving the pages to Archie, but do you think I should look at them with Al."

This caught me by surprise. I was worried that I had been critical of Hector, but then said okay. "Please understand that I am under a lot of pressure." I explained to Hector how he could put the pages back in order.

Ed and Drew made one more trip to Follamento around the 16th of September. After looking at detailed work orders, Drew was satisfied that the infrastructure could be maintained. Ed reviewed the financial data, and with some cross subsidies among the businesses, he was confident that the big picture would be slightly above break even.

Their one odd observation, outside of their formal analysis, was that the townspeople's parking lot had almost exclusively late model cars, some SUV's and sports cars, and a few BMWs and Audis. There were only a couple of older cars and only a few of the lower priced Fiats. With so many issues in play, it didn't raise a red flag.

Cathy was complaining to me almost daily, but despite the griping, she and the outside lawyer, Luigi, were making good progress on a draft agreement with Angelo.

I also learned from the Law School that despite Drake's histrionics at the last meeting, he would attend the faculty global committee meeting on September 22nd.

Nancy called me several times, worried about whether she would be viewed as a flunky for the administration.

"In a place as complex and loosely connected as Olmsted, there will always be naysayers. The goal is to make the right decision with a consensus among those who have an open mind. Drake was off base to walk out. The other two faculty members who spoke about the process questions, George and Stacey, remain involved, and you should engage them."

I am unsure whether others could see this, but Nancy lacked her usual self-confidence at the start of the meeting. She said, "I appreciate that the process questions were raised, but I believe after the last meeting the committee now desires to consider the substance, is this good for Olmsted." She asked Angela, Edward and Paula to hand out the two-pager that they developed on a hypothetical curriculum. I think many of the faculty felt as I did when they saw it; they wanted to be a student at Follamento.

After about half an hour of positive discussion, Drake changed the topic knowing that this could be his last chance to kill the project. "How do we know that the University will control all of the academic and non-academic aspects of the site, especially with the son still involved in the decision making?"

Nancy said, "I met the two principals, the lawyer/executor and the son, and they understand that the University will have full control over the town." Edward, Paula, and Angela all agreed that control would not be an issue in their judgment.

Drake, being the good lawyer, then asked if the committee could see the will, and on this matter Nancy turned to me.

"I heard both the lawyer and the son say specifically that the University has complete and absolute control over everything and this will be in the gift agreement."

"Will we see this agreement?"

"If it's sharable, the committee will see it."

Never one to give up easily, Drake had one more line of attack. "I assume that if Olmsted accepts the gift then we will not have another site somewhere else in Italy. Aren't we depriving our students of an Italian urban experience?"

Angela jumped right in. "I was worried about this, too, but having visited and thought about it, the immersion of students in the town and its proximity to Rome, Florence, Venice, Bologna and Milan will permit the best of both worlds."

For the rest of the meeting, Drake was quiet. As time was running out, Nancy asked, "How does the committee want to express its advice?"

Edward said, as though he was waiting for this question, "We should say that we have examined the potential academic value of the gift, and based on this, even though we have not finished our work to scope out a global agenda for Olmsted, the committee believes we should accept the gift if the due diligence meets the University's high standards."

I could not have said it better myself. That statement was supported in the ensuing discussion with three related amendments. First, at Paula's suggestion, the recommendation was to start small, limiting the number of students to fifty per semester in the first year. Second, Angela thought we should start in the next academic year, eleven months from the meeting, so that some current students could experience the site. And finally, David thought that the University should name a faculty and administrative committee to oversee the site with representation from the faculty global committee.

Nancy said, "I will draft the recommendation to the University and circulate it to the committee. Can I see a show of hands from everyone who supports the recommendations?" All hands went up except for Drake's. He said, "I am leaning to oppose but I want to see the recommendations in writing."

After the meeting I thought, *Olmsted is going to do this and its success will rest on me.*

Day 46

Though I was not expecting anyone, I was taken to a conference room straight from breakfast. When I arrived, a fiftyish, slick-looking, gray-haired man in an expensive suit was there. "Good morning. My name is Peter Nicolson. I was a lawyer in Washington, DC but I moved to Panama twenty-five years ago and now I am a partner in a small, specialized Panamanian law practice, Moreno, Cardoza and Nicolson."

"Why are you here?"

"Charles briefed me on your situation and I spoke with Archie in the Embassy. I take it you are using a small-time, minor leaguer, Hector Mendoza. It's no wonder you're still in prison. Hector is no match for Guzman and Quintero. Unless you have an attorney who can influence them you are completely at their mercy. Hector is not the one to do this. All you have to do is sign this paper that makes me your new attorney."

I almost freaked out but I held it together. I could not figure out where he was coming from. If Charles is connected to Guzman and Quintero, was this an attempt to get Hector out of the way? Was Charles actually trying to protect Olmsted? Because Al is arriving soon, I decided my best course was to put off Nicolson until Al could check him out. I said that I would get back to him in a few days. He gave me his business card, and on his way out he said, "I am sure you will make the right choice."

When I got back to the cell, Ernesto was very eager to know who was visiting, and I told him that it was another attorney recommended by the University but I was not likely to switch. No sooner did I explain this to Ernesto than we were interrupted by an unannounced inspection. Ernesto said, "I am surprised. Maybe it is the work of the other family. These occur every two months or so but usually I know before."

The inspectors were guards who worked in another cell block and they were not familiar to us. About four cells were opened at a time, we stood outside, and two guards per cell went through all of our stuff. I was lucky on two counts. First, I had gotten all of my pages out of the cell by Hector's last visit. All I had in the cell was last night's writing, which did not interest them. Second, we were not doing pick-ups and we had no extra cigarettes. Ernesto kept an eye on the guards because they were not beyond planting something, but we were given the all clear.

Between the slick attorney and the cell inspection, I was exhausted, but the most consequential event was yet to come. We were in the yard for about fifteen minutes after lunch when individual prisoners were pulled out and frisked.

It was terrifying, knowing the guards could plant something at any time. At dinner, Ernesto said, "The other side could have flipped the guards against us. Fortunately, that did not happen." He hoped that the raid would serve as a catalyst for renegotiation, rather than a declaration of war.

With many things falling into place on Follamento, I did a lot of base-touching, especially with a possible start-up in eleven months. Melissa was increasingly distracted and had moved on from the gift. "You do not have to check in with me on minor matters." At the time I attributed her hands off approach to confidence in me, but it was a precursor to her deterioration. I am usually the last person to notice this kind of thing. Franny is usually the first one to notice, which is why I'd give anything to be able to talk to her now.

Charles asked me to come to his office. He was thinking out loud about the Board. "We have the first board meeting of the academic year coming up on September 30, but all the pieces will not be in place by then. If we wait for formal approval until the December board meeting, there is no chance to have students in Follamento by September."

"We need to meet the faculty's timetable. Would you consider a detailed presentation on September 30th where we could summarize the outstanding issues, and assuming all were resolved satisfactorily, obtain approval via a newly scheduled conference call?" I knew that Charles did not like doing board business on the phone, but he agreed. I asked if two faculty members could be part of the presentation, and he reluctantly said yes, assuming they left during the deliberations. I thought that it would be awkward, but better than no faculty.

At the end of our meeting, Charles surprised me by asking, "If you were the only one to make the decision, knowing only what you know now, what would you do?" My mindset was to get all the pieces in place for others to make the decision, so I needed to think for a few seconds. "I would accept the gift." I knew my role made me biased but it went unsaid.

"I agree."

"Do you think we should hire a private investigator to find things we cannot find? The internet search by the law firm and Stephanie, my assistant, found nothing of consequence. I am surprised that someone like Roberto Follamento could have so little about him online."

"If we use a private investigator, it will become public and I'm uncomfortable with that."

"But they might find something important that we can't." I did not raise the late model car finding by Ed and Drew because it was speculative.

"Please take no for an answer." I dropped it.

The only real bump in the road was Laura's reemergence as an angry camper. She had not been to Follamento and said, "It will be humiliating for me to have Olmsted's largest gift reviewed by the board without playing a key role."

"At this point you have no role," but that just made her angrier. She was calling and emailing me three or four times a day and finally I told her to go to Melissa if she was not happy, knowing that she probably would not do that and she did not.

I dislike PowerPoint presentations as I believe they repress careful listening, so I just handed out an agenda for the Board discussion that I emceed. Melissa introduced the broad parameters of the gift with some but not as much enthusiasm as I thought was appropriate. Marshall made up for it with an impassioned explanation of the key academic benefits. Nancy and Paula spoke longer than necessary about the process of the committee, but the committee's strong support was important for the Board to hear. Both Ed and Drew explained their analyses and the positive conclusions. Cathy was more cautious, but actually quite balanced, saying that we were still working on the role of the donor's son. The entire presentation took about forty minutes.

I asked if there were any questions for Nancy and Paula before they departed. A board member asked each of them individually if they thought acceptance of the gift was a good idea and both said yes. Just as Nancy and Paula were about to leave, Mel Fineman, a University board member and a leading Law School donor, asked Nancy, "Do you think this will undermine the credibility of the faculty global committee because you have not completed your work?" While Fineman was speaking, I watched other board members connected to the Law School. They clearly knew that Fineman doing Drake's bidding. Nancy held her ground and said, "One Law School member of the committee raised this very question but the rest of the committee voted to consider the gift."

Melissa then asked if any others had questions and there was silence.

Charles thanked both Nancy and Paula for coming on such short notice. After they departed, the board discussed Angelo, and I thought for a moment that they would not move ahead without an agreement from him not to litigate. The tide turned and the sentiment was to get a solid agreement that made it clear that the University was in charge. Cathy added that while litigation could delay our finalization of the gift agreement, she was confident, based on advice from Luigi, the University would prevail because Angelo had witnessed and signed the will.

The board voted to have a telephone conference call before the end of October, with the agreement with Angelo the most pressing undecided matter. After the meeting, Marshall approached me and asked, "Do you think we are moving too fast?"

"We might be. Do you want me to slow it down?"

"No, but do not take short cuts just to meet the agreed-upon schedule. Do you think Melissa is okay? She seemed off."

"I think she's uncomfortable with Charles."

"I hope that's it."

Day 47

With any luck, as I write this on Sunday morning, Al is on a plane flying from New York to Panama. If and when I see Al, it will give me confidence that at least one honest person is on my side. I'm approaching seven weeks in this place and am unsure how much longer I can hold it together.

The day after the Board meeting, a Saturday, I met with Cathy in her office and she was exasperated. Angelo was changing his demands via emails and phone calls, going back on several key points. "Angelo has not come to grips with the fact that he will no longer be in charge. Increasingly over the past week he has mentioned litigation."

I called Lorenzo who suggested that Cathy and I come to Italy to try to reach an agreement face to face. We booked our flight to Rome for the next day. We would meet with Luigi and Lorenzo Monday evening and then work with Angelo on Tuesday.

Before we left, Melissa wished us luck, and Charles said, "You should be fair minded, but you have little maneuvering room. We will walk away without an agreement from Angelo not to litigate."

Franny was pissed, as we had some commitments during the week with family and friends, and she suggested I video conference instead. She was much more assertive than usual, and she had a point, as this was my fourth trip since July. We talked it through and I explained that increasingly, I saw this as *my* project for once, as opposed to working on other people's projects. She kind-of understood and said she would see if the kids and friends could reschedule.

Cathy and I had dinner with Lorenzo and Luigi at Conte Matto restaurant in Trequanda, as we did not want to run into Angelo in the Osteria Buona Fortuna. Lorenzo said, "The issue with Angelo is more psychological than legal. I predict you will fly home on Friday with a signed agreement if you can allay his fears that he will be nothing more than a clerk. The more the new job looks and feels like the old job the better."

Just as we were finishing our pasta and waiting for the main courses, in walks Angelo, alone. He spotted us and waved like he was going to eat at the other end of the restaurant, but Lorenzo signaled him to come over and join us. We stopped talking business and turned instead to the upcoming US presidential election and who we thought would win. After some polite back and forth, Cathy and I were feeling the wine and jet lag, and on the way back I wondered whether Angelo's appearance at dinner was orchestrated.

When we met in Lorenzo's office the next morning, the convivial Angelo was replaced by the angry one. "I am strongly considering litigation. The two of you are wasting your time and money trying to get an agreement." Lorenzo was taken aback, even turning a little red, or was it all just an act? Cathy rolled her eyes.

I asked Angelo to go for a walk with me. We did not speak going down to the piazza and he was agitated as we walked. I started. "I know how disruptive this must feel to you and I'm not surprised by your reactions. As generous and significant as this gift is, if the University is not in total control and if you do not agree to abstain from litigation, then we will walk away. You should hear us out about how we will form our relationship with you, who will be involved, and then compare that to the unknown of the next possible recipient in line."

I thought at the time how ironic it was writing about a situation where I held all the cards, but today I have no cards whatsoever. I don't even know what game we're playing.

We walked for about three minutes in silence. Angelo said, "I appreciate your directness. I am disappointed that the University does not recognize the difficult position I am in but I have watched you and I think we can work together."

"If we are going to invest in building a first class study-abroad site, then we need to know that our presence here is not in legal jeopardy." I did not say that our legal team would win the litigation as I thought it was piling-on.

"When I signed my father's will I thought I had plenty of time to get him to change the part that related to me, but he went downhill faster than anyone thought."

We had walked around the piazza twice and were back in front of Lorenzo's office. He asked "Can I have some time to myself and meet you back in the office at two p.m.?"

"Fine."

I went back to Lorenzo, Luigi and Cathy and reported on the details and the flow of the conversation. They were relieved that Angelo had calmed down. I thought it was likely an act to strengthen his bargaining position but I kept that to myself.

I asked Lorenzo, "Will Angelo show up?" "Yes." We spent the rest of the time before lunch outlining the key points in the agreement: Angelo was the town manager and his accountability was to the University. The University could fire Angelo without cause and name his successor. After lunch I said, "Maybe it will not take all of Wednesday and Thursday to get a working draft."

"Do not rush. Let Angelo get used to his new future." This was a microcosm of the difference between New York and Italy.

Lorenzo was right. The five of us worked the rest of Tuesday, all day Wednesday and Thursday to hammer out a draft. Angelo lost his temper a few times and wanted everything explained in agonizing detail. He didn't understand why the University needed strong control over the businesses as opposed to the academics. I tried to explain the interrelationships; he was not convinced but finally agreed. He insisted that if we fired him without cause in the first three years, he could litigate and Cathy thought that was acceptable.

My opinion of Cathy rose over the three days, albeit starting at a low level. On the way to the airport early Friday morning, both Cathy and I agreed we likely would not have gotten to the finish line long distance. A week after we arrived in New York, Cathy shared with me drafts of both the agreement with Angelo and the gift agreement. This was a world's record for her.

Day 48

The minute hand was not moving after breakfast but finally, at around 10:30 a.m., a guard came by to take me to the visitor area. The good news was that Al was with Hector, and the surprise fantastic news was that Franny was with them.

I was supposed to stay on one side of the table with no touching but I had to hug Franny until the guard came into the room and pulled us apart. "I miss you so much."

"What have you done?" she said. "I'm worried you'll be here for a lot longer."

After getting the call from Hector, Franny called Al and she was not taking no for an answer. Against his better judgment, he allowed her to accompany him on the condition that she return to New York the next day. Al did not want her to come because the people who had it in for me could find and use her, but he figured that he could keep her safe for a day. She said that I looked "skinny but okay," but that even the public area of the prison scared her.

"Are you safe in here? Are you sick? What are you eating, obviously not enough? What's that smell?"

I tried to answer in a reassuring way, but she saw through that.

Finally Franny said, "Are you going to make it?"

I fought back the tears and said I was going to be fine, trying to convince us both.

Hector asked, "How do you want to spend the next twenty minutes or so?"

"Franny should stay the whole time, but I want a few minutes with Al, Franny and me, and then just Franny and me."

"It took a while for Al and Franny to understand that you still have no charges filed against you." He described the likely role played by Guzman and Quintero and then told Franny and Al about his idea to try to use Ernesto's family to get me out. "I should hear back from my family contact this week, and Al and I will come back to see you when and if there is a way to move ahead with the arrangement. We will try to come on Friday or Saturday, no matter what."

Franny wasn't happy about the idea of using the family, sensing that I could get deeper into trouble.

Hector tried to be reassuring and said, "One of Al's roles is to assess the risk."

"What about the Embassy?" she asked.

"They have no real power in this situation," which she found hard to believe. She kept asking if there were some people with clout who we could enlist but Hector said no. The time seemed to zoom by and Hector said, "I'll go to the waiting area and you can spend a few minutes with Franny and Al."

As quickly as possible, I explained to Al and Franny my concern that everyone was connected and working to keep me in prison. "I'm reasonably sure that Hector is not involved, but it is easy to get paranoid. I want verification that Hector is working for me."

"I sense that Hector is on your side, but I will know more over the next few days," Al said.

"I need you to evaluate the plan to use Ernesto's family."

"I'll know by the next time we see you. Anything else I need to know?"

"My imprisonment is likely due to some problems at Olmsted's study abroad site in Italy but I do not think that matters for now." I quickly explained what I was doing on the cigarette side, which made Al very nervous.

Franny went nuts. "Do you realize that your well-being is at stake and nothing else is so important? Focus on getting out and staying safe, for your family's sake as much as yours."

"You're right."

I then told Al and Franny about the visit from Peter Nicolson. "Can you check him out, at least initially without going through Hector? And did Hector mention anything about information from my assistant, Stephanie?"

169

"I'll ask Hector about Stephanie. I know several retired New York City police officers who are living in Panama. A lot of them retire here. I'll see if they know Nicolson. Will you pay them to help you?"

"You need not ask, just keep a running tab."

"I have a good feeling about Hector, but I will check him out. Here is my cell phone number. It is working in Panama."

"Thanks, but I do not have phone access here."

"I understand about the phone. My first order of business is to get Franny safely on the plane to New York tomorrow and then I can begin working for you." Al left as the guard was coming in and he signaled one more minute.

Franny said, "You are not thinking clearly. Maybe this Nicolson guy has more clout than Hector."

"Al will check out Nicolson, and I love you."

"Do not give them a reason to keep you here. I love you too."

Lorenzo and Angelo called me the day after I returned, Saturday. "Do you think we could be done by the beginning of October? Lorenzo said,"

"There's a chance."

Angelo's call was different: "I hope you see that I agreed to the University's conditions in a helpful and civil way. I'm glad you understand that the businesses will not need the University's constant attention." I never said that but I was all praise nonetheless, and he also asked about timing. I gave him the "chance for a mid-October agreement" answer.

Charles called me into his office first thing Monday and pressed me very hard for details. "The conditions you set enabled us to blunt most of Angelo's attempts to gain control," I said. "He's only interested in the businesses, not the academics." I praised Cathy's work and Charles wanted to know if I had a fever.

Before the staff meeting on Tuesday, Nancy sent me a draft memo to Melissa that had been endorsed by the full faculty global committee except for Drake. As expected, it said that process-wise the timing of the gift was unfortunate as it preceded the committee's proposed articulation of Olmsted's global agenda, but when all aspects of the potential gift were considered, the committee voted to accept the gift with only one negative vote, assuming that all due diligence was completed and positive. The memo thanked the administration for its openness and transparency. The last paragraph underscored the need for faculty control of the academic program.

I did not change a single word. Nancy wanted my confirmation that it would be a public document and I said it would.

Also, before the staff meeting I received a call from two student reporters at the *Olmsted Oracle*. After being tipped off by an unnamed source, they were writing a story that the faculty global committee was divided on its support of the gift and that the University was going to push ahead despite the faculty opposition. I assumed the source was Drake. I asked the students, "Have you spoken to Professor Nancy Wright?"

"She doesn't want to comment yet."

"Your article is factually incorrect. I will ask Professor Wright to contact you." I called Nancy. "You need to let the students know that their article is wrong, and then ask them to delay it until your memo is released in a few days. You can explain how an incorrect article will damage the *Oracle's* credibility."

Nancy let them know off the record that the vote had been nearly unanimous with only one dissenter, and then promised to send them the memo at the same time that she sent it to the President.

The senior staff meeting had that "we won the election, now what do we do?" feel about it. I passed out a draft of Nancy's memo and everyone was pleased. We all knew that Drake was doing the Law School Dean's bidding. Cathy explained the work we did in Italy and how it was resolved. She turned to me about the marching orders from Charles and how it changed the negotiations, and Melissa said, "This was one time Charles's meddling had a positive effect." Cathy hoped to have a draft agreement with Angelo in a few days and a draft gift agreement would follow that. Ed and Drew thought that the Follamento staff people in their respective areas such as the bookkeeper/accountant, Sabrina Marchetti, and the capital projects person, Paolo Tavente, should report directly to them, not to Angelo, but both Cathy and I explained Angelo's sensitivity on this issue and that they would need to report to Angelo.

Melissa then asked me to comment on my assessment of Lorenzo. "He appears to be doing what he is legally bound to do, represent Roberto Follamento's estate. He has a complex relationship with Angelo, and I am unsure of its full dimensions. He certainly coached us well on how to deal with Angelo, but I do not know how much was orchestrated with Angelo himself." I took a leap and said, "Overall I think we can work with him."

Day 49

Ernesto had no news this morning at breakfast, though he did speak with his uncle for 15 minutes. As we were lined up to return to the cell, they announced that there would be no yard time today and tomorrow. Ernesto said, "Negotiations are on-going. If there are going to be fights among the families it will have to be at meal time. Don't stray too far from me."

Over the next six days, three critical elements came together sequentially. Nancy formally submitted her memo, which signaled strong faculty support. Drake maintained his opposition, which made the positive vote from the other twenty members of the committee all the more impressive. I spoke with Gabe as the *Oracle* was now free to write their article, which they did almost immediately. Though written as news, it was more of an editorial in favor of the study-abroad site.

I was the first to see Cathy's draft agreement with Angelo. She had the legal part correct, but she didn't include text that described Angelo's broad role in terms of its scope and importance. The agreement gave us an opportunity to bolster Angelo's pride. I drafted the appropriate language, Cathy added it, and I sent the draft to Lorenzo for his comments. Ironically, he thought the language on Angelo was weak and sent me five additional sentences that further celebrated Angelo's role. Once all the edits were included I sent it to Charles, Melissa, and Marshall for comments.

Then, about two days later, Cathy sent me a copy of the gift agreement. I had just started to read it over, when I got a call from Melissa's chief of staff, Alyssa White, letting me know that about twenty students had taken over Melissa's office. She said that she and David Goodman, Al's successor as chief of Olmsted's security, were heading to my office. Several other security officers were placed outside of our suite to prevent additional students from joining the protestors. Fortunately Melissa was not in her office. We were all caught flat footed.

Despite the overall rise in student protests on American college campuses over the past several years, up until now, Olmsted had no protests since the Viet Nam war days. While we were aware that we would not be immune forever, we had been lulled into thinking that issues could be worked out without protests at Olmsted.

The protest was well planned. The elected student leadership group had a regularly scheduled meeting with Melissa that morning, her first of the day. About ten students in the group regularly met with the President, and it was common for them to bring one or two additional students to speak about a particular issue. In this case they each brought a guest, and because they staggered their arrival, the security guard did not realize the crowd was about twenty students instead of the usual ten or twelve. Their backpacks contained food and blankets in addition to the usual books and laptops.

At 9:30 a.m., about five minutes before Melissa's normal arrival, the students announced that they were taking over her office. Her chief of staff phoned her before she entered the building and she went back to her apartment. The students announced that they were not leaving until all the demands were met. Included on the list were the absence of fossil fuel stocks in the investment portfolio of Olmsted's small endowment, support for Palestinian students, and, what may have been the precipitating event, the promise of financial aid so that all Olmsted students could utilize the study abroad-site that was described in the *Oracle*. The students went live on Twitter and Instagram. One of the students actually worked for the *Oracle* and she was feeding real time information to the world through their website.

Soon, about fifty additional students congregated at the guard station outside the suite of leadership offices chanting "Hey, hey, ho, ho, not just rich kids get to go," over and over at high volume so that Alyssa, David and I could hear it clearly in my office, some distance away, and it was also being broadcast on social media.

We had a protocol for this kind of student protest. It was stale and did not fit the circumstances, as we never thought it would occur in the most obvious place, the President's office. The protocol called for someone in authority to let the students know that we wanted them to be safe and that we would get back to them soon. Marshall joined us in my office and he, Alyssa, and David all thought that I should be the one to establish contact with the protestors, as each of them had relatively lame and self-serving reasons why it should not be one of them.

I agreed to meet with the students at around ten. I entered the President's office and to my surprise, everyone stood up. The students were extremely nervous and polite, none of them even sitting at Melissa's desk. They were dressed up, the men in jackets and ties and the women in smart looking clothing, no jeans.

They wanted to state their demands, with all of it being broadcast live, but they let me speak first.

"We want to engage with you civilly and within the University's Code of Conduct. This requires a two way understanding. You can have access to a restroom. No one from the outside will be permitted to join you. If you leave you cannot come back in, though if we move to a neutral site, you can come and go. It is the occupation of the office, not the protest, that is a violation of the University's code of conduct, but no disciplinary action is contemplated *at this time.*"

They then recited their demands and stated that they were not leaving until all of them were met. After they were done, I thanked them and said I would be back in a while, and I took all of the papers on Melissa's desk, none of which they had touched. They were faculty tenure documents with Melissa's odd post-its visible, and I placed them in a safe place in my office.

I went back and reported to Marshall, Alyssa and David who were in my office and with Melissa and Charles via phone though they watched it all on the web. Melissa had forgotten about the tenure papers, Charles was surprisingly calm, and Marshall was rightfully worried about the safety of the students. We all agreed to wait a little while before we got back to them.

Day 50

Yesterday, I thought I might get a visit from Al and Hector, but it was probably too soon. I miss Franny and our kids more than ever. Franny told me that the kids are more worried about me than she was, and she is off the scale. I asked her to tell them that I'm doing okay though her description of me and this place is likely to scare them. Meanwhile, we weren't allowed in the yard, and there were extra guards in the cellblock and cafeteria. When Ernesto is as worried as he is, I am really worried.

Melissa wanted Alyssa, David, Marshall and me to meet in her apartment at 11, before I went back to the student protesters. She was as angry as I have ever seen her, fuming that her space had been violated and she had been betrayed. To me, she was much more upset than the situation warranted. A few times she almost lost her breath and spoke incomprehensibly.

"This is not about you," I said. "This is what students do today."

"I spoke with Charles and he favors their immediate removal with disciplinary action." Both she and Charles thought we should meet none of the demands. This was the first sit-in of her office during her career and it showed.

Marshall and I wanted to de-escalate the situation amicably. We went over each of the student demands, most of which we would not and could not meet. In terms of fossil fuels, the trustees were not about to change the portfolio's investment strategy. All students, including Palestinian students, were eligible for financial aid but our leadership and trustees would not permit singling out one group. The demand for financial aid for study-abroad was one area where we had some wiggle room.

Marshall explained to Melissa, "We are better off ending the protest, certainly without any violence, but also without having to discipline our students. Student protests are part of their education and can shape their world-view more than most classes."

"I don't buy that. We have a reasonable governance system that enables students to address all of these issues."

"You are missing the point for today's young adults. These are not students on the 'fringe of ideology and action' but the elected leaders, maybe egged on by others, and they are a thoughtful, mainstream group."

Melissa got a phone call and went into the other room and Marshall asked me what I thought we should do. "The students' culture values spending a night in protest, and I think we can work with that to end the protest."

"We are likely to give financial aid to study abroad anyway," Marshall said, "so it will do no real harm to announce that." We knew that Melissa and especially Charles would see this as capitulating, but in the long run it was best to end the protest peacefully and we were not doing anything we would not do. My tombstone will say, "He was a pragmatist," and I am not ashamed of that, though I hope decisions on my tombstone are some years away.

When Melissa returned, Marshall, with a smirk on his face, said, "Bill has an idea."

"I can go back to the students and say that they first need to leave the office in order for us to negotiate," I said.. "I could give them a number to call and then say that I'm available to talk at any time.

"We would then play a bit of a waiting game. If they do not call me back, and I don't think that they will, I'll go back in tonight and let them know that anyone in the office at eight a.m. will be subject to student discipline, which will place a note on their record," I said. "I do not think this will end it. I will go back at six, explaining if they agree to leave by eight, no discipline will be imposed. I will remind them that discipline will show up on their college record. We will agree to provide $1,500 for each student with documented need who enrolls for a semester at Follamento, which would cover their plane fare plus a little more, and they would continue to get their existing financial aid. With housing costs less than in New York, finances should not be an issue for study at Follamento."

"I will also remind them that the program is going to start small but we will keep the offer in effect for at least five years. I will explain that the current governance mechanisms can deal with the other demands, and I will be back at 8 a.m. to see what they want to do." I pointed out to my colleagues that the $1,500 per student would be from the Follamento endowment and even for 200 students per semester it would only be $600,000 per year, clearly supportable from the $100 million endowment income, and we would have implemented something like that anyway.

Marshall said, "This balances the students' need for a victory of sorts and our need to end the protest without giving up anything real."

"I don't like the students in my office overnight, and I'm not convinced that giving the financial aid as a result of the protest is right."

"We can hedge a little on the offer by saying that it needs to be endorsed by the Board of Trustees but we will present it with our recommendation."

Melissa thought that was better but still too much of a capitulation.

Marshall pushed back. "There is no guarantee that they will accept this," and that sobered Melissa's thinking.

She asked, "Should we run this by Charles?"

"You can but Charles will say no and we could be in for a long sit-in."

Just then, Charles called, and Melissa put him on speaker. He said, "We should give them nothing and throw them out of school."

Melissa shifted our way and said, "Remember, Charles, student protest to a limited degree can be seen as positive, and we have disciplinary rules that we need to follow."

This made him grumpy and he hung up with the sage advice, "Do not give them anything and get them out of your office."

Melissa agreed we should implement the first part of the plan and then reconvene in her apartment at 5 p.m. if nothing forced us to intervene earlier. I went back to the administrative offices with Marshall, Alyssa and David. The protestors were still there chanting and they booed as we walked through the narrow lane the security guards forced them to keep open. David said, "When you meet with the students, please take all of their Olmsted IDs for safety reasons and ascertain that there were no non-Olmsted students in the President's office."

The students were active on social media when I walked into Melissa's office. A few were sitting in the guest chairs, and most were seated on the floor. It looked relatively untouched and no one was sitting at her desk. The apparent leader asked, "Are you ready to meet our demands?"

I ignored his question and said, "We are willing to discuss the demands but you need to leave the President's office first. We will identify a conference room in the student center which you can use, and here is the phone number you should use to call us." The number was a land line programmed to go to David's cell phone. "Our rules of conduct require that each of you give me your ID card," and several students began handing them over but a couple said that they would not. I collected eighteen of the twenty with no real problem and then said, "Students are subject to immediate expulsion if I do not have your IDs," and the two remaining students handed them over. I walked out while they were still shouting questions at me.

When I got back to my office David was there with Alyssa and Marshall and I gave my brief report though they watched it live on the *Oracle's* feed. The student protestors expressed frustration that I was not prepared to engage. After I left they argued about meekly handing over the IDs, but one student looked up the code of conduct and it was there in black and white. A minority of the protestors wanted to move to a different location so that we could negotiate, but the majority did not want to give in, and it was clear that they were prepared to spend the night. The good news was that all the students were enrolled at Olmsted. We have little leverage over outsiders and they would have changed the nature of the sit-in. David relayed the absence of outsiders to the NY Police Department, as the Police were monitoring the social media sites and they told David that they were available if we needed them. Frankly, if we called in the NYPD we would lose total control and it could have jeopardized the students' safety. The NYPD would not enter the picture unless we asked them, or if there was a breakdown in public safety, and then they would engage without asking.

I now had a few hours before we were to reconvene in Melissa's office, so I read the draft Follamento gift agreement. It was dated tentatively as October 15th and this was a stark reminder that, once signed, the planning for the study abroad site and the management of Follamento would commence in earnest.

Our kids were alerted to the protest on social media and called Franny. They were all watching and kibitzing among themselves they told me later. Franny called me once to make sure I was okay and asked rhetorically why I was on point.

Franny was very supportive of my work, including taking on the oversight of Follamento. But as she was teaching full time and doing her art part-time, she would not be accompanying me on what I thought would be the visits to Follamento every couple of months. With both our kids out of college, I pointed out that in many cases I could schedule my trips at times when she could go with me. She said, "it's not about me travelling but us being apart. I know this's important to you."

After checking in with Melissa, we reconfirmed my plan to meet with the protestors around 9:30 p.m. The crowd outside our offices shrunk during the day but it had grown to its largest size, maybe 100 students, at about 6 p.m. when I headed home for dinner. In an email, our daughter, Ruth, told me to get rid of my suit and tie when I went back in to meet with the protestors, as it highlighted me as part the establishment. Our daughter lovingly referred to me as "the man."

Day 51

It was announced at breakfast that time in the yard would start tomorrow. Ernesto was surprised because he did not know of an imminent deal. On the way back to the cells word was passed to Ernesto that business was still on hold.

I assume Franny made it home safely, as I think I would have heard if she had not. I really want Hector and Al to get along and put their minds together for my release. There is only so long I can go with 60 second showers once a week.

I met with David, Alyssa, and Marshall in my office at around 9:15 p.m. There were about thirty-five students at the guard desk, though they had stopped chanting. I'm sure my arrival was relayed to the students in Melissa's office, which made me wait a little longer before going in. The buzz on social media was about spending the night.

I met with the protestors at 10:15 p.m. They looked tired and seemed eager to hear what I had to say. I was wearing jeans, as directed by my daughter. "I'm disappointed we are not in a conference room and talking. You are violating University rules and must be out of the office by eight a.m. tomorrow, or face disciplinary action. Please keep in mind that the University has the right to invoke emergency disciplinary procedures which involves suspension." Many students shouted at once, asking if we planned to do this. "It's our right and if you do not leave by eight tomorrow morning, we will. Remember that the suspension could affect your financial aid. The offer to negotiate at a neutral site is good until eight a.m., but if you do not leave by then we will begin the disciplinary process."

"If we are still here at eight will we be physically thrown out?"

"President Wakefield needs her office back and letting you stay effectively twenty-four hours is generous on our part."

They interpreted that to mean we would physically throw them out, but I doubted that we would do that. "When you are ready to negotiate, call me on the number I gave you, but once eight a.m. rolls around I will be back without any opportunity to negotiate." I was counting on the fact that some time in the morning they would want to talk but when I left the room I was unsure.

Immediately I received texts from Franny, Ruth and our son, Eliot, saying that I did very well. Eliot said that many of his former classmates texted asking whether he wanted to organize a protest. Alyssa, David and Marshall were complementary when I got back to my office. About five minutes later Melissa called and said, "Charles and I watched on the *Oracle* internet feed and we both feel that the students will stay through the deadline. Charles threatened me with my job if this does not end soon. This is terrible." Hysteria is not a good solution to a student protest.

"The discipline is a serious threat, at least to the student leaders," but she was unmoved. I felt like saying that second guessing is easy when you are holed up in your apartment, but I did not say that either. I thought both Melissa and Charles were over-reacting.

We all went home at about 11 p.m. and I tried to get a few hours of sleep. My phone vibrated at 4:45 a.m. and I took it into the living room to avoid disturbing Franny. It was David "I have been monitoring the *Oracle* feed since four and a rift has developed among the students. The guests who accompanied the student leaders are from several groups who focus on issues like financial aid for the Palestinian students and disinvestment in fossil fuels and are much more militant and radical. They want to stay in the office past the deadline, while the student leaders want to go to a conference room to avoid discipline. The only thing they agreed on was to resolve this democratically with a vote."

I'm sure the students preferred to argue in private but because they had made such a big deal of being fully transparent to the world on social media, they were forced to argue in public. David and I watched for a while and agreed to speak again at 6:30 a.m.

Close to 6 a.m., the stress was mounting. At around 6:15 one guest suggested that the student leaders, who hoped to protect their resumes, could leave and the guests could stay, but this idea was voted down fifteen to five with a lot of loud arguing. At 6:30 I went to David's office to avoid walking through the roughly twenty protestors who had spent the night at the guard desk outside of the university administrative offices.

In what seemed like a choreographed move, three of the student leaders' phones rang and it was their parents who were watching on social media. In all three calls, the parents reminded the students that they were not paying several hundred thousand dollars for four years that ended in reduced job prospects because of disciplinary actions on their records. The student protestors had not thought of this when they opted for transparency on social media.

At 6:45, the student council president took a risky approach and asked for a non-binding straw vote on whether to go to a conference room by the deadline or stay and face discipline. I think that she sensed there was not unanimity among the guests. She was right and the vote was twelve to eight to go to another room to negotiate. At that point the more militant guests again tried to argue that they could stay, but the fact that they'd previously voted to stay together trumped their desire to split off from the other group. Finally, at 7:30 they took a binding vote on the issue and voted thirteen to seven to move to a neutral conference room and negotiate. They called David's phone and he said I would be there in ten minutes.

I went in to talk to the students at 7:45. "We have another room and we can negotiate your demands if we move there immediately." They asked for a few minutes to gather their things and then sheepishly asked if we could provide coffee in the conference room. I said yes to both. By 8:15 Melissa's office was amazingly neat and clean and the students walked out to "thunderous applause" from the roughly eighty students by the guard station and the 100 on the street outside the building. I told them that I would meet them at the conference room at 9 a.m., giving them some time to have coffee and me some time to confer with Melissa, Alyssa, David and Marshall.

At 8:30 we called Melissa, who was still in her apartment, gun shy about returning to her office. She had just spoken with Charles who said, "Give them nothing." Everyone is a big shot when they are some distance from the actual protest and they are not immediately accountable for safety. My opinion of Melissa and Charles was at an all-time low and trending down.

In the half hour or so before I went to meet with the students, I grabbed some coffee and sat by myself in my office. I had a sense of relief that we had ended the Presidential office sit-in with no real histrionics and no injuries. Now my job was to get it all wrapped-up.

When we convened, the ever present social media was turned on. I debated whether to ask them to turn it off, but up until now it had actually worked to our advantage so I did not say anything. I told them that I had about two hours. I actually had all day but knew it would fill the time if I allowed it. There was clear fatigue visible to me across the board. They asked if we could spend a few minutes on each demand and I agreed.

The issue of disinvestment of fossil fuel stocks was in front of the AUC and I said it was inappropriate to usurp their opinion. Last year the AUC voted with a strong majority to disinvest, but that was rejected by the trustees. The AUC then voted to reject the trustees' response. whatever it meant to reject a response when it was clearly the trustees' decision to make, and were developing a new resolution. The protesting students agreed to send a message to the trustees, which they could have done without the protest.

I sensed that the students were looking to say something on each of the issues and I was nervous about financial aid for Palestinian students. I allowed the spokespersons for this issue, two of the guests, to speak for about ten minutes. I guess we were lucky that they were not calling for a boycott of Israel, but they were the most militant of the entire group. They outlined the oppression and discrimination suffered by Palestinians world-wide and in their homelands and jumped immediately to special financial aid to improve their chances in life. I chose not to question their statements and went immediately to my main argument that we do not single out any nationality in terms of financial aid eligibility. They smartly asked about donors who, for example, wanted to give aid to first generation students and I said that was not based on their nationality. We went back and forth for about thirty minutes when the student council president spoke up and offered to consider the Palestinian issue in the student council, where consideration had been rejected previously. This was a way out, but down the road it could exacerbate the Palestine-Israel differences among the students. I made a judgment that we could live with it and the student leaders agreed to take up the issue.

Finally we got to the Follamento issue, the first where I had something concrete to offer. The students had pretty much stayed awake for nearly thirty hours, except for some short naps on the floor of Melissa's office. The student council president had prepared his "demand" as a review of the Follamento gift to see if funds could be set aside for financial aid for needy students. Amazingly, they were asking for less than I was prepared to give and I helped them shape their ask so that it went to Melissa with a recognition that whatever she supported had to be approved by the trustees and consistent with the yet to be signed gift agreement. The students then asked me to step out of the room for ten minutes so that they could confer among themselves which seemed pretty silly given the coverage on social media but I left for ten minutes and took the time to summarize what I thought we agreed to during our two hours together.

I went back in, read my summary of the three points, which they accepted, and then they announced on social media that they had gotten something from the University on each of the issues and they were ending the protest. They all wanted to shake my hand and they left the conference room to join with the roughly 400 students who had gathered two floors below in the lobby of the student center, and they came out of the elevator with great pride and a rightfully earned sense of accomplishment. Spontaneously, all 400 voices erupted in a new verse, "Hey, hey, ho, ho, all Olmsted students will get to go."

Day 52

Hector and Al visited this morning, and Al let me know Franny arrived home safely.

"Seeing her was my best time in the past nine weeks. I miss her and our kids so much that it hurts."

"I don't need time alone with you," Al said, "unless you want it. Hector and I are in agreement on all issues." This was a good opening signal. "I want to take care of the Peter Nicolson issue first. I found out through several contacts that Nicolson was disbarred in New York State for securities fraud and then moved to Panama where he is permitted to practice. His firm, Moreno, Cardoza, and Nicolson, appears to do all securities work."

Hector added, "I checked with my closest colleagues and no one heard of them."

Based on this, I asked Al to contact Nicolson and then Archie on my behalf and say, "I will not be using Nicolson." It made me think that Charles surely does keep interesting company.

Hector had heard from Stephanie. "She said that she learned that when the SEC investigates a matter and there are no charges, there is nothing on their website. She did find an article on the internet in an investment newsletter on tax schemes in the Caribbean from several years ago that mentioned Guzman and Quintero as one of the firms that courted American business. She was ready to stop searching when she found a photo of Charles and Jose Guzman taken at a fund raising dinner for cancer research three years ago in New York." Hector gave us time to take this in and then said, "This pretty much eliminates any doubt of the connection."

The fact that they are linked and I'm still in prison was surprising to all three of us.

Hector continued, "My contact with the family was inconclusive. He had an encouraging response about a week ago, but then he could not get the top people's attention." I wondered whether this was because of the sharing arrangement negotiations, but they probably had bigger things to worry about. "Al has come up with another option and I will let him explain."

Al knew two fairly high ranking retired NYPD officers, Kevin O'Neil and Greg White, who had served with him and were living in Panama. Neither was surprised about my situation and one of them knew how powerful Guzman and Quintero was. Kevin and Greg said that they could contact the Ministry of Government, for whom they'd done some work as private investigators, to see if they could gain my release.

"It makes sense to work both approaches, as both have longish odds and Kevin and Greg will not be intimidated by Guzman and Quintero," Hector said.

"Should I discuss any of your dealings with the family with Ernesto?"

"No. We are dealing pretty high up in the family. Ernesto's intervention could only confuse things, plus we do not know if he is in favor of your release." I ended the meeting by giving Hector all my new writing to today, and asked that he retrieve the papers from Archie and give them to Al to bring back to New York to give to Franny.

"Can Al and I continue to read your writing? It provides additional information on Olmsted, Follamento and prison."

"Of course."

Later in the yard, two groups started shouting and then shoving each other. As soon as it started Ernesto told me to stay close to the basketball court while he moved closer to the shoving, but by the time he got within ten yards of the fracas, it had broken up on its own. Ernesto came back and said, "Both families are freaked out by the stoppage of business but they know that fighting will only prolong the problem." I could not help myself and I muttered so Ernesto could hear, "I really want to be out of here."

After dinner, Ernesto said, "The pick-ups will resume on Monday."

My work with the students was appreciated by my colleagues, if not by Melissa and Charles. Charles thought that I gave them too much. Of course the student protestors made a big deal about their "victory" and Charles was serving as my research assistant sending me the postings from the internet and the articles in the *Oracle*. Gabe was able to reach the *New York Times* before the reporters wrote a short article, which was factual and favored neither the protestors nor the University. Most of the article focused on the pervasive internet coverage and its effects, including the call by the parents.

Within hours of the end of the sit-in Laura popped into my office unannounced, and as soon as I saw her I realized that we had progressed very far on the gift agreement with virtually no input from her or her office and that was a mistake. Before she could say anything I said, "The gift agreement is in draft form and I was remiss in not sending it to you."

"How did you know what I was going to say?"

"I knew as soon as you walked into my office that we should have sent it to you sooner."

She appreciated my candor and some of her edge seemed to have worn off. I printed out copies of the draft agreement with Angelo, the draft gift agreement and the will, gave them to Laura, and asked her to send her comments to Cathy and me.

Laura had one more important issue that I should have seen coming but I did not. "Now that the gift was close to being finalized, how do we value it for purposes of reporting on Olmsted's fundraising totals?" Most university fundraising professionals live and die by the amount they raise and are famously fastidious about valuing and counting gifts to the University. While a cash gift is straightforward to value and it comprises most of the gifts, we get a few other assets from donors including land, buildings, artwork, stock, and sometimes odd collections like weather vanes or candelabras, to name two recent gifts. I was surprised that Laura was asking me because we had standard methods for independently appraising each type of non-cash gift, though this gift was unique.

"The value of the two endowments, 100 million euros and 50 million euros, is straightforward. We will need an appraisal in Italy of the land and buildings."

Laura agreed and asked, "Can you do a back of the envelope estimate? My office gave me an estimate but I would like to hear yours before I tell you mine."

I felt like I was on *The Price is Right.* I went online to get a rough value of land and buildings per square meter, then did some math to guesstimate the area in square meters and did the same for the land. Though I was not very confident in my number, my estimated value of the non-cash assets was about $350 million when converted to U.S. dollars, and that plus the endowment at 1.15 dollars to the euro, gave me a total close to $500 million U.S. dollars. I had never thought of how much this was all worth, and I was a little surprised at my own number.

I said to Laura, "I am in the ballpark of $500 million."

She said, "My office estimated about $650 million," so we were in the same galaxy if not solar system, admittedly a nice place to be. Olmsted's fundraising is about $85 to $110 million a year, and no matter what the eventual valuation, the inclusion of Follamento would make this a record- setting year. I could see the dollar signs flashing in Laura's eyes, and I almost made a comment about how she did not have to do much for this gift but that was left unsaid.

"You should work with Cathy and the Italian law firm to get an independent appraisal once the gift agreement is signed. I will figure out a time for you to visit later in the fall." She appreciated that and I think most of her ill will was behind us, at least for now. It's amazing what adding $500 million to the fundraising totals will do.

To get a final gift agreement, there was back and forth over Charles's requests and then Lorenzo's responses. It was largely a clash of egos over fairly trivial matters, with Charles trying to be the big man on campus and Lorenzo reminding him that he represented the estate. By

October 7th we were in agreement and the board conference call was scheduled for Friday, October 14th. Cathy pointed out that there was still the matter of the paperwork in Panama to transfer the Follamento stock to Olmsted, but that could wait until after the gift agreement was approved by the Board. At the time I thought it was a formality.

Cathy, Marshall, Ed, Drew, Laura and I all took the board call together on speaker phone in Melissa's office. Cathy walked the board through the three key documents, the will, gift agreement and agreement with Angelo. A board member asked the total value of the gift. "We have not yet received the independent appraisal of the land and property but the total including the two endowments are in the neighborhood of half a billion dollars." After a few questions about minor details, one board member who was a smart alumna who had made her fortune in real estate asked, "Do we really know that this is as good as it looks with no hidden surprises?"

Charles said, "I looked both Lorenzo and Angelo in their eyes during our entire visit and I think it is, but Melissa should weigh in."

Melissa was caught a little short and seemed lost, as she was not paying close attention, so she hemmed and hawed while she regained her footing, and then said, "Bill has been there the most."

I was thinking of the comments that Ed and Drew made about the late model cars, but that was very speculative so I didn't bring that up. "I agree with Charles and Melissa that this is the real thing," and with that, the board accepted the gift unanimously.

Day 53

Ernesto and I were thrown a curve-ball today when his uncle reported that Ernesto may be transferred to another prison, which often happens before release. I know that Ernesto is part of my predicament, but the news felt like a blow. Uncle Eduardo said that he would try to prevent any move.

After the board call, I connected to Lorenzo and Angelo on their cell phones, and let them know that we voted to accept the gift, though it was not yet public. I told them to expect a call from Cathy or Luigi about signing the papers, and added my personal excitement about Follamento.

Charles called both of them right after I did but Melissa lost some of her initial enthusiasm and did not call immediately. Her spirits picked up after Laura told her how much both of their fundraising reputations would be helped by the gift. She eventually called Lorenzo and Angelo but the conversations were brief and almost perfunctory according to both of them. Lorenzo actually asked if she was okay.

An hour after the board call, Gabe came to my office and asked how soon he could get out a press release. "You should start to work on the draft, review it with the Olmsted leadership, and then run it by Lorenzo."

"Can I call Lorenzo and Angelo while I am working on a draft?"

"Use your judgment. It's our press release, not theirs. Start with Lorenzo and let him provide advice on how much to involve Angelo."

"It's important to include a positive quote from Angelo as his absence could imply opposition."

Cathy came by my office and said that she had an unusual conversation with Lorenzo, the Italian law firm, and the Panamanian law firm, Guzman and Quintero. She described some of the complexity of American ownership of an Italian property that is incorporated in Panama, the upshot of which is that it could take almost a year to formally transfer the ownership to Olmsted.

"Can we push this along?"

"I pushed as hard as I could but the Panamanians are not budging, blaming it on bureaucracy in Panama. I spoke privately with Lorenzo and Luigi and they agreed to draft a time limited agreement covering the period between the signing of the gift agreement and the formal transfer." This was already more complex than I had imagined. Cathy ran this by Melissa, who said it was all fine, though Cathy felt that Melissa was zoning out.

The AUC meeting was six days away and Cathy's conclusion was that neither a gift nor the establishment of a study abroad site came under their purview. I called Nancy and let her know that the gift had board approval, but we would not be issuing the press release until after the AUC meeting.

Gabe worked expeditiously on the draft press release. Everyone signed off on his or her quotes and Angelo's was viewed as a signal that he was on board. "My father always had great ambitions for Follamento and the study abroad site that Olmsted envisions gives generations of students the opportunity to learn and work in this wonderful setting and have an experience of a lifetime." Melissa and Charles thought we should send out the release within the hour after the AUC meeting, around 1 p.m., and Gabe was ready.

The AUC meeting was a circus. The students wanted some acknowledgement of their sit-in and the promises that the University made, and Melissa was not going there. The students had prepared a summary of the agreed-upon items and when Melissa could not repeat them from memory, the students distributed the summary. Melissa was shaky, going point by point using the summary from the students, sometimes calling on Marshall or Cathy for clarification, but after this she totally lost it. "No one appreciated how the sit-in violated my space and betrayed me," she said. "You destroyed all the trust that had been built up between the students and administration during my presidency.

You were wrong for breaking the rules and not coming to me before you sat in my office." The students were taken aback, as were the rest of us. I caught a glimpse of Marshall and Gabe who were sitting next to each other and they looked like they were watching a train wreck. It took some time for anyone to respond, but finally the head of the student council said, "We believed that our requests were not being heard, and peaceful student protests are part of Olmsted's tradition." It was clear to all that of the two, the student council head was the grown-up in the room and Melissa did not realize that she had overreacted.

Melissa's speech put a damper on the meeting. But when she announced, "The Board has accepted the bequest from an alumnus, Roberto Follamento, and Olmsted will be establishing a study-abroad site in the Tuscan town of Follamento," there was a brief pause and then a rousing round of spontaneous applause which surprised me.

Right out of the box the student leaders asked if we would commit to financial aid so that all students at Olmsted could have a chance to study at Follamento.

Melissa turned to me. "We share the students' goals and that's our plan." There was another round of applause.

I thought that the presentation was completed but then came the biggest shocker. Despite the position endorsed by Melissa and the rest of the senior leadership that there would be no vote on the part of the AUC, Melissa then turned to Cathy and asked, "Should the AUC take a vote on the acceptance of the gift?" When this blunder was added to her earlier rant, I'm sure I was not the only one in the room to think that she was losing it. I had never seen Cathy openly disagree with Melissa, but I knew she needed to do it now.

After a significant pause, Cathy rose to the occasion and said, "A vote is not in order at this time as the AUC does not approve either gifts or the establishment of a study-abroad site."

When Melissa did not respond immediately, Marshall said, "Thank you, Cathy, for the clarification. My reading of the AUC's role is in agreement with Cathy's."

Melissa barely got through the rest of the AUC meeting.

Day 54

After fifty-four days I feel like a kid trying to hold my breath under water as long as I can and I have to surface. I feel that a reason for me to stay in prison will be manufactured. At breakfast a few hours ago Ernesto's uncle again raised the issue of my movement to the other side of the business. Ernesto was able to resist on the grounds that too much was in flux, but that just underscored that it was not a matter of *if* but *when.* I know that Hector and Al move at a pace that is largely out of their control but I'm frightened. Ernesto has shown no signs that something is brewing on the release side with his family and he confirmed after breakfast that if there's one more day of calm in the yard today, business will be on for tomorrow.

I miss Franny much more after she visited than before I saw her. Seeing her here reinforced that I do not know when I will see her again, and all these thoughts feed on one another. It's a cliché that family is most important, but it is. I'm sure Franny will be on Al's case relentlessly and she will weigh in whether or not Al and Hector consult her. I have always been a workaholic and now I'm not sure it has been worth it. Olmsted would be just fine if I had spent less time at work. I'm not sure why I needed to solve all the problems at Follamento without any help. I think of myself as a careful decision maker but now I'm not so sure.

The day after the AUC meeting I stopped by Marshall's office to get his take on Melissa. "I have not had a meaningful and coherent conversation with Melissa in weeks," he said. "I bounce back and forth between Melissa suffering some kind of temporary, acute, PTSD-like reaction to the student sit-in, versus a more chronic issue with her mental health. I hope it's the former and Melissa will emerge from her funk. Her career has been a series of five year stints in various positions where she was fortunate to move on before something like the student sit-in occurred. Her charmed career may have produced a sense of invulnerability and the sit-in was so disconfirming to her self-identity that it brought on the aberrant behavior."

"That seems plausible, I'm not sure."

While I was with Marshall, I ran by him my ideas on staffing the start-up of the study-abroad site. "On the academic side, I believe the Italian department and its chair, Angela LoPresti, should be in the lead. I would like Ed, our CFO, to take the lead on the non-academic side as the finances are a key issue. Drew should also be involved given the importance of Follamento's real estate, but he can report to Ed." Marshall was agreeable on all of this, but cautioned me to stay on top of Ed's budgetary forecasts.

After the AUC meeting we learned that Lorenzo countersigned the gift agreement, and Angelo had signed his agreement, making them both final. Just before Gabe made the press release public, he sent it to the entire Olmsted community. faculty, students and staff, with a short cover note from Laura. I had failed to let Gabe know that Laura was not involved with this gift so it was my fault, as previous community-wide gift announcements were sent out by Laura. Ironically, Laura called to thank me for letting it go out under her name.

Gabe hit the send button on the external release, but at Charles's direction, without disclosing the gift's valuation. This angered Laura and Gabe because they thought it would be mentioned as one of the largest gifts in higher education. We ended up getting good coverage, though each article was fairly short. The *Times* gave us four paragraphs in the section on New York and ran the piece in the national editions as well. They reached out to a more critical Olmsted faculty member, who was quoted often in the *Times*, and he said, "It is a wonderful gift for Olmsted, and maybe it will jump start our lagging global programs."

The academic planning needed to move quickly if we were going to meet the tight time line. Angela LoPresti agreed to be on point. Lucy Arguello, a second year post-doctoral fellow in the Italian department, who was doing research on 20th century Tuscan literature, agreed to coordinate the academic program, under Angela's direction.

Ed initially balked at being on point for the non-academic side, but when I said that Drew was my next choice he changed his mind. Ed asked Nate Zito, an Italian speaking analyst, to handle Follamento. Justin Casciano in student affairs agreed to cover student housing and health, and live in Follamento during the first year of operations. Cathy was handling the legal side which was focused on getting the Panamanian shares transferred to Olmsted. The complaints from Cathy came in like water in a fire hose. "It's going to be months before we see the actual transfer. I consulted with different Panamanian lawyers who confirmed that a process involving three countries, an estate and a gift is likely to be a long one."

"You should aim to get the transfer done before the students and faculty arrive in the fall." She made no promises but this is one she kept, sort of.

We realized that students needed to be recruited in January when they would be planning the next year's schedule. This marked a point of no return. I agreed to travel to Follamento once before Thanksgiving and again in January.

Franny and I continued taking private lessons in Italian one night a week at home. Our tutor was excellent, though neither Franny nor I had much of an aptitude for languages, making the going quite slow. He came to the apartment for an hour one evening each week and afterwards both Franny and I were exhausted.

I asked Ed and Nate to develop a placeholder budget for the rest of this academic year and one for following year. Sabrina Marchetti, the Follamento accountant/bookkeeper, was their primary point of contact along with Stefano Contrato, the accounting partner in Florence. Ed, Nate ad Drew would also need to rely on Paolo Tavente, who managed the capital projects.

Once I set my trip for mid-November and made sure that Lorenzo and Angelo would be there, Ed, Drew, Lucy, Justin and Nate decided that they would get there a few days before me and then report on what they had accomplished.

By our November visit, Lucy had made great progress on the academic program. She and Angela decided on Italian courses, and two courses each in art history, literature, economics, and political science. All of the courses except Italian would be taught in English, at least for now.

On my November visit I spent time with Lorenzo and Angelo, both separately and together. It seemed to me that once we had the formal agreements behind us, they were much more open, forthcoming and helpful.

Day 55

After breakfast Ernesto confirmed that we would resume our collections. "For now you are to continue with the three you've been working with before," Ernesto said, emphasizing *for now*. "Be alert and if you spot any trouble just stop. If trouble takes place after you do the pick-ups, quietly discard the cigarettes if you can do it without being caught." He was uncharacteristically nervous. I asked him if anything was wrong; he said no, but not convincingly.

A few minutes ago, Ernesto was taken to the administrative offices by a guard. I had a pit in my stomach thinking that it could be related to his transfer.

When I returned to Follamento in January for a five-day visit, it was the first time that the weather was not welcoming, though it was about twenty degrees warmer than in New York. Through the entire visit the sky was gray, it rained occasionally, and there was fog until noon. It was damp and the rudimentary heating systems in the old buildings made it feel colder inside than outside.

Lucy with Angela's help did an amazing job constructing the course schedule for September and even roughed one out for the next semester. She identified a mix of faculty from Olmsted and the University of Siena. This enabled us to announce the courses before the students applied to spend the semester at Follamento.

One of the most surprising calls I received was from New York University. A staff person in their community affairs office, Loretta McKay, called and invited me to stop by NYU's villa in Florence when I was next in Italy to both understand how they structured their study abroad site and to see if there were any opportunities for collaboration. I actually felt that they wanted to show off their magnificent facility in Florence but that was okay too. There were some at Olmsted who considered NYU as a competitor, though that was a stretch for Olmsted and no one at NYU thought we were the competition. Even if nothing came from the visit, I accepted their invitation and drove to their villa in Florence, La Pietra, about an hour and a half away.

I was determined to practice my Italian and when I got off of the Autostrada at Firenze (Florence) Sud. I tried asking the toll taker for a receipt in Italian, and of course I did not know the word for receipt so it took a lot of hand gestures and shouting. After about thirty seconds and some horn blowing behind me, he figured it out and gave me the receipt. As I was trying to create a learning moment, I asked in Italian, *"come si dice receipt,"* or how do you say receipt? He gave me the word and he laughed.

After I got off the Autostrada I drove to La Pietra, at 120 Via Bolognese. The NYU villa had a closed iron gate. I rang on the intercom and they opened it. Once through the gate there was a dirt road, lined by giant decades-old cypress trees, that went straight to La Pietra, originally a 15th century villa built by Sassetti, a banker to the Medici family. About 200 students from NYU study at La Pietra every semester and it was truly amazing. I was given the grand tour by the director, and I left thinking that with La Pietra in Florence and Follamento in the Tuscan countryside, collaboration could add significantly to the experiences of both Olmsted and NYU students.

I drove back to Follamento by the same route, skirting around Florence to the Firenze Sud exit, and then 85 kilometers south on the Autostrada to the Valdichiana exit. My comfort in Italy in general and with driving in particular was increasing and I was proud that I had navigated through a complex maze.

I exited at Valdichiana and at the toll I used the one lane with a person, instead of the automatic ones, in this case staffed by a young woman. I paid the toll, and then, feeling good and confident, I asked for a receipt using the word I had learned just that morning, "per favore, fica." The woman looked aghast and closed her sliding glass window, and she must have pushed a button because lights started to flash, sirens went off and gates were lowered behind and in front of the car. After about thirty seconds of noise and lights, two officials from the building next to the toll booth emerged and one signaled the cars behind me to go to another toll lane and the other told me to turn off my car and get out and give him my keys. While standing by the car I was asked for my license. I gave them my New York license and the international driver's license that I had purchased through AAA. They took my licenses and grabbed my arm and ushered me into the building next to the toll booth, then into a small, four-person conference room and told me, "Sit and wait." It was about 6 p.m.

I had no clue why I was pulled from the car and there was no one to ask. In a couple of minutes an Autostrada regional supervisor arrived. "Do you know what you did wrong?"

"No."

"What did you say to the toll taker?"

"I asked her for a receipt."

"Please repeat the actual phrase you used."

"Per *favore, fica.*"

He said, "The word, fica, is a slang word for a woman's vagina, something like the word, pussy, in English."

I was dumbfounded and then suddenly realized why the toll taker who gave me the word earlier that day at the Florence toll was smiling. My mistake was obviously compounded by the fact that the toll taker was a woman.

I explained what had happened and he asked, "Can I see the receipt from the Florence toll?" He went and made a copy of it and said, "The toll taker was obviously playing with you and if I can identify him from your receipt then he will be reprimanded. "You should be more careful in the future. The woman who you insulted just finished her shift and I want you to apologize to her. The word in Italian for receipt is *ricevuta.*" I apologized in English and the supervisor translated. I felt like I was in the principal's office. I drove back to Follamento fairly slowly, a little shaken, embarrassed and duped.

When I drove to the Rome to catch my flight to New York, I asked for a *ricevuta* at the toll booth.

Day 56

When Ernesto returned to the cell yesterday he was agitated. He said that the deputy warden advised him that he was on a transfer list and could be moved to a different prison any day now. His family is working to keep him here but there are no guarantees.

In the yard, everyone, including the guards, was on edge. I went to my "safe" place by the basketball court and watched out of the corner of my eye as Ernesto moved about discretely. Instead of standing in small groups around the perimeter, some of the guards were circulating, which made Ernesto much more cautious and it took twenty minutes instead of three. Once I saw that he was back with his uncle, I waited a couple of minutes and then walked circuitously to my first two pick-ups. No words were exchanged. After I left them, I walked in the direction of my third mark, who came bounding over. He said, "I am very pleased things have started up again," and he gave me the two packs. "Why did the pick-ups stop?"

"I do not know, but we should separate."

He reluctantly returned to his normal spot.

When we were set to go back, I lined up next to Ernesto. He said, "I am disappointed you did not confide in me that you reached out to the family about your release and I had to find out from my uncle."

I was ready for this. "I did not want to put you or your uncle at risk. I want my lawyer to do the legwork. This way you are not in the middle of my problems."

"Once I arranged the call I was in the middle. My family cannot go against Guzman and Quintero. The next time you should come to me." I was not about to tell him that I was working the prison bureaucracy through Al and Hector and the retired NYPD officers.

At dinner Ernesto's uncle told him that if things went well for a week, he would move both Ernesto and me to the other side of the business. Hector and Al had better hurry.

Soon after I returned from Follamento in January, the enrollment period for the fall and spring semesters began and I was anxious about whether we would hit our enrollment target. We announced that all students with financial need at Follamento would receive a supplemental $1,500. The *Oracle* ran an editorial that gave all the credit to the students in the sit-in, and Melissa demanded we say that we were going to do this anyway. Charles weighed in, "Unless we let the community know that we were going to do this without the sit-in, we will have a sit-in on every issue." Gabe, Marshall and I prevailed and we were silent, enabling the students to feel that they accomplished something.

There was no reason for me to worry about enrollment, as more than 300 students, about 20 percent of the College of Arts and Sciences, applied to go in the fall. Demand was so high that we needed a lottery.

In March, Ed and Drew stopped by my office and said, "We continue to feel that we are missing something in Follamento."

"Is this related to your comments about all the late model cars in the parking lots?"

"Yes and no. The numbers tie together but we feel uneasy."

Given Ed's history and Drew's hard-nosed nature, I knew that this was not fanciful or frivolous, but when I asked for evidence they admitted that it was weak. "Some of it has to with the residents' cars and clothing, which seem more upscale than their earnings suggest. Nearly everyone takes two or three trips a year to places all over Europe and to America, Australia, Japan, China, and South Korea. We do not want to bet our lives on what we are telling you."

I was planning to visit Follamento the following week, and said, "I will keep an eye out for anything unusual. Have you spoken to anyone about this?" Both said "No," quite emphatically and in unison.

"Please keep on the lookout and report to me anything that you spot, but keep it to yourselves, for now."

I tried to convince Franny to come with me this time, but with the wet and cool early March weather, she decided to stay in New York. I chose not to confide in her about the possible missing piece because it was too speculative. That was a mistake. I left on a Sunday, arrived Monday mid-morning, and drove to Follamento in time for a late lunch by myself. I got my ricevuta on the Autostrada without insulting anyone. In the afternoon I had meetings with Lorenzo and Angelo separately and then I had dinner with them together with Lorenzo's wife, Nicoletta. We had a very cordial and upbeat conversation but I could not help viewing everything through the lens that Ed and Drew put in my head.

This visit was timed to coincide with Justin's work on housing. On Tuesday and Wednesday, he and I toured all the apartments for students, faculty and staff, accompanied by Paolo Tavente, who would be responsible for upkeep and repairs.

At dinner on Wednesday I indirectly probed Justin for any observations linked to Ed's and Drew's comments. The only thing he noted was the high level of foot traffic around the piazza, especially in the evenings and on the weekends. He said that the pizza shop did a huge business and even delivered in vans to nearby towns. All of this seemed normal and innocent at the time.

Lorenzo was relaxed when I met him in his office for our final meeting on Friday afternoon. He asked, "How were the apartments?"

"I was favorably impressed and assuming Justin and Paolo take care of the punch list, housing should be all set." I then asked him a very general question, something like, "I have been coming to Follamento for almost nine months and I think that I am knowledgeable about how things work, but is it possible that I am missing something?"

I expected a no you are not missing anything but it was like I flipped a switch and he went from easy-going and calm to questioning and tense. "Why, did you find something? Is there something that you want to talk about?"

204

In that split second, I was surer that Ed and Drew were on to something. I remained calm and matter-of-fact, and retreated. "There is nothing specific, but if there is anyone who could tell me what I do not know, it is you."

On a scale of ten this brought him from a 9.9 to a 9.0 and he said, "If ever there is ever something important that you need to know I will tell you. If you have any questions, please come to me."

"I am now responsible for the lives of students, faculty and staff, and I want to be sure."

He calmed down a little more and said, "The students, faculty and staff will have the time of their lives."

Day 57

Hector started this morning's visit by saying, "There is movement but no breakthrough. We even toyed with the idea of waiting before we visited, but we knew that you are anxious for news." Al said, "Kevin and Greg will consider it a personal failure if they did not get you out."

But Hector said, "Enthusiasm and commitment can go only so far in Panama. The people who want you in jail are clearly very powerful. Kevin and Greg have contacts in the right places. But too much pressure could backfire."

"The family is trying to pull me deeper into the business, and this makes me very nervous."

"Resist this move at all costs, even to the point of going to the infirmary." He further confirmed that the approach through the family was dead. "It goes without saying but I will say it anyway. you should not reveal any of the Kevin and Greg approach to Ernesto." I felt like I was walking on a high wire with a growing crosswind.

Al has been speaking with Franny at least every other day. She and our kids are nervous. I think being out of touch and far away may be even more difficult for Franny than for me. This is the first time in our forty-year marriage that we have been apart and not speaking. Al said, "Your kids want to come, but we told them it's too dangerous."

Al and Hector were trying to bolster my spirits, but frustration showed on them. They were able to decipher and read my writing, and wanted to know if the circumstances in Italy that got me in prison could change in such a way that I would be released. I told them I didn't know.

Ernesto has been acting cooler and visibly annoyed. On the line back from dinner he said, "My uncle thinks it's time for us to graduate." As if I did not have enough to worry about, later that night he said, "My family is trying to prevent my transfer but even if I stay here the prison officials can change our cellmates every sixty days." Of course, he waited until day fifty-seven to spring this on me.

I used the plane ride home from the March visit to try to organize my thoughts. I had Ed's and Drew's observations and the over-reaction from Lorenzo as the most obvious data points and I fantasized that perhaps there was a secret drug business. But as soon as I thought of this, I chalked it up to watching too many police dramas.

I woke up from a brief nap with an obvious idea. David Goodman, Olmsted's head of security who worked with me on the student sit-in, mentioned that if I was so inclined, he could come to Follamento to do a "safety check." He said it in a "if you want to send me to Italy I would be willing to endure the hardship" way but he is a smart professional and I could ask him to assess the safety for students, faculty, and staff without any hint at my concerns.

When I returned to New York I asked David if he could accompany me in April. He not only agreed but also made the case for bringing along one of his senior deputies, Ralph Williams, who speaks fluent Italian. Meanwhile, Melissa's strange behavior continued to get worse. She met with as few people as she could, cut short public ceremonial occasions she used to enjoy and blew off several fund raising appointments and a gala where Marshall was being honored. She was forgetting basic things I had told her over the preceding week and was nasty at times in ways I'd never seen before. I was not surprised when Marshall told me that he was quietly going on the job market. "I think Melissa's presidency could end badly and I don't want to go down with the ship. Because the job search is taking up a lot of time, you should bother me only with highly consequential issues. Otherwise you should handle them yourself." I always thought of myself as a "lifer" at Olmsted but Marshall's perspective was food for thought.

The visit to Follamento was scheduled first week in April. We had a large contingent this time, with David and Ralph; Lucy, Nate and Justin, and even Angela. Before we arrived, I called Lorenzo to let him know about the safety check. "This visit is a typical American misjudgment and it stems from negative stereotypes of Italians," he said. Angelo got wind of it and acted even more insulted. He tried to talk me out of the safety check, but I wasn't backing off.

Day 58

In the middle of last night Ernesto woke up feeling terrible. He vomited several times and had diarrhea. He spent the entire night on the toilet. With no circulation in the cell, I felt like I was stuck in a port-o-san. By 6 a.m. he was weak and pale and we called for a guard. The guard said, "There were five cases of this last night, probably food poisoning." Initially, Ernesto said that he would ride it out in the cell, but when I returned from breakfast he was worse and a guard took him to the infirmary. Despite his complicity, his absence drove home how much I counted on him. Even breakfast alone was nerve racking. His uncle came over to me on the cafeteria line and said, "I will let you know about the pick-ups at lunch today."

On the first day of the April trip, Lorenzo sent an email to all the businesses and town officials with a copy to me to let them know that David and Ralph would be in town through Thursday, and to answer all of their questions and show them anything that they wanted to see. I worked with Nate, Justin and Paolo on the punch list for the apartments.

At dinner David and Ralph said that they had not found anything really unusual but they had several questions for Sabrina, the bookkeeper/accountant, especially about the compensation of the employees.

I spent the next day with Lucy and Angela, who toured me through the classrooms and reviewed the academic program. Then I met with David and Ralph for a drink at the hotel before dinner. David, who did most of the talking, reiterated what he said the day before, "Follamento is a very safe place and this was confirmed by our visit with the Carabinieri who were very friendly and offered to show us anything that we needed to see."

After this good news, they mentioned two things that were a little unexpected. First, apparently without having spoken with Ed and Drew, David, said, "The cars in the parking lot seem to be higher end than the families could afford on the salaries reported to us by Sabrina. Perhaps Italians spend more of their budgets on cars, but all the new Mercedes, BMWs and Alfa Romeos don't fit what they're earning. Second, when we were having lunch outside at the Osteria, we noticed an unusual amount of carry-out pizzas. Would it be okay if, tomorrow, we follow the van making pizza deliveries?"

"Okay, even though it seems far-fetched." Not as far-fetched as me being in a Panamanian prison for over eight weeks.

On our last day, I had lunch by myself in the Osteria and then went to my meetings with Lorenzo and Angelo, scheduled for 3 p.m. to be followed by my meeting with Lorenzo alone, at 4:30. Angelo and Lorenzo were in Lorenzo's office when I arrived and it appeared from the espresso cups that they had been there for a while.

There was a chill in the room at the start. First up, they wanted to know what David and Ralph found. "In my briefing last night they concluded that Follamento is very safe."

Angelo asked, "Did they find anything unusual or worrisome?"

"No."

"Was David and Ralph's visit necessary given that they did not find anything?" Lorenzo asked.

I purposely paused before I answered, partly to calm myself, and partly to see if Angelo would say anything but when he was not going to answer, I said, "Student, faculty and staff safety is paramount to Olmsted and while Follamento appears to be safe, I wanted the Olmsted security professionals to make an independent judgment."

"You have subjected us to an unnecessary inquiry and our meeting is over." Lorenzo's voice was cold.

The last dinner for the Olmsted contingent was scheduled for seven o'clock at the Osteria. Angela, Lucy, and Justin were already there and Nate arrived when I did but there was no sign of David and Ralph. They finally arrived as we were ordering dessert at 9:15. We all headed back to the hotel around 10 p.m. and I asked David and Ralph if they wanted to go for a walk.

David said, "We staked out the pizzeria all day with nothing to show for it until we were ready to quit. At 6:45 the van drove across the piazza, parked in front of the pizzeria, and loaded ten unusually large pizza boxes in the van, one at a time, which seemed strange as they are easy to stack. At that point Ralph went to get the car and I stayed just off the piazza watching the van which sat for fifteen minutes. It was clear that they were in no hurry. Finally the two young men who loaded the pizzas drove the van north across the piazza toward the San Giovanni-Torrenieri road. I called Ralph and we followed. After about two and a half kilometers the van turned left up the hill to San Giovanni D'Asso and stopped in the middle of town. Ralph let me out and parked out of sight.

"The two men started to unload the boxes one at a time. The address was Via XX September #30." That seemed familiar to me and when I looked in my phone it was the same address where I had initially met with Lorenzo in July. "Each of the trips to unload the boxes took about five minutes. Just before the van left, a man walked up and said hello to the two men and then entered the same address. I used my cell phone to snap a picture of them." When David enlarged it for me, I could see clearly that the third man was Lorenzo.

"What do you think is happening?" I said.

"Our only conclusion is that the boxes do not contain pizzas." I explained that Lorenzo had a small office at that address, which was where I met him in July. By this time we were back to the hotel and David asked, "Should we change our flights and look into this over the next few days?"

"No, if something develops I will ask you to come back," and they emailed me the photo. We each had a glass of wine and went to our rooms but I could not sleep. I decided to call Delta and changed my flight from Friday to Sunday, giving me two more days in Follamento, and I let Franny know I would be staying. She wanted to know why and I explained that I needed to tie up some loose ends which may take a day or two. Franny said, "It's okay if you don't want to tell me the details but don't make up a story. I'm no longer so sure this Italy thing is a good idea."

Day 59

At lunch yesterday I ate alone. Ernesto's uncle approached me and said, "You should do your regular pick-ups and keep the cigarettes in your cell." But when I got back to my cell, I threw up and had diarrhea and lay down to sleep, skipping dinner. At breakfast Ernesto's uncle asked, "Why weren't you in the yard yesterday?" I answered, "I had a case like Ernesto's," and he just rolled his eyes, grunted and walked away.

On Friday in Follamento I watched the pizzeria during the morning. The bar had a small outside seating area and I slowly drank a couple of cappuccinos. Over the course of three hours about fifteen people went into the pizzeria and only two came out. At about 11:30 a.m. I went into the pizzeria and no one was there, which meant at least thirteen people must have gone out the back door. I decided to go to the Osteria for lunch and to warm up.

As soon as I sat down, Paolo and Sabrina came in and asked if they could join me. "I thought you were leaving today," Paolo said. This made me nervous; maybe he had been watching me during the morning. I said, "It's so beautiful in Follamento that I decided to stay the weekend," and he and Sabrina seemed to buy that. Toward the end of the meal there was a short lull and I asked, "Where do folks in Follamento buy their cars? I don't see any dealers in town."

Paulo replied, "There are a couple of places in Buonconvento, but most people go to Siena. Cars are important to Italians."

As we were getting up to leave, Lorenzo came in for lunch. He spotted us, came over, and said, "I thought you were leaving to go back to New York."

"I decided to stay the weekend."

He paused, and said, "If you have some time at five you should stop by my office."

During the next two hours I walked around the piazza and every twenty minutes or so I went through the two passage-ways from the piazza to the grassy area behind the shops and then to the upper street and back. There was plenty of foot traffic but at no time did I see anyone leave the pizzeria from the rear door.

At Lorenzo's office his assistant greeted me by saying, "He is expecting you." I entered and he said, "I sense that we are not communicating clearly. Your so-called security check is an insult that conveys to the world that you do not trust me." There was some truth to that.

"The visit was not intended to be insulting. We now have confirmation that Follamento is safe and we are looking forward to the students' arrival in September."

"I accept your apology," even though I did not apologize. We shook hands and he offered me a glass of wine which we drank and things seemed to be a little better between us. As I left he said, "Please come to me with any questions rather than try to play detective." The way he said this made me very nervous.

My flight was Sunday and I now had Saturday on my own. I decided to take the 80-minute drive to San Gimignano, which is a beautiful town between Siena and Florence. After lunch I headed for the car and as I passed one of the several galleries on the main street there was a blue van parked outside and two men were delivering what appeared to be pizza boxes. At first I thought it was a lot of pizza for a gallery and maybe they were having an opening. Discretely I took a photo and then walked away to compare it with Thursday's. It was clearly the same men, though a different van.

I waited until they left before I went into the gallery, which had an eclectic collection of modern paintings, sculptures, ceramics, and photographs. There was no sign of pizza boxes. One of the gallery staff came over and asked, "Can I help you?"

I wanted to ask what they did with the pizza boxes but I did not opt for the direct approach. I walked around, saw a watercolor artist that I liked and asked, "Do you have any others?"

She said, "I have a couple in the back." I followed her to the back of the gallery as she entered a store room and brought out two unframed watercolors. I looked at them and said, "I'll think about it." I could see partway into the store room but did not see any pizza boxes. I left the gallery no closer to figuring out what was going on. But the first watercolor I admired was special and I went back to the gallery to purchase it for Franny.

As I drove back to Follamento, I asked myself whether I had any real evidence that would jeopardize the program in Follamento. The worst case scenario was that there was some kind of clandestine drug business but I had no hard evidence.

Once I convinced myself that the semester in Follamento should start as planned, I thought through my next steps. Melissa was deep into some other world and Marshall had one or two feet out the door. Lucy and Angela were busy starting a new academic program, Nate was working on finances, and Justin was responsible for the fifty students. None of them had time to play detective. I decided to keep the information to myself until I discovered something more dispositive, as the lawyers like to say. Looking back, I should have asked for help or at least spoken with an Olmsted colleague. I was fearful that something could kill the program and that clouded my judgment.

At least I did one thing right. Franny loved the watercolor.

My next visit to Follamento was in May, and Franny came with me so we could visit Florence and Venice after my meetings. I told myself that visit didn't lend itself to further sleuthing, and anyway, I was going to come back in late August when the students arrived. It was a combination of procrastination and delusion. I desperately wanted this to be *my* project.

Day 60

At around 10 this morning, Ernesto returned to the cell, still looking pale and weak and he confirmed my amateur diagnosis of a forty-eight-hour flu. I told him, "I had a mild case two days ago but I was able to sleep it off."

He guided me to the corner of the cell where we were off camera and said, "Your mark, who works in the infirmary, took good care of me."

"I skipped the pick up the day before yesterday, but resumed yesterday and I have the cigarettes in the cell."

"Did you speak with my uncle?"

"Yes, he wondered why I missed a pick up and when I told him I had a bug he walked away."

"My uncle thinks there is no valid excuse for missing a pick up." It may be my imagination but some of the tension that I sensed between us before he got sick appears to have lessened which, if true, is a good thing.

Ernesto was extremely talkative. "Was there was any news on the 60 day rule to change cellmates?"

"No and I didn't see any movement among the other cells."

"I asked my uncle to use his influence to keep us together and he said that he would try, as that will be more important when we switch to the other end of the business." Was that the good news or the bad news? "When will your lawyer visit again?"

These were a lot of questions from Ernesto but I could not read anything particular into it except that he was pleased to be back in our cell with someone he could talk with. Even if Ernesto is using me, I hope we stay in the same cell, perhaps a case of Stockholm syndrome.

Shortly after I returned from my April trip, Charles asked to meet in his office for an update. I told him that everything was close to schedule, but decided not to discuss my concerns. Now that I suspect he's connected with Guzman and Quintero, who knows what might have happened if I had leveled with him.

Charles asked, "How is everything with Lorenzo and Angelo?"

"We are doing okay, considering everything. Lorenzo and Angelo, but especially Lorenzo, asked whether the safety visit by David and Ralph was necessary."

"Was the visit necessary or were you just covering yourself?"

"I wanted other professionals to look things over."

"You were covering yourself."

I decided not to argue.

"Are you glossing over any problems with Lorenzo and Angelo?"

"We are getting used to working together."

Charles let it drop there. As he walked me out of his office, he asked about Melissa and Marshall.

"With my travelling to Follamento quite often I don't see Melissa as much."

"I don't see her much either and when I do see her, she seems to be in another place."

"I know Marshall told you he's looking at presidencies. He will be tough to replace but we should be able to attract a strong pool of candidates."

As we said goodbye Charles repeated, "If anything does not seem right in Follamento, please contact me immediately."

Nate met with me a couple of days before Franny and I departed for the mid-May visit. "When I did the financial review with Sabrina," he said, "she seemed edgy, and one category labeled 'other revenues' had declined by about 50,000 euros a month. When I asked Sabrina about it, she said, "that it's a catch-all category of one-time items, such as the sale of a piece of artwork in Roberto's collection or the sale of land or a building. Now that the collection is owned by Angelo, any proceeds went directly to him." Neither Ed nor I had seen this coming, but now the budget is tighter. He suggested I meet with Sabrina and I said I would.

Before Franny and I left, the student newspaper, *The Oracle,* published its annual review of the academic year. It took an unusually harsh view of Olmsted's leadership and called Melissa the absentee president who had done a disappearing act. The story also noted that Marshall was interviewing for presidencies elsewhere. The article, which was more of an editorial, said that if not for the Follamento gift, the previous year would have been a lost year. It went on to lament the fact that other universities such as NYU were gearing up their global program and that all of Olmsted's eggs were in Follamento. They complained that the long-awaited report from the faculty committee on global articulation was a non-event.

After the faculty committee had endorsed the Follamento gift, I stopped attending their monthly meetings but I heard from colleagues that they were bogged down over how specific to be in their final report. They wanted to encourage Olmsted to move more aggressively in the global area, and to do so with strong faculty leadership, and they wanted the global initiatives to be prudent and to allow all students to participate. They did not reconcile how to be aggressive and prudent at the same time and no examples or specifics were included. Ironically, they praised Follamento as an important first step and commended Olmsted's leadership for putting faculty in the lead in designing the academic program. I found it a shame that after the faculty made such a big deal out of faculty leadership that they proved unable to actually lead.

Rightly or wrongly, I felt tremendous pressure for Follamento's success, and felt it was all up to me. In retrospect I wasn't thinking clearly.

Day 61

While nothing seems to be a sure thing in my case, Hector and Al identified a promising pathway for my release. Hector thought it was our best chance, though Al worried that we were being shaken down with no guarantee of success. Hector and I had to explain that without some pro-active moves on our part, I could be in prison for a long time.

"According to Kevin and Greg, with about $15,000 in U.S. dollars we could get the Department of Corrections to issue a release order," Hector said. That was the good news. The less than good news was that we needed the signoff from the prison warden, who might be in the pocket of one or both families. "To get the approvals of the family and warden, we would have to pay more, but I am not sure how much."

During this discussion I thought Al and Hector would handle the approval, but Hector said, "Bill is in the best position to try to gain the support of at least Ernesto's family and also determine whether that's all we need." When I tried to push back, Hector argued, probably correctly, "You are much closer to the right people."

I asked about Guzman and Quintero, and Al and Hector looked sheepishly at each other. Finally. Hector said, "We believe that if we follow the plan, your release might not be contingent on their approval."

Sensing that I felt worn down and depressed, they tried to help me think through the right approach to Ernesto. I explained again, "They're pushing me to participate in the 'other side' of the business, which makes the timing awkward."

But Al actually thought that this was a good time to try to get the family approval. I could claim that I could never participate in that side of the business so they might as well reap some profit from my release.

I asked Hector, "Do you have any idea what the family approval would likely cost?"

"I suggest that you start by offering $10,000, saying that it's coming from your pocket, and see what happens."

I wondered if I could put the payment on a university reimbursement form. There was also the warden but I did not want to go there.

When I returned to the cell, I told Ernesto, "My attorney found a possible pathway but I need your help. We can talk over dinner."

At dinner, Ernesto's uncle pre-empted my discussion by coming over as soon as we sat down. Their private conversation took all of the time in the cafeteria. On the way back to the cell, Ernesto said, "The conversation was about a prisoner who was skimming and needed to be replaced." This was not the news I was hoping for.

Franny and I arrived in Follamento on a Tuesday afternoon, May 24th, the most dazzling time of the year. The countryside was green, the sky a deep blue and many flowers and trees were in bloom including the red poppies and the yellow genestra. We had an early dinner at Osteria Buona Fortuna and slept a full eleven hours.

First thing Wednesday morning I met Sabrina. Her self-confidence was gone, she was upset, and initially she could not make eye contact. I did not know her that well but I took a chance and asked, "Is everything okay?" She started to sob. When her crying went on and on, I became downright scared. I wanted to reach out and hug her but in this day and age that was off the table.

Finally, she said, "There is something important that you do not know but I cannot tell you more. You have to find out from someone else."

"Does it have something to do with the shortfall that you discussed with Nate?"

Sabrina held firm. "I cannot tell you anything more."

I tried asking her a dozen different ways but she had made up her mind. When I realized that my pushing was making her more uncomfortable, I stopped and asked, "Do you agree with Nate's assessment that Follamento will still break even?"

"I think so."

As a way to keep her talking and prolong the meeting, I said, "I'm meeting with Lorenzo and Angelo tomorrow. Are you working well with both of them?

"I work for Angelo and see him several times a week but I rarely see Lorenzo. Sometimes he will have a question but most of the time he goes through Angelo." She was regaining some of her self-confidence. "What do you think of Angelo?"

Realizing that was a loaded question, and wanting to keep her talking, I added, "I feel that we have a decent relationship though there is always some kind of edge."

Sabrina smiled. "What you see with Angelo is an act, admittedly a good one, but in reality he is furious."

I decided to take a chance with my next question. "Do you have any idea why Roberto did not give Follamento to Angelo?"

"I do not know for sure but I suspect that Roberto was worried that Angelo would manage for his own benefit. I hope that Olmsted will steer Follamento in the right direction." It was gutsy of her to speak this candidly. At the end of the meeting she came surprisingly and uncomfortably close to me and said, "My fate is in your hands and you need to keep my confidence."

Although I tell Franny practically everything that goes on in my life, I did not tell her. In no uncertain terms, Franny would have implored me to discuss the situation with my colleagues and enlist their help instead of trying to be a big shot and solve what was turning out to be a mess completely on my own.

Day 62

I did not sleep all night thinking about what I would say to Ernesto over breakfast. It was neither as good nor as bad as it could have been.

I thought that I was pretty composed when I started talking but I realized that my hands were trembling. "I'm at the end of my rope, and I'm doing all I can do to hold things together. When I was feeling sick and you were in the infirmary I almost thought about giving up, but I rallied and blamed my depression on the stomach bug." This was true, though I was overstating it to get some sympathy.

"My attorney, Hector, is working to gain my release and one approach is through contacts with the Department of Correction." I did not plan to say "one approach" but when it came out that way I realized that it was a good way for Ernesto to think that I had more options. "I have thought long and hard about your uncle's desire to get me involved in the other side of the business, and even if it jeopardizes my safety and well-being, I will never do that. If I'm caught with the merchandise, I could spend years in prison which I can not handle. I realize my refusal could be dangerous and create bad blood between us, which is not what I want to do, but I know myself and I will not get involved in the other side of the business."

"That is really unfortunate. Because a key player is now out of the business. I am sure my uncle will want you involved as soon as possible."

Ernesto had a serious and menacing look, but I held firm. "I have a proposition to make. The option with the Department of Corrections is promising, but Hector believes that support from your family relayed to the warden will increase the odds of success even more. I'm prepared to pay $10,000 U.S. to the family if they support my release."

Ernesto, who had his elbows on the table and his head resting on his hands, leaned back. He said, "I do not know exactly how to say this but my family, particularly my uncle, do not like to be presented with problems. Your refusal to work with the family is a problem and your suggestion of buying your way out of prison is risky and can go wrong in many different ways." As unbelievable as this will sound, I was pleased with Ernesto's answer because it was not an outright refusal. "I understand if the family will not support my release but perhaps they would not oppose it either."

"You probably realize this already, but you could pay the money to the Department of Corrections and still not get out."

"My dealings with you and the family have been truthful, and while I know there are no guarantees, I'm sure that if the family agrees to help me, they will."

"I will bring your proposal to my uncle, but I am not optimistic about the response." As soon as these words were out of Ernesto's mouth, as if on cue, his uncle came over to the table. Unlike all previous times, he did not come to sit down and did not ask me to move away, but he whispered something to Ernesto and left. Ernesto turned pale and he said, "The matter that my uncle described yesterday is taken care of." Right after that, before the end of breakfast, an alarm sounded and we were lined up and marched back to our cells. On the way back to the cell Ernesto said, "The inmate who wanted out of the drug business is in the infirmary with several stab wounds." Back in the cell Ernesto said "I will wait a day or so until things have calmed down and then raise your proposition with my uncle." I was glad that the interaction was over, at least for now. As soon we got back to the cell, the guards announced that there would be no time in the yard at least for the next two days, which was fine with me.

Franny and I awoke on Wednesday to another crisp and clear spring day in Follamento. We had cappuccino together and Franny drove to Siena. I arrived at Lorenzo's office right at ten, early for Italy. He was ready for me nonetheless and Barbara offered me the obligatory coffee.

Lorenzo dutifully asked about Franny and then he got right to business. "I am sorry to say this but Olmsted's take-over of Follamento is changing the town's culture for the worse. Angelo and I believe Ed and Nate's oversight of the finances is too controlling, and their demand for monthly reporting is too onerous. We should change to quarterly reporting."

I knew from Ed and Nate that this was a non-starter. "The time commitment will lessen once everyone is familiar with the process, but given the absence of any real-time computer system like we have in New York, monthly reporting needs to stay in place." I thought that Sabrina told me they did monthly reporting already but at the time I was not sure. "The bequest of Follamento affects our finances and we are too close to break-even."

"Are you seeing Sabrina on this trip?"

"I met with her yesterday," which seemed to surprise him. He asked if she brought this up and I said no, and then he suggested, "You should see her again to check on the specific issue of quarterly reporting."

"I will but I know if it is important to her she would have said something yesterday."

"My second issue is more delicate than the first," and he gave himself some time by asking Barbara to bring us another cup of coffee. Once Barbara left his office, Lorenzo said, "I know that you are looking around and asking a lot of questions, and that it is making everyone very nervous."

I had thought my sleuthing was pretty subtle and unobtrusive, but apparently I was mistaken. "Follamento is all new to Olmsted and because I'm the most responsible administrator, I need to learn as much as I can. I don't think that I am asking an inordinate number of questions, but I will be mindful of my presence going forward." Going through my head were Sabrina's words that I did not know what I needed to know.

Lorenzo reiterated what he had said many times only this time I heard it differently. "If you have ANY questions, you should not play detective but instead come to me."

Instead of the "yes, sir," I'm sure he wanted, I said, "I'm not giving up my right to ask questions, to establish relationships with people such as Sabrina and Paolo."

"You are not really listening to me."

"I hear you. I will ask my questions with more sensitivity."

Lorenzo then stood up, ending the meeting very abruptly and early, saying, without meaning it, that he was looking forward to our dinner that night.

I was sufficiently put off that I felt like leaving Follamento for lunch. It seemed to me that I was followed by a white Fiat 500 from Follamento to San Giovanni which then reappeared behind me after lunch.

To say that I was edgy going into my 3 p.m. meeting with Angelo is an understatement. He met me in his office above the hardware store, greeted me cordially, asked about Franny, and then said, "Have you spoken to Sabrina on this visit?"

"I met with her yesterday."

"Is your time in Follamento living up to what you thought it would be?"

This was actually a question that I considered over lunch and I was a little worried that my answer would sound too rehearsed, but I used it anyway. "The gift by your father is so unique and magnificent, it was impossible to form any expectations going in. During my time here I am impressed with the way the town functions and I'm confident that the students and faculty will benefit immensely."

"Good. I think you can relax a little and not try to manage every little detail."

"We are managing at the same level of detail as in New York."

"It is probably inevitable that Follamento will change with Olmsted's involvement, but I hope that once you gain confidence that everything runs smoothly, things will operate more like they were before my dad passed away."

After our meeting, I wandered over to the town offices to see if Sabrina was in. She was glad to see me. I sat on a couch in front of her desk and she asked, "How did your meetings go with Lorenzo and Angelo?"

"Both of them alluded to you when they told me that the monthly reporting was too onerous."

Sabrina laughed and said, "They are hiding behind me. I did monthly reporting before Roberto died." Then, she came around her desk and sat close to me on the couch, lowered her voice and said, "Thank you for being so understanding yesterday when I fell apart."

"I appreciate the pressure you're under and you should know that I would never reveal the things that you told me."

"I know. Thank you."

Day 63

Yesterday after lunch, Ernesto told me that his uncle was very angry. According to Ernesto, his uncle said I still owe the family and it's essential for me to work on the other side of the business, at least to fill in while they are short-handed.

"I repaid my debt for the phone call. My refusal to work on the other side of the business is absolute and we will pursue our option without your family's support."

"You will cave, but give me a chance to speak with my uncle over dinner."

About an hour before lunch, five cells were opened and one inmate in each cell was removed and rotated to another cell, part of the plan to prevent inmates from becoming too close to each other. Ernesto believed we would be exempt.

At lunch, three inmates started to pummel a fourth until the guards broke it up. The men who instigated the fight were taken away and the fourth inmate, covered in blood, was removed separately, presumably to the infirmary. On the way back to the cell Ernesto said, "The inmate who was attacked lost his support from the family."

The time before dinner was an eternity, with cell-mate changing in five additional cells. I read a few chapters in the Truman biography but I was really thinking about how it would go at dinner with Ernesto's uncle. On the line Ernesto asked, "Can you do a few days on the other side of the business as a gesture of good will?" Maybe he thought that I was moved by the beating at lunch, but I would never do it.

Ernesto's uncle came over, I moved away, and they talked for a bit. On the way back to the cell Ernesto said, "I made a case for the family to help you out. I used your line about being a good worker since you were brought into the business and also used the argument that if you were released and returned to New York you could continue to be useful to the family."

I never would have suggested such a thing but I had to trust that Ernesto knew better than I did how to work his uncle.

"My uncle is worried about going against Guzman and Quintero."

"Once Guzman and Quintero are ready to release me then I really do not need the family's support."

This must have hit a raw nerve for Ernesto. "Do not ever say that again. You are playing a dangerous game with a very tough crowd and trying to pressure my uncle is a sure way to get on his bad side. If I repeat the idea that Guzman and Quintero could release you without the family support, my uncle will feel that you are disloyal and you will be seen as a liability." Just before we got to the cell Ernesto said, "My uncle will think about supporting you. I was surprised that I did not get no for an answer."

Franny returned from Siena a little before I got back from my meeting with Sabrina, and we went to the small bar in the Hotel Buona Notte for a glass of wine. She could see that I was in a funk and implored me to snap out of it so we could tolerate or even enjoy the upcoming dinner. We arrived fashionably late, and we were the first to arrive. The next guest was a surprise, Sabrina. I introduced her to Franny and she told us that Angelo and Lorenzo invited her. Maybe they wanted to keep an eye on her. Lorenzo and his wife, Nicoletta, arrived next and a little of the chill I felt in the morning was diminished, but not totally gone. Angelo made his grand entrance last and announced that he was going to the cellar to get a few bottles of his dad's 1997 Brunello wines to make this a celebratory dinner. He offered a very long toast to the growing relationship between Follamento and Olmsted. "My father made an excellent choice." I could not help catch Sabrina's eye. We both knew he deserved an Oscar. We had a fabulous meal and the six of us finished three bottles of the incredible wine. After some grappa and coffee that Franny and I passed on, Angelo invited us all downstairs to see his father's wine cellar, or as Angelo corrected me, one of his wine cellars.

I did not know what to expect but whatever I was thinking it paled in comparison to the vast expanse of wine cases as far as the eye could see. The basement extended well beyond the foot-print of the restaurant on both sides and I asked Angelo whether it was also under the piazza, and he said, "It is. With the strict rules in Tuscany, the only new space we can build is underground. I do not have to purchase another bottle of wine for the rest of my life. As my dad's wine collection grew, it was too large for the palazzo. To hold more wine, he expanded the basement under the piazza and appropriated the basements from the art gallery and town offices."

On the way back to the hotel, Franny commented about how pleasurable the dinner was, but then took a jab at me and said, "You were really eyeing Sabrina." She is attractive but other than during Angelo's toast, I was not at all aware that I was looking at her more than at anyone else.

Franny is quick to pick these things out and it left me no choice but to say, "She's half my age."

Franny looked at me and asked, "Why does that matter?"

"I'm in love with only you," but she only chuckled and said, "Gottcha" as we arrived at the hotel.

Day 64

Hector and Al were very interested in Follamento and even though I wrote about it in the pages that I gave them, they wanted me to go over everything. "Franny is freaking out," Al said. "She's pressing harder to visit and is calling all over the US State Department." Hector asked, "Should I see if the warden will allow you a phone call to her?"

I thought about it and said, "As much as I want to talk with her, I don't want to use a chip on a phone call."

"Right answer."

"Ernesto delivered my message to his uncle, who was angry and insisted that I get involved in the other side of the business. An inmate was badly beaten at lunch. Ernesto told me that this inmate had fallen out of favor with the family and I'm sure that this beating was a message to me."

"I am surprised. I assume Ernesto's uncle has many people he could trust to do this work. In addition, you are not likely to be good at it, for a variety of reasons, foremost being your limited knowledge of Spanish. It is unfortunate that an inmate was beaten simply to teach you a lesson."

"Ernesto said he argued on my behalf a second time and his uncle agreed to consider my request. As part of Ernesto's argument, he said that I could be valuable to the family in New York which makes me really nervous but I'm not worrying about it for now. I tried to tell Ernesto that if Guzman and Quintero want to release me, then I will not need the family's support, and he went berserk. I thought it was an overreaction but then Ernesto said that if he repeated this to his uncle it would have been interpreted as a threat and I should never do that again."

Hector asked, "Did you raise the idea of getting the support of both families?"

"No. It would greatly complicate things and also give his uncle another reason to get me to do the other business."

Hector said, "You are right, but if you see an opening you should go for it."

Both Hector and Al thought that my interactions with Ernesto and his uncle went better than they expected. Al said, "His uncle may be the kind of person who says no to everything the first time." Al asked about alerting the U.S. Embassy and Hector felt that we should do that when we actually heard that there was movement to release me; the Embassy could not be helpful in the process we were counting on. Finally Al and Hector told me that they were not going to contact Guzman and Quintero until we knew more about where the current options were going.

Before they left, they spent a few minutes trying to build up my spirits. "One way or the other we will get you out," Hector said. I knew that they were bluffing but it was good to hear it anyway.

Franny and I left Follamento and drove through a classic part of Tuscany and then up the hill to San Gimignano. After we had porchetta sandwiches for lunch, I wanted to show her the paintings in the gallery where I purchased the watercolor. The gallery owner had excellent taste, or more accurately had our taste. This time, there were about a dozen new works by the same artist, only now the paintings were more in the range of 8,000 to 10,000 euros instead of the 1,500 euros I had paid. As we were admiring them, the gallery owner came over to us and said she remembered me.

"I'm surprised that the prices are so much higher."

"The artist just passed away, and these are her last works."

We gave her our condolences. As we left the gallery, Franny said, "I like the painting you bought, and now it turns out to be worth a lot more than we paid for it."

Back in New York, Melissa wanted to meet with me right away. She asked me a lot of basic questions that she should have been able to answer herself, at times mixed up Lorenzo and Angelo, and had no clue about the academic program. I tried to straighten her out but I had the feeling that nothing was retained for more than a minute. What she did know was that with the Follamento gift, her fundraising totals were among the highest nation-wide.

I also met with Marshall, who gave me details on his two recent university president interviews. He would hear from both before Thanksgiving, and it was obvious that his attention was far away from Olmsted.

Charles was now the only one who wanted to know all the details. He pressed me repeatedly on how soon we could complete the stock transfer and when I said that he should ask Cathy he said, "I thought you are in charge of this project. You should know something this important."

I thought that entire interchange seemed out of character but at that point I didn't know about his connection to Guzman and Quintero.

As if that wasn't enough, he had more. He brought up the subject of Melissa, and we had an awkward and inappropriate conversation because he was thinking about firing her. "She seems to be losing any ability to focus on her job," he said.

"Perhaps she deserves some kind of medical review. Should you urge her to get a check-up?"

"I'll think about it."

I had gone into the meeting with Charles thinking I might confide in him about my mystery, but with his comments on the stock transfer and Melissa I changed my mind.

Day 65

There were more cell switches today and each cell had to remove all newspapers and magazines. We were told to clean our cell and were given buckets with soapy water and brushes and ordered to scrub. Ernesto and I keep a pretty neat cell so there was not too much to throw out but the water in the buckets immediately turned a dark brown. After five minutes we were moving the dirt around instead of removing it.

In New York, the demands of Follamento diminished and I needed to pay attention to other matters. We had several issues with individual faculty members including two charges of sexual harassment and one possible case of financial fraud. There were two new deans who were recruited from outside of Olmsted and both seemed overwhelmed with the university's complexity and being in New York. Also there were three programs with significantly declining enrollment and we were faced with the difficult question of whether to shut them down. Each of these actions required a nuanced approach which meant many meetings and conversations. At least the issue of controversial speakers on campus that plagued Olmsted and many universities during the past academic year was quiet over the summer.

I was confident that we were ready for the arrival of the fifty students and five faculty members in Follamento at the end of August. We directed the students to fly to Rome on August 21st, with orientation beginning on August 23rd.

I had planned to return once more before the students and faculty members arrived but I reconsidered because Lucy and Justin had things under control. I convinced myself that if something was seriously wrong, they would spot it. Why I thought that, I have no idea.

Every ten days or so, I spoke with Charles, who spent most of the summer at his house in the Hamptons. He enjoyed telling me that as an investment advisor, he could work from home or anywhere. During each call he asked me the same set of questions about Follamento and the stock transfer in Panama and then went into a riff on Melissa. He kept saying that he had to confront her face-to-face rather than over the phone. Of course, he knew that I knew he was coming into Manhattan a couple of times a month, but I was not about to tell the board chair to bite the bullet and fire the president.

Melissa simply disappeared over most of the summer. She was probably in the office for a total of eight or ten days during June, July and August. It was a classic case of absentee leadership, which in her case was probably more effective than if she had been there.

My false sense of equanimity was shaken in early August when Nate stopped by my office. He had been to Follamento on his regular visit to review the finances. "I'm alarmed about Sabrina's unsteadiness," he said. "She told me that she had given you some important information and you are ignoring it." I told Nate that it was nothing to worry about even though by then I knew that Sabrina was right.

I left for Follamento on Saturday evening, August 19th. Franny mildly protested my missing some of the nicest days in New York, but she could not travel with me. On the 20th I hosted a dinner for the five faculty members and their families at the Osteria and it was festive and fun. They were hoping to meet Angelo, which I said I would arrange.

I didn't have much involvement in the week of student orientation and the first few days of classes, but I thought that I should be there in case something went wrong. I was scheduled to give an overview for the students on August 24th.

On Monday, August 21st I met with Lorenzo, Angelo, and Sabrina. Lorenzo wanted to know if I was continuing to play detective.

"My goal is to make sure that the academic program gets off to an excellent start."

He let me know that I didn't answer his question. His parting words were, "Be careful."

The meeting with Angelo was much more enjoyable. He insisted that we drive to San Quirico D'Orcia to have lunch at Trattoria Al Vecchio Forno. He said, "My father's death affected me much more than I thought it would, and with some distance, I appreciate his desire to share Follamento with Olmsted."

The meal was wonderful, even better than the one time Franny and I had eaten there. Angelo was a bit of a celebrity and the owner came over to pay homage and ask how he was doing. Towards the end of the meal he said, "I think we have reached a good accommodation regarding my authority."

I arrived back in Follamento a little before my scheduled meeting with Sabrina at 3:30. I checked my email and there was a long rant from Cathy. The bottom line was that Guzman and Quintero were unlikely to meet their target of September 1st for the official transfer of the stock. "Guzman and Quintero claim they are getting closer but not at the finish line. They blame Panamanian bureaucracy that worsened after the publishing of the Panama Papers. I'm hoping for a transfer in early September. At least in the eyes of the laws in Italy and the U.S., Olmsted controls Follamento. Charles has been checking with me daily, sometimes twice a day, and he blew up on the phone when I gave him the news. I don't mind saying that I was shocked by the vehemence of his response. When I mentioned the interim agreement he simply said that I didn't get it and hung up."

It seemed like an overreaction to me.

Sabrina and I spoke for a few minutes about the budget but it was clear that neither of us thought that was important. I went over all of my odd observations and interactions of the past few months and she said, "Unless and until you can come up with more information, I'm not in a position to help you. The clues are right under your nose."

Day 66

This morning, Hector started by asking, "Have you made any progress with the families?"

"As of dinner last night, Ernesto's uncle was unmovable. He told me directly that I was making a huge mistake and that I could be in prison for a long time. But at breakfast this morning he changed course and said that I needed to do the other side of the business for just two weeks to gain his support for my release. I stood pat with my refusal.

Hector and Al thought my responses were exactly right, though I reminded them that they were not going to bear the consequences. Al said, "Ernesto's uncle is not as powerful as he portrays himself."

I asked Hector and Al if they were telling me everything, and Al said, "We are telling you what you need to know."

As they were getting ready to leave, they both implored me to keep out of trouble for a little while longer.

After my meeting with Sabrina I decided that I would use the next day to observe the piazza. I wrote a detailed description of each person who went into the pizzeria. Of the forty-five people who I observed going in during the morning, only four came out. I had lunch in the Osteria where I was able to get an outside table and continued to watch the pizzeria. After lunch I rotated where I sat in the piazza, sometimes at the bar and sometimes in the outdoor space of the pizzeria itself. I did some reconnaissance when I went inside to use the 'bagno' and saw three doors in addition to the back door to the outside, the only one marked with an 'uscita' (exit) sign. One was for the unisex bagno, one was for a storeroom, and one appeared to go to the basement.

I gained new respect for law enforcement personnel who stake out locations for hours. It was difficult for me to maintain my concentration and alertness, especially in the middle of the day when I was sleepy after lunch and the foot traffic was in and out, sometimes with pizza, sometimes not. About five times after lunch, I reread the forty-one descriptions of the people who went into the pizzeria in the morning but who had not yet exited. Then about 3:45, the first person from my list of came out, followed over the next ninety minutes by a total of thirty-seven people. At about 6:05 p.m. I went in to order a small pie to eat on the piazza and a thirty-eighth person emerged. I ate the pizza slowly and no one else from my list left from six to seven. I may have missed a few people but I thought my count was close. I was tempted to tell Sabrina but I worried that it was insufficient to move her.

On Wednesday, the 23rd, I decided I would again watch the pizzeria and when I thought that most of the people who were entering for the day had arrived, I would follow one inside to see where he or she was going. Olmsted owned all of Follamento, true in spirit if not legally, including wherever these folks were going. I didn't want to enter too soon and have someone right behind me, but I also didn't want to go too late when no one else was entering. I decided to go in after the thirty-fifth person.

To calm myself, I repeated that "we" owned the whole town. I recognized the thirty-fifth person from the day before, a woman in her early thirties, and I walked into the pizzeria about twenty yards behind her. I followed her down a steep single flight of stairs, keeping my distance. I hoped the staff, who had seen me enter, thought that I was using the bathroom. At the bottom of the stairs, which was lit by a single bulb, she walked across the basement. There were about twenty large bags of flour raised off the floor and three dozen boxes of tomato sauce stacked against the far wall next to a large refrigerator. Next to the tomato sauce was another unmarked door and she entered. I gave her a little space and then went through this door and down another single flight of stairs lit by one bulb. At the bottom of the stairs she went through another door.

I waited twenty seconds and then followed her. When I opened the door, coming out of the relatively dark stairway, I was nearly blinded by brightness and it took me a few seconds to adjust my eyes and get my bearings. I was in a hallway that was about twenty yards long and beyond this hallway was a huge open space, extremely well-lit with dozens of work stations, each of which contained a table and chair and an easel. Each work station was surrounded by partitions and there were many paintings leaning against each. If my underground sense of space was correct, the basement was partly under the piazza. Fortunately, I could stay in the hallway and observe most of the room without being conspicuous. One other person entered after me but I was able to move and he blew by me quickly without making eye contact.

My first impression was that this was some kind of art school. There was a row of offices along the far wall, each with full glass windows that looked out into the large space. The art school impression was somewhat dispelled when I saw, along the wall to the left, what seemed to be stacks of various-sized pizza boxes in shelves that looked like they were labeled.

As I was trying to put everything together, a bell rang and Angelo, along with a person I'd never seen before emerged from an office. Angelo had a microphone and the room quieted when he started to speak. He spoke in Italian but I was able to get the gist.

He thanked the people in the room for their excellent work. He seemed to be saying that their business was growing and would continue even though Olmsted was here. He mentioned that the students and faculty were coming to town, and he told people not to speak about their work to them. He emphasized this point by repeating it. He gave the microphone to the person next to him who called out names and each person came up and received a lanyard, which appeared to have a key attached. After the lanyards were handed out, he said that everyone would need to start using the key tomorrow. Angelo and the second person thanked everyone again and people returned to their easels.

At that point I felt that I stayed as long as I could without being seen and I headed back up the first stairway, went across the basement, and then up the stairs to the pizzeria itself. As I was heading up the second stairway I saw two men installing new door knobs and locks on the doors at the top. I tried to nod at them as though I was doing something I should have been doing and went past them and headed for the bar. I ordered a cappuccino and went out to the piazza feeling completely wiped out.

I took about an hour and half and nursed two cappuccinos, trying to process what I had observed. All through the day, I drank about four times my normal coffee intake, and it gave me a buzz. Initially, I was relieved because I feared that the secret involved drug dealing. I tried to combine the morning's observations with what I observed previously but I could not come up with a coherent narrative. After lunch, I decided to seek out Sabrina.

I went to her office about 2:30 and she was meeting with Angelo. She seemed surprised and annoyed to see me, and because Angelo was there I asked her, "Do you have an idea about the year-end finances?"

"That is the topic of this meeting with Angelo, and because you are changing Follamento's fiscal year to coincide with Olmsted's, there is an incredible amount of work I need to do before Nate's visit next Tuesday." She almost shouted at me, "I will not know about the year-end until after I meet with Nate. Please do not bother me anymore until I am finished," and she practically slammed the door in my face.

Day 67

This morning Ernesto broke our rule about talking in the cell before breakfast and said, "You are being foolish, the two-week request from my uncle is a good deal."

"I am not going to be bullied."

He rolled his eyes and shrugged his shoulders. "You will hear from my uncle at breakfast," and he was right about that.

As soon as Ernesto and I sat down with our food, his uncle came over, already red in his face. "Ernesto and the family have protected you throughout your stay, and that is about to end. Though you think you may be close to getting out, it will be unfortunate if you are unprotected for the remaining time." To me, one interpretation was that if I did not play ball, then he could alter the release date, but he never said that explicitly. Instead, what I hoped he meant was the release date was coming soon, but that I could be beat up between now and then.

I tried to reconcile this statement with yesterday's comments from Hector that Ernesto's uncle was not as powerful as he made himself out to be, and I was confused. As we were nearing the area for the line, a large inmate walked in front of me, intentionally tripped me, and I fell hard to the ground. I felt like more was coming but Ernesto bent down and helped me up. The large inmate just glared at me and offered no apology.

After we got in line a guard came over to see what the disturbance was, and it turned out to be Officer Tejada, whom I had not seen for many weeks. He asked, "Are you okay?"

"Yes," I said though the words caught in my throat.

"I am surprised that you are still here."

"I am hoping to get out soon."

As he was walking away he said in a low voice, "I will be working this cell block for the next few weeks," which offered me some minor encouragement.

On the way back to the cell, Ernesto said, "Do not collect any cigarettes in the yard," effectively firing me from a job I did not want to begin with. Before I could conjure up any celebratory thoughts, he said, "I have never seen my uncle this mad. You need to be very careful as he probably has some kind of bounty on you and the trip in the cafeteria was just the beginning. You are on your own." How long could I go without a shower? My next thought was almost humorous. As a vice president at Olmsted, I have fired more than a few people. No matter the circumstances it is not pleasant. This was the first time I'd ever been fired, but it felt like progress.

I knew that Sabrina would be at my morning meeting with Nate and Lucy to go over the Follamento work assignments. But just before the meeting, she called Lucy to say she was working on the year-end budget and would not be able to make it. As I scanned the list of student work assignments, the only thing that stood out was no one was assigned to the pizzeria, and I asked about that. Nate said, "Sabrina told us not to assign anyone there."

After lunch, I met with the students. My scheduled talk went well and I was able to put aside my trepidations about the "art school." I began by saying how lucky the students were to spend a semester in Follamento. All they needed to do was look around the piazza and take in the incredible learning opportunity that was in front of them for the next fourteen weeks.

Afterward, I called Sabrina on her cell. Before I could say anything, she said, "You should do your homework," and hung up.

On the spur of the moment I walked into the bike shop and rented a hybrid bike. I had hardly exercised at all while in Follamento. As I was leaving, I got a call from Stefano Contrato, the partner in the accounting firm in Florence, who said that he would like to go over a few things. We agreed to meet the next day, Friday, in Siena for lunch.

I went for a short ride beyond Torrenieri to a winery, Citille di Sopra, ate an early dinner at the pizzeria in Torrenieri, and then rode back as it was getting dark.

I awoke early Friday morning and I decided that I had time to ride to Torrenieri, then to Buonconvento, and then back to Follamento through Chiusure and San Giovanni D"Asso, about 20 miles or so. I was able to think about my situation, especially as I pedaled slowly up the hill from Buonconvento past the Monte Olivetti monastery to Chiusure. During that climb I decided that I needed to tell someone what I'd found and I thought the lunch with Stefano was the perfect opportunity. I returned the bike when I arrived in Follamento, showered, and headed to the car to drive to Siena for lunch.

When I got to my rental car there was a flat tire and a note in English that said, "Stay out of the basement if you know what is good for you." I called Stefano to let him know I would be late, and called the car rental company who sent a repair man. He put on the temporary tire and I followed him to Asciano to get a new tire. I arrived in Siena about two and half hours late, yet Stefano was still there waiting for me.

After the usual pleasantries, Stefano said, "Sabrina and I used a number of one-time items to make the budget balance for the fiscal year including the sale of a piece of unusable land that was 'owned' by Follamento and several surplus cars, and a payment from a family friend who had used the town for their daughter's wedding. These items are legitimate but they will not likely recur, and we need to make some fundamental changes in revenue and spending."

I agreed, and as we were having dessert and coffee, I scrunched up my courage and said, "I have seen unusual activities in the basement below the pizzeria."

All of the color drained out of Stefano's face and he could not bring himself to speak for about a minute which seemed like an eternity. When he regained his composure, the first thing he did was ask the waiter for a check. Then he leaned over the table so that he could speak softly and said, "You have two choices. One is to realize that this is Italy, not the United States, and things are done differently here. The underground economy rivals the legitimate one, and neither of us can change that. From my limited knowledge, the basement activities should bring no harm to the students and faculty, and you should ignore it."

"What about the other choice?"

"Option two is to continue to pursue the issue and face the consequences."

"Consequences such as?"

"Use your imagination."

"Do you know what's going on in the basement?"

By then he had paid the bill, left a small tip and as he was getting up to leave, said, "I do not know much and do not want to know more. You should go with option one." He thanked me for coming and left in a hurry.

When I returned to Follamento and looked at my phone, I saw a missed call. Lorenzo's anger jumped out of the voice mail: "You must meet with me tomorrow at eleven a.m."

Day 68

At lunch yesterday I sat by myself, no Ernesto, no uncle. Unlike my first day in prison, everyone was actually watching me. Despite the small size of our cell, all afternoon yesterday Ernesto avoided me and never made eye contact. In the yard where I tried to stay in a visible public space, mostly by the basketball court, I was followed around by three inmates who never left me though they never got closer than about ten feet. It must have been their way of telling me that they could pummel me any time they wanted.

Dinner yesterday and breakfast today were the same, as I ate by myself and spoke to no one. When I returned from the cafeteria there was a guard waiting for me and I was moved to a cell on the other side of the block, where I have no cell-mate. I assume the move was courtesy of Ernesto and his uncle.

It may be my imagination but I feel that there are more guards in the prison. Now that I am on my own, knowing the location of the guards is a survival technique. Maybe I'm going crazy.

The voice mail from Lorenzo bothered me, especially his "demand." I decided that I needed to think ahead. After dinner at about 8 p.m. in Italy, six hours later than New York, I emailed Cathy and asked her for the cell number of Luigi, the outside attorney in Rome. Cathy immediately wrote back and wanted to know why I needed to contact him and whether she should be on the call. I lied and wrote that it was a technical matter, and not a good use of her time. She sent back his cell number and asked me to keep her in the loop. My plan was to call him after I met with Lorenzo.

When I showed up at his office, I was greeted by two stern, accusing faces: Lorenzo, who was expected, and Angelo, who was not. There was no small talk at all and no coffee. The three of us were standing and no one made a move to sit down. Lorenzo spoke first. "I am sure that you know that the stock resides in Roberto Follamento's estate. One call from me to Guzman and Quintero in Panama and the deal will be on hold, with Olmsted looking foolish and fifty students plus faculty and staff at a study-abroad site you do not control. I can easily tie up the transaction in the Italian courts for many, many years."

I was very tempted to say "go ahead, be my guest" but I did not.

"You are playing with a fire you know nothing about. I know you were eavesdropping in the basement, your security guys spoke to the Carabinieri, and you met with Stefano yesterday.

Angelo took over in a tag-team. "I can still challenge the will in the courts, and though I may not win, it will take at least thirty years or more for the case to be resolved."

"The law in both countries is firmly on Olmsted's side. You can use guerilla legal tactics but Olmsted has deep pockets and we will not be intimidated." It was pure bluff as I actually had no clue what Olmsted would really do if Lorenzo stopped the transaction and Angelo contested the will. For all I knew, Olmsted would just walk away, but I doubted it. "You need to tell me what is going on in the basement." They just looked at each other and I almost thought one of them was going to pat me on the head and say, "now, now" but instead Lorenzo said, "You are turning a winning hand into a losing one. It's time for you to terminate your faux detective work."

I turned and walked out. Neither of them said a thing or tried to stop me. As I walked to the hotel, I had difficulty controlling my emotions. With seemingly everyone connected to Follamento complicit in whatever was going on, I was glad that I asked for Luigi's phone number. I called and reintroduced myself and asked, "Do you have a few minutes to talk?"

"I am with a client but if it is urgent, I have a minute."

"There are several unusual things going on here in Follamento and I am being stonewalled."

He abruptly stopped me and said, "You should not say anything more on the phone. Can you come to Rome tomorrow?"

"I will go to the Rome Airport Hilton tonight."

"Come to my office near the Spanish Steps around eleven in the morning. I will text you the address."

I went to my room and though I was scheduled to stay in Follamento for another five days, instinctively I packed up my things as though I was leaving for New York. I made a reservation at the airport Hilton and was on the road by about 8:45 p.m.. When I got to the airport it was close to 11:45 p.m.. Despite the air conditioner in the car, with the temperature close to 100 F, I was sweating heavily when I parked and checked in. Before I went to bed I called Franny. "I'm meeting with an attorney in Rome. There is a small chance I will come straight back to New York but I think that is unlikely."

"What's going on? You're hiding something."

"I do not want to speak on the phone. I will fill you in when I see you."

"I know you're totally dedicated to making Olmsted a better university but I hope you will not do anything to jeopardize your well-being. It may be time to rebalance the equation in favor of our family."

"I will be home in a few days and I will tell you everything."

I arrived at Luigi's office right at 11 and took the small elevator to the fourth floor. He offered me coffee but, having walked over in 90-degree heat, I asked for water instead. It is funny how over ten weeks later I recall the taste of that icy cold water.

Luigi's clothing looked about a couple of sizes too big.

"Thank you for coming in on a Sunday."

"I was recently diagnosed with pancreatic cancer and tomorrow I am flying to Switzerland to get an experimental treatment."

I felt horrible. "I'm sorry."

"They think they got it early."

I doubled down on my apology for taking his Sunday and he said not to worry. "We have as long as we need before my flight tomorrow, though my preference is to be home for dinner."

"I promise you will be home for dinner."

"Take as much time as you need."

"Do you have any relationships with Lorenzo and Angelo, and is our conversation protected by attorney client privilege?"

"I have no relationships with them, I know only what I learned from the advising role with Cathy, and for the most part our conversation is protected."

"Can you treat this specific conversation as between us and keep it confidential?"

He said "Okay. I expect to be in Switzerland for some time."

Day 69

Yesterday the number of guards in the yard was probably doubled. Again I was followed by four inmates but I stayed near the guards in a very visible place. My third mark approached me and asked, "Are you okay?"

"The family is pissed off at me."

"Stay as much as you can in an open area near the guards," which was what I was doing. When he left he said, "Stay safe."

Then all hell broke loose. Whistles and sirens started blasting and about 50 additional guards stormed into the yard, some with helmets, riot-shields, and visors, and I saw Officers Tejada and Nieves near the door to the yard. We were told to freeze where we were and a small group of guards started going through the yard with lists. Right away I saw them grab Ernesto's uncle and place him against the fence near the entry. Shortly after, they did the same to Ernesto. When they had about fifty men of the roughly 250 in the yard, they placed the rest of us in a line on the opposite fence. Senior-looking people came into the yard with photographers, and these new people, some uniformed, some in suits, posed for photos in front of the group that included Ernesto and his uncle.

They shackled all the prisoners in the smaller group and marched them out. Officer Tejada found me and said, "The federal government has been observing the drug trade for months. You are lucky." After about ten minutes they had us line up and we went back to our cells.

At dinner you could hear a pin drop. No one spoke, no one made eye contact. I heard people breathing, coughing, sniffing, and sighing. We went back to our cells in silence.

Today after breakfast I was ushered into a conference room where Hector's and Al's happiness filled the room. Hector said, "You are most likely getting out tomorrow," my seventieth day in this

Panamanian prison. "All you need to do is to stay safe for the next twenty-four hours." I was smiling broadly as I gave them my recent writing.

My initial explanation to Luigi took about three hours; he knew about the gift and its parameters and restrictions. I spent some time on Lorenzo and Angelo, and explained my evolving, up and down relationships with both of them. After the generalities, I turned to the list of suspicious questions, starting with the abundance of late model cars, through the delivery of the pizza boxes, my discovery of the basement and my last meeting with Lorenzo and Angelo. I said, "Sabrina would not give me the entire picture but she confirmed there is something going on."

Sometime after 2 p.m. Luigi asked his assistant to order in salads. He asked me to describe what I saw in the basement three times, in each case asking questions, many of which I could not answer. He did the same on the delivery of the pizza boxes. He tried to get me to recall exactly what Lorenzo said at our last meeting. By five he concluded, "You and Olmsted need to get to the bottom of this. Something is not right, even for Italy. I am not positive but it does not appear to be drug-related. What can you say about the quality of the paintings in the basement?"

"I was snooping and just trying not to get caught. I did not focus on the types or quality of the paintings at all."

Before we broke at 6 p.m. he said. "I am speculating but it could be something to do with art forgery. But I admit that the scale of the operation works against my theory. I recommend that you return to Follamento and try to convince Sabrina to help you and if not, you should return to New York and let Cathy know. Do not confront anyone while you are in Italy, as that could be dangerous. If Cathy and Olmsted want to use the firm on this matter, Cathy should ask for one of the other attorneys as I will be away." We said goodbye and we each wished each other luck, though Luigi needed all the luck for the two of us.

As I was heading back to the airport Hilton in a car service provided by Luigi, my phone rang and it was Cathy. "Where are you?"

"I just met with Luigi and now I am heading back to the airport Hilton."

"Please call me as soon as you get to the hotel."

When I returned Cathy's call, she said, "I have just had a long conversation with the lawyers at Guzman and Quintero. They called in many favors and they are now ready to do the closing and transfer the stock certificate from Roberto Follamento's estate to Olmsted. For many reasons we should do the closing right away, before the end of the university fiscal year on August 31, and before anything else interferes." Given that Lorenzo had threatened me with delaying the closing, I agreed fully.

She continued, "The only way to do this before the end of the fiscal year is to do it all in Panama."

"That's fine with me," thinking that Cathy would be the one to go.

"The attorney at Guzman and Quintero specifically requested that you be the signatory."

I was puzzled by this and protested. "We should dictate who will sign, not them, and besides, New York is closer to Panama City than Rome."

"I agree and I called Charles to find out if it was okay for me to go. He told me to just do as they request. "Tell Bill he has to sign it.""

Reluctantly, because I wanted the deal done, I agreed to fly to Panama City and then to New York. I said I would contact our travel agent to get me a ticket for Tuesday. I wanted to try one more time to get Sabrina to open up. Cathy said, "I will set up the closing for Wednesday, August 30th."

After driving back to Follamento, I sent Sabrina an email asking to see her early the next day. I woke at about 6:30 and there was no email from Sabrina so I went for a walk around the piazza, had a cappuccino and tried her cell around 8:30. She did not pick up and I left a voice mail message.

I emailed Franny my change in plans. I could hear her saying, "Why does it always have to be you?" Finally, around 11 a.m. Sabrina called and said, "I am booked all day on the budget, and I cannot talk now on the phone."

"I can walk over to your office in under five minutes," but she said no, quite adamantly. At that point I wondered if someone else was there and I was on the speaker phone.

After I hung up I was caught in a mental tug of war; one part of me was in total agreement with Luigi's admonishment to stop my investigation and the other part of me desperately wanted to get to the bottom of whatever was going on. I went back and forth many times, but the signing of the stock transfer on Wednesday would put whatever was going on in a new light, one where I could be sure that Olmsted was in charge and I did not want to screw that up. I had lunch in the hotel, put my stuff back in the car and headed again for the Rome. I called Franny before I went to bed and got her voice mail. Cathy emailed me while I was on the flight that Guzman and Quintero would have a car waiting for me and had booked a room at the Intercontinental Mirimar Panama, walking distance from their office. I was in the hotel room by 8:30 p.m. on Tuesday, 2:30 a.m. in Rome and I think I was falling asleep when I heard that fateful knock on the door.

Still Day 69

Just after dinner I was trying to make the clock move faster when Officer Tejada arrived at my cell and said I that had a visitor. I was confused but I thought that we caught a break and the timetable for my release was moved up. I asked Officer Tejada, "Should I bring everything with me?" Of course, everything was a few pages of writing and a toothbrush.

"I do not know. I was just told to bring you to the administrative area. Maybe take everything."

My heart was pounding. As I walked into the conference room I was fantasizing about getting out when I was greeted by Peter Nicolson, the disbarred securities lawyer, who said, "I have some good news." Now I was really confused.

"I have been in touch with Jose Guzman and he has arranged a 'back-door' release for you but we need to move quickly. I want you to go to the infirmary tonight. Maybe the officer who brought you here will take you there; I have some cash on me. Once you are in the infirmary, a doctor who makes nightly visits will take you to the hospital, where I will meet you. The security at the hospital will look the other way and you will be out. This is a way for the prison officials to let you out without a lot of paperwork and explanations. You can fly to New York tomorrow. I do not know what your local lawyers are cooking up but this is the most immediate and fool-proof way to go."

"Have you been in touch with my lawyer?"

"No, but the prison officials we are dealing with said that they were working with your lawyer on another plan to get you out."

Why is this one better?"

"You're still here, aren't you? Later tonight you will be out. Have they arranged for that? Don't tell me that you want to stay longer. Both

Jose Guzman and Charles Mannford want you to do this." Again, Charles.

I never liked Nicolson and liked him even less for invoking Guzman and Charles. I did not want my feelings for Nicolson to cause me to make a mistake. I wanted to be out in the worst way but something about him and the offer did not feel right. "I have no way to verify anything you're saying. I appreciate the offer but I will continue to work with my attorney." If I was wrong I could pay a huge price.

"You are nuts. The deal with your attorney may never happen and I doubt Guzman will go through the trouble to do this again. Trust me and you will be eating breakfast at the airport tomorrow and having dinner with your family."

"Why isn't Guzman here?"

"He needs to have some deniability." Not a ringing endorsement.

For an instant I thought about taking the next step and going to the infirmary and then deciding if the plan looked good. But once in the infirmary, if the plan was bogus, then I might not get back to my cell for Hector's plan.

I have never had such a high-stakes decision with so little information. I went with my gut. "Thanks for taking the time to come out here. I'm going to stick with my attorney."

"Suit yourself. You are making a terrible mistake."

Day 70

This morning, time was standing still. Five minutes felt like a half an hour. The pall that fell over the prison yesterday was just as strong today. I hoped the target on me was suspended because of the raid. I ate by myself and was constantly looking around. I thought of skipping breakfast but I wanted the coffee and toast. As unbelievable as this sounds, I missed Ernesto. He is smart and had he been born in another setting, he would have had many more options. I wonder if I will ever find out what happened to him and his uncle.

The two hours in the cell after breakfast were the longest two hours of my life. I thought each set of echoing footsteps was coming for me. It was shortly after 11 a.m. when Officer Tejada came to take me to the administrative area and again I brought my writing. While we were walking he said, "I hope this goes better than last night." When I reached the area where I checked in and saw the clothing I had worn ten weeks ago, I realized that my release might be real and my heart started to race. An assistant warden opened a changing room and I put on my clothes, which were way too big on me. The assistant warden gave me my wallet, keys, dead cell phone and passport, and then I signed about five papers, all in Spanish, that I did not read or understand, but it did not matter. He then said the words I had been dreaming about for seventy days, "You are free to go." I thanked Officer Tejada, said goodbye, and walked out of the triple exit doors, each one buzzing and opening one at a time. At that point, I kept waiting for something to happen, to wake up from a dream, for someone to yell to *stop that man*, but I continued on and stepped outside.

In a small parking lot outside of the last gate, Hector and Al were waiting for me along with Archie and a man I did not recognize. I was surprised that Franny and my kids were not there. I hugged Hector and

Al, shook Archie's hand and then I was introduced to Jose Guzman of Guzman and Quintero. He was the only one in a suit and tie, and he was about sixty, very thin, with well-groomed black hair and moustache.

Hector said, "We should get right in the Embassy van, in case they change their minds." I was not sure if he was kidding or not. We all got in the van except for Jose Guzman who drove his own car to the Embassy. As we were driving away from the prison I kept thinking that something bad was going to happen. I had visualized this ride dozens of times and there were many days when I was positive it would never come.

"I am sorry you were not released sooner," Archie said. Hector and Al can vouch for my efforts. Many people at the Embassy worked on your behalf and they were incredulous that nothing happened. The Ambassador and I are very pleased that you are out."

"Thank you and your colleagues for all of their efforts. I could not have made it much longer."

Hector said, "I pleaded with Franny not to come and she was hard to convince. Even up until the last minute, your release was uncertain and I did not want her here if things went badly. I bought you and Al plane tickets to New York for tomorrow. You have your passport?"

"Yes." For a second I wondered how I would have gotten my passport in Nicolson's plan.

Hector handed me a cell phone and I called Franny from the van. "I am a free man. I'm okay and coming home tomorrow." The cell connection was not great and Franny said to call her when I got to the hotel. "I love you," I said.

Hector said, "Jose Guzman called me this morning, claiming that your imprisonment was a bureaucratic screw-up and that he'd been working for your release the entire time, undoubtedly a lie. Guzman will meet us at the Embassy, but he was insistent on coming to the prison today. He said that the stock transfer had not been finalized and he wants you to sign the papers this afternoon."

"We should not meet with Guzman until I speak with Olmsted and get the okay. Do you know that Guzman sent Nicolson to the prison yesterday evening and he used Charles' name? He offered me another way to get out, through the infirmary last night. It was a tough choice but I turned him down." Hector shook his head. "Nicolson claimed that his way out was better and more certain, but I stuck with our plan."

"You are out now and that is what matters. I'd say you made the right choice."

"I agree." Archie said. "Guzman will wait in a different area in the Embassy. I want one of the senior security people to debrief you as soon as we arrive."

I wondered what had happened in Follamento over these ten weeks. I tried Cathy from the car and she picked up. She said, "Everyone at Olmsted knows you are being released today. I am elated that you are out and safe. How hard was it?"

"It had many scary moments and I need a real shower, but I survived largely intact."

She turned right to business and asked, "Are you willing to sign the stock transfer before you come to New York?"

"Why didn't Charles sign the papers when he was here a month or so ago and visited Guzman and Quintero's office?"

"No idea. I didn't know he visited the lawyers. I thought he visited you."

"Have you been in touch with Lorenzo?"

"He's been calling me once or twice a week both to report on how well things were going and also to check on you. The first semester in Follamento has been amazing. Everyone asked after you. I will send an email out announcing your release."

"Did you receive a report from Luigi?"

"Luigi passed away in Switzerland."

That explained why no one at Olmsted knew anything I told Luigi. I thought after he learned of my long imprisonment he may have broken our confidentiality. I asked Cathy, "Given that it has been ten weeks, should I come back to New York before we sign the stock transfer?"

"Charles insisted that you sign."

"Okay, I will sign." I figured it was better to deal with Lorenzo and Angelo when Olmsted was legally in charge. Dealing with Charles was a different matter.

When I got to the Embassy, about twenty staff members in the lobby greeted me with a joyous round of applause. Apparently, I was a cause célèbre and all these people worked on my release. I thanked them and shook all of their hands. There was a guest room with a bathroom for me to take a shower, and Hector had claimed my suitcase with some clean clothing from the hotel. I took a shower without any fear for the first time in ten weeks and I felt like a different person wearing my own loose-fitting clothing. Archie said that he had arranged for a nice lunch and wanted to know whether we should eat and then meet with Guzman, whether Guzman should be invited to the lunch, or whether I wanted to sign and get Guzman out of the way, and then eat. Despite being famished, I chose to sign and then eat.

I met with Archie and a senior State Department official for a de-briefing. I asked if Hector could be present and they said no. They asked about my health, my treatment, conditions at the prison, people I was most in contact with, my personal safety and whether I had been involved in drugs. After saying that I was okay and treated reasonably well, I took about 15 minutes and described Ernesto and our relationship and what I did and did not do. They asked if I thought that Hector had served me well and I said, "Yes. He was very good to me and I felt that he was on my side." I told the interviewer why I had summoned Al and who he was. "Did you promise money to anyone to get out?"

"I will know more after I speak privately with Hector and Al." He asked how much I paid Hector and I said, "Nothing yet." At the conclusion I said, "Both Officers Tejada and Nieves were helpful to me on the inside."

This took about forty-five minutes and despite being very hungry, I wanted to get the paperwork with Guzman behind me. First, I asked to meet with Hector privately. "Thank you for being there for me, for your work as a lawyer, and now as a friend."

"Your release became a mission for me and I am almost as pleased as you are that you are out and safe. You had a few close calls." I asked him about his fees and he said, "Let me take care of that with Cathy."

"Did we end up paying anyone else?"

"We were prepared to pay, but it was not necessary."

"Can I give Jose Guzman a hard time about my imprisonment?"

Hector thought about that for a moment and said, "While it may make you feel good for a while, you have nothing to gain by doing so."

"Can I let Guzman know that I know that he was the one who imprisoned me?"

"Why not, though he'll likely deny it. I doubt we can ever prove Guzman and Quintero's complicity."

We met in a small conference room and I introduced Hector as my attorney. Immediately, Guzman began by saying, "Guzman and Quintero were looking into your release as soon as you did not show up for the signing. It was likely some kind of mistaken identity and we thought it would be resolved much sooner."

"Why and how was I singled out to begin with?"

After it became obvious he had no answer, I continued. "Guzman and Quintero were the only ones who knew that I was coming to Panama and where I was staying."

"Your passport was in the system when you entered the country."

"Why didn't Charles sign these papers when he was here a month ago?"

"His visit to our office was on personal not Olmsted business."

At that point I got a look from Hector signaling me to move on and I did. "We should complete the paperwork."

Guzman then took the papers from his briefcase and asked if Hector would witness the signing. We got Cathy on the speaker phone and she had a set of the papers. I probably signed my name twenty times with Guzman explaining each of the documents. I read carefully the one that described the stock transfer, and I asked Hector to read it as well. The others I just skimmed and checked with Cathy that it was okay to sign. While I knew I had to do this for Olmsted, I was fuming and after the signing I could not help myself. Without expecting an answer, I told Guzman, "I know that Guzman and Quintero were behind my imprisonment."

"Absolutely not. I have worked with Charles Mannford for many years and you can check with him. I was in touch with him often during the ten weeks." He gave me the Olmsted copies of the papers, we grudgingly shook hands, and he departed.

I knew my conversation with Charles was going to be interesting.

It was about three in the afternoon when Hector and I went into the room where lunch was served. Archie, Al and three others from the Embassy were there, along with Kevin and Greg. It was a great leisurely lunch of minestrone soup, steak and fries, salad and chocolate ice cream. It was a feast fit for royalty and more than my weekly food intake in prison. So much so soon was probably too much.

Al and I agreed to meet for breakfast before our 9:30 flight to New York. I was about to call Franny when Charles called: "How are you doing? I was working continuously behind the scenes to get you out."

Yeah, I bet you were, but instead of saying it, I cut it short, thanking him and saying that I needed to call Franny. I was not yet ready to deal with Charles.

Franny and I spent three hours on the phone, catching up. She said that she wanted to come to Panama with the kids but Hector was dead-set against it. She asked if she should come to JFK to meet me and I said no, I would get home as soon as I could. She said, "I hope the ordeal did not create any permanent damage to you." I was crying as I said that I loved her at least a dozen times.

New York

It feels liberating and wonderful to be in our apartment in New York. Waking up in a bed next to Franny for the past two days is worlds apart from waking up in a bunk bed with Ernesto. Our kids were here at the apartment when I arrived and they pumped me for information.

Between Archie and Hector, all of my daily writings made it out of the prison and were in a large file folder that Hector gave me yesterday. Al was impressed that I was able to write every day, but I told him that it kept me from going crazy.

Al filled me in on some details on the flight back, including a few I didn't suspect. He confessed that they withheld information from me, in part because circumstances would often change rapidly between visits, but also because they believed it would reduce my stress. No one in the group of four, Hector, Al, Kevin and Greg, had any doubt that Guzman and Quintero were behind my imprisonment. Several people in the Department of Corrections acknowledged this at least tacitly, and Al implored me not to trust them going forward.

My response was that we could reincorporate Follamento as an Italian or American corporation and eliminate the need for Guzman and Quintero.

One puzzle piece they had been unable to find out was the precise relationship Guzman and Quintero had with Ernesto's family. Al said, "Hector and I thought it was a marriage of convenience, not a premeditated arrangement, but we were never sure who had the upper hand. Both Ernesto's family and Guzman and Quintero were bigger deals than we originally thought. Ernesto's family is powerful in Panama City and has ties to other countries including the U.S. There was a time when Kevin and Greg were close to securing your release, involving several payoffs, but as that was nearing the finish line, their contacts in the Department of Corrections volunteered that the forces who wanted to keep you imprisoned, they assumed Guzman and Quintero, backed off, and I was pleasantly surprised that no payoffs were necessary.

"Hector had his own contacts in the Department of Corrections, different from Kevin's and Greg's, and his contacts warned him about the pending drug raid two weeks before it happened. This is why we were so adamant for you to stay out of the drug business. Also, Hector's contacts were connected to Officer Tejada who was asked to keep an eye on you. Officer Tejada was a double agent in the drug investigations, a dangerous assignment.

"I think the most likely scenario is that, for some reason, Guzman and Quintero wanted you out of the way and in jail, and they were familiar with Ernesto's family. Initially their objectives were complementary. But at some time during your imprisonment, Guzman and Quintero began preparing for your release while Ernesto's family wanted you to work in the drug business. This created a conflict and whether coincidence or not, the raid allowed Guzman and Quintero to okay your release without going against Ernesto's family. The worst case scenario would have been that you got caught in a raid just when we had set the stage set for your release."

Al thought Nicolson's first visit was to get Hector out of the picture, as he was independent of both Guzman and Quintero and the family. He had no idea about Nicolson's last minute plan for my release. Was it real or not? We'll probably never know.

Al was curious about my discoveries in Follamento that I described in my writing. I shared a few additional details including my meeting with Luigi. "Who else at Olmsted knew what you discovered?"

"No one."

"How can that be?"

"It was a combination of factors. Melissa and Marshall were not paying attention. Initially, Charles was too intrusive and directive but once I was in Panama I learned that his role was probably more complicated. Cathy was too officious and would not allow us to work things out. Most importantly, I kept thinking that I was always one step away from solving the mystery myself, after which I could present the full facts to Olmsted's leadership. But each time I thought the time was right, something else would intervene. I was convinced that I could right the ship alone, but I was wrong. I wanted Follamento to be *my* accomplishment but I allowed my personal ambition to cloud my judgment. "

Of course Al asked the obvious question, "What are you going to do now?"

"I don't know for sure. We own Follamento free and clear, and Lorenzo reported to Cathy that the semester went well. My initial instinct is to return to Follamento and confront Lorenzo and Angelo, find out what exactly they're doing, and stop whatever is detrimental to Olmsted's interests."

"You continue to be unrealistic and naïve. You should give Olmsted's leadership the full story and let others sort it out."

"I'm not sure. I worry that the study-abroad site will be closed."

When I got to the apartment, it was very emotional. Franny and I cried and our kids made fun of us. All of our fears came rolling out and we both admitted that we thought we would never see each other again. We called a few relatives and friends, and then all four of us went to dinner.

I was able to explain what I thought had happened, and Franny and our kids thought that I was nuts to have kept it all to myself and try to play the hero.

"You can go into the office tomorrow," Franny said, "but after that you and I are going to our country place for a few days."

I protested a little but then realized that she knows me best and this was exactly what I needed. While one part of me wanted to dive right back into work, the other part was on emotional life support.

The Olmsted IT department had not put an "away" message on my email until my third week in prison, and there were thousands of emails. I had no clue how I was going deal with them, but Franny was not negotiating. I let Melissa, Marshall, and Cathy know that I would be stopping by the next day and then Franny and I had the best night's sleep for ten weeks.

When I went to Melissa's office, she greeted me as though I'd been away on a two-week business trip. "Bill, I am glad you are back. When are you going to Follamento?"

"I need a little time with Franny. Are you doing okay?"

"I hope you can go to Follamento before the end of the semester. I expected you to report to me more regularly."

She didn't even ask about my imprisonment and I got out of there as fast as I could.

Marshall had left word with my assistant for me to stop by. He gave me a warm welcome. "I was very worried about you," he said.

"I was frightened for a lot of the time, but other than the intense emotional strain, I didn't suffer physically."

"Do you know why you were imprisoned?"

"It relates to Follamento. I will try to sort it out when I go there in a few weeks."

"Do you think that our students and faculty are at risk?"

"No, not at all. How is your search going?"

"I'm in the final stages of two searches right now, one at a large public university and one at a smaller more prestigious private college, and both have promise. If you're still up for it, you said you would be a reference."

"I'll be pleased to be a reference though we'll be sorry to lose you."

When I got to my office Gabe was waiting for me and he just shook his head asking, "What the hell happened?"

I rarely hold back information from Gabe but this time I did. "It was a problem related to Follamento, but I think I can address it when I return there after a few days in the country."

"Some problem! That explanation makes no sense. People know about your time in prison and I want to put out a statement."

"A statement is the last thing I want at this point. If anyone wants to know what happened just say that I'm safe and we believe it was a case of mistaken identity."

Gabe was not buying it. "I'll call you if and when anyone in the media contacts me."

I ate the best BLT sandwich of my life at my desk and rapidly went through emails but I did not know whether to start with the ones from ten weeks ago or the most recent ones. I was able to get through about five days of the oldest emails in about an hour and then I went to see Cathy. Surprisingly for her, she greeted me warmly. "Tell me about the signing. It was strange that Charles insisted that you go to Panama."

"It went fine."

I gave her all of the papers and she said, "Everything will be complete in about ten days. It's very sad that Luigi died." Then she asked, "Why do you think you were imprisoned?"

"I saw some things at Follamento that may not have been on the up and up.

"Is it something illegal?"

"It could be. David and Ralph spoke with the Carabinieri when they were there and the Carabinieri said that nothing was wrong. Maybe they are in on it. I also spoke with Stefano from the accounting firm in Florence and he said not to worry. Given the success of the program, I'm not worried about the students and faculty. I'll tell you more after my trip to Follamento. I need to go back there after a few days at our country place to unravel it."

"I think you should level with me about what you found. If you were imprisoned because of it, something is going on."

"I'll give you everything when I return. It's all written down in case something happens to me."

"I am going out on a limb, but I'll give you the benefit of the doubt. Yesterday Lorenzo called me about retiring." At least one positive emerged from my ordeal.

Charles called me and while I always take his calls, I didn't feel like speaking with him after what felt like a very long day. "I'm going to the country for a while. Can we talk tomorrow?"

New York and Follamento

I must have been going on pure adrenaline because when I woke up the first day in the country I could hardly move. I felt like I was underwater and my arms and legs weighed five times more than usual. I was finally out of bed by eleven, right when I was supposed to call Charles.

He began with new-found concern about my well-being and the circumstances that led to my ten-week imprisonment. "I didn't realize that Panama is a place where you can be imprisoned with no charges for ten weeks. Why were you locked up?"

Charles knew much more than he was letting on. Despite the advice from Franny and everyone else, and even with my fogginess, I wanted to get to the bottom of this myself.

"Please hear me out without interruption so that I can give you a complete picture." I knew that was unheard of for him.

"I'm listening."

"I found some unusual things going on in Follamento. I'm sure that in your career, there were instances where you wanted to solve a problem by yourself rather than seeking the help of others and this was the case for me. I peeled back the layers of an onion and when I thought that I was pretty close to finding out what was going on, some people who didn't like me snooping around got me to Panama and were able to keep me in jail for ten weeks."

True to form, he interrupted. "I find this unbelievable." I reminded him of his promise to let me finish. I was amused because I knew he was lying.

"At times I thought I was close to solving it, but I never did. I sought out several sources in Italy who I believed would be helpful to me but they either refused or were likely complicit. Apparently, our students and faculty had a great semester in Follamento so the things that I discovered did not affect that. After a week in the country I'm going back to Follamento to clear everything up."

"Who besides you knows the details?"

I wanted to say "you" but I didn't. "No one knows everything, but it is all written down and if something happens to me, Franny will give the written material to Cathy."

"Your secrecy and failure to confide in me are disappointing. You are not the one to go to Follamento."

"I'm responsible for Follamento and I intend to have the entire picture before I discuss it."

"How does your imprisonment relate to what you found?"

"I'll find out the answer to that in Follamento."

There were a few moments of silence before Charles spoke again. "The more I hear the angrier I get. I don't like the way you handled this, and I don't want you to return to Follamento. You have to give me the details and I will work with Lorenzo to sort it out."

"I must address this myself. I was the one who spent ten weeks in prison, and I know the most about Follamento and the players."

"That is not happening."

I let that soak in for a few moments as I realized the next few sentences were extremely risky and could cost me my job, but I plunged ahead.

"Charles, I know that you had a connection with Guzman and Quintero and you were in touch with them over the course of my imprisonment. I believe you were involved with them prior to your SEC investigation. I want to solve this myself but if I can't, then I will have to tell people about your complicity." Impulsively I had gone all-in, not knowing if I really had a winning hand, or what winning actually meant.

Charles was quiet for so long I asked if he was still there.

"Bill, the SEC matter was resolved without any charges. It would be very difficult to prove your groundless accusations. I should probably fire you right now."

I was actually more nervous than I thought I would be and it was not time for bravado. I was almost surprised at what I just said to the board chair. There was another long pause. I was acting more like a criminal than a university administrator. Maybe the person who was released was not the one who was imprisoned?

Finally he said, "I will permit you to go to Follamento to bring this to a close but then you need to enlist Cathy and the lawyers in New York."

"Okay."

He could not resist saying, "If you had used Peter Nicolson, the lawyer I sent to visit you in Panama, you would have been out of prison a lot sooner. You do not know what you are doing," and he hung up.

He blinked.

When he hung up, my mind turned immediately to my obligation to Olmsted regarding Charles's questionable actions. I know I should probably confide in Cathy first, but I decided to wait until after my trip to Follamento.

I told Franny about my conversation with Charles and she was adamant that I should not be the one to unravel the mystery in Follamento. Our disagreement turned into one of our rare fights. She asked to read my pages from prison and I could hardly say no. Her verdict was that I was totally out of my mind. "You're asking for a lot more trouble by taking on Charles and going back to Follamento. You could go back to jail, this time an Italian one. Olmsted should hire a security firm and let them find out what's going on." She kept googling Amanda Knox.

"Bringing in outsiders could end the study-abroad program in Follamento."

"Do you hear yourself? If it's that bad it should be closed."

I disagreed. For most of the next few days we went at each other and neither of us was backing off.

The argument became more intense when I suggested that I go by myself. "No way. If you're going then I'm going with you." I couldn't talk her out of it. "Should we should stay in Montisi to gain some distance from Follamento?"

"That will raise more questions than it's worth," and we booked a room in the Hotel Buona Notte.

I planned to go into the office one more day, Wednesday November 15th, then fly to Rome on Thursday, November 16th, landing on the 17th. We booked an early return flight on Thursday, November 23rd so that we could have Thanksgiving dinner that night with our kids. I emailed Lorenzo and asked to meet first thing on the morning of the 18th and even though it was a Saturday, he agreed. During the time at our country place, I exchanged several emails with Sabrina, and explained the call to sign the papers and my imprisonment. Once I told her this and sent her the dates of our visit, she wanted to pick us up at the airport so she could talk to me before I got to Follamento.

"Can't we talk on the phone?"

"No." When I reminded her that we needed a rental car, she said, "I'll take the train to Rome, meet you in the airport, and then drive back with you as far as Chiusi, where I will leave my car at the train station."

In our rental car, Sabrina said, "The entire time you were in prison in Panama, I felt responsible."

Maybe she was responsible indirectly, at least. "I don't blame you."

"My entire life is dependent on Lorenzo and Angelo, and, except for a little savings, I could be homeless if I cross them in any significant way. I tried to point you in the right direction, but looking back I should have been more helpful."

"I realize how powerful Lorenzo and Angelo have been in your life, but Olmsted is in charge now."

Sabrina then filled in some missing pieces. "Over a decade, what started as a small forgery scheme grew into a complex enterprise involving around fifty people in Follamento and many art galleries around Europe. It began fifteen years ago when Roberto hired a well-known Tuscan art conservator to maintain his collection. The conservator worked on the most damaged and vulnerable paintings first and after about five years the collection was in much better shape. The conservator himself was a painter and he told Roberto that he could copy virtually anything. Roberto dismissed his claim and said that he could spot a fake a mile away. To prove Roberto wrong, the conservator copied three of Roberto's paintings and hung them side by side with the originals in a well-lit room. He gave Roberto a chance to pick the real painting and he got only one of the three correct. Roberto was amazed but left it at that.

"Angelo watched the conservator fool his dad and thought that there was an opportunity for him, though it started out as a lark. He made a private deal with the conservator that his father may have known about but if he did he looked the other way. Angelo began by purchasing some paintings from an older local artist who was reasonably well-known and directed the conservator to paint original pictures in the style of this artist. The conservator was so meticulous that after he completed four paintings, Angelo could not tell the originals from the new, fake ones.

"Shortly after the four paintings were complete, the artist died and Angelo was amazed at the rapid increase in the price of this artist's paintings. Angelo thought that if he could get a gallery owner to sell these paintings, then both he and the gallery could profit, but it was the thrill of it, more than the money, that Angelo liked. He did not think that the executors of the artist's estate would figure it out, but if they did he would share the profits."

Franny said, "Remember the prices of the paintings in San Gimignano?"

"It turned out that there were many galleries in the towns near Follamento where the owners had a hard time earning a living and he quickly found one who would go along. The paintings sold relatively quickly and he and the gallery owner made out quite well. Angelo split his end with the conservator."

"What started out as a lark soon became a more premeditated scheme. Angelo and the conservator knew that the plan would take time because each artist needed to die, but they did not care because, at least in Angelo's case, he had all the money he needed. Also, the conservator was limited to only a few paintings a year so he started to train local Follamento residents and about one in four, once trained, produced a credible facsimile. The scheme grew slowly as additional older artists were identified and the number of participating galleries increased. Each time one of the artists died, their "new" paintings would be sold at the elevated price. At the start Angelo handled the selection of the artists and the recruitment of the galleries but soon some of the residents took over that part of the business and the transport, and Angelo was just the 'CEO.' When the conservator was in his eighties he recruited his successor, who jumped right in.

"Seven years ago, the business became so large that Angelo created the basement space and linked it to the pizzeria. Because it was difficult to maintain total secrecy, Angelo arranged for the complicity of many people including the local 'painters,' Lorenzo, the accounting firm in Florence, the Carabinieri, and residents like me, all of whom benefitted financially from the scheme. Then Olmsted entered the picture and you started playing detective. I was incredulous that Angelo thought the business could continue.

"A few days before you went to Panama, Angelo told me that you were snooping and he needed to do something. After you left, he began dismantling the basement operation and I think they moved it to a location outside of Follamento, but I don't know where. It took close to nine weeks because they had to move everything out slowly to avoid attracting attention, but I do not know if they are up and running in the new location. I did not know whether you knew enough to blow the whistle on the operation from Panama while they were moving out, but that did not happen. I now think the call to get you to sign the papers in Panama was engineered by Lorenzo and Angelo to get you out of the way long enough for them to move the operation. It was easier to get you to disappear in Panama than in Italy.

I could feel Franny in the back seat reprimanding me for trying to do it all by myself.

As Sabrina was explaining all of this, I wondered whether, if Luigi had not died, things would have turned out differently. I said to

Sabrina, "You really didn't have much of a choice. I won't involve you in my meeting tomorrow with Lorenzo."

We dropped Sabrina at Chiusi and drove to Follamento. Franny could not stop shaking her head.

Follamento

After Franny and I checked into the hotel yesterday, I met with Lucy, Justin, and Nate. They were bursting at the seams to tell me how wonderful the past twelve weeks had been. They stopped at one point to take a breath and asked about me, but youthful exuberance overwhelmed concern for me, as it should.

"It was amazing how well the Follamento residents and Olmsted students bonded," Lucy said. "At first there was a language barrier but that was an effective incentive for the students to learn Italian."

Justin said, "Our biggest problem revolves around the 30 or so students who do not want to return to New York. To give other students a chance, we decided that one semester is the limit."

Franny and I went to Trequanda to have dinner at Conte Matto, in part to avoid seeing either Lorenzo or Angelo. Franny looked at me across the table. "There were times when I did not know whether we would ever be able to do this again."

"I felt the same every day in Panama."

"What do you expect in your meeting with Lorenzo tomorrow?"

"I plan to challenge him."

"Do you believe Sabrina's entire story?"

"Yes."

Then Franny switched gears. "I have to ask you, how did you agree to get into the drug business so easily?"

"It certainly wasn't easy, but I was going insane knowing I had no outside lifeline, no phone calls, no one who even knew what had happened to me. And I only did cigarette pickups, not drugs. But you're right. I wasn't the same person in there as I was out here."

"I hope you return to your former self."

In the morning, after we had a cappuccino together, Franny drove to Pienza and I went to my meeting with Lorenzo. As I expected, Angelo was there.

"We were so concerned with your well-being," Lorenzo said, looking concerned. "Have you recovered?"

Angelo said, "I know that the criminal justice system in Panama is quite backward."

Yes, he was good, definitely an Oscar-worthy performance.

I let the silence drag on for fifteen seconds. "Nice try, but I know that you both were involved in my imprisonment. Now that Follamento belongs to Olmsted, each of your roles will be reduced to the legal minimum. Lorenzo, you are the executor of the estate and we cannot change that without a lengthy court battle. As for you, Angelo, you will no longer serve in your mayoral/city manager role. I know you put me in prison to give you time to dismantle the art forgery business, and I hope you have permanently closed it down."

I knew I was acting beyond my authority, but my emotions were taking over, and I no longer cared.

Lorenzo and Angelo were briefly taken aback. But Lorenzo quickly regained his composure and went on the offensive. "The moment you thought something was going on, you should have come to me. By continuing to play detective you were breaking the trust that had been established between us, and you were disrespecting the legacy of Roberto Follamento."

"Did Roberto make his fortune through art forgery?"

Angelo immediately jumped in. "My father was one of the most respected men in Tuscany. You are insulting our family name and I want an apology."

"Apology! You sure have some gall. You're the one who should be apologizing for demeaning his legacy. Was he involved before he died?"

Almost unbelievably, Angelo wilted right before my eyes. "He did not know much about the full extent of it. Because of your snooping

273

around, many of the residents who came to rely on the income from the art business will need to find other jobs."

I thought for a few moments about what he'd just said and what he didn't say. "Is the business shut down?"

"It is no longer in Follamento and that is all you need to know. You will never understand Italy. Artwork is forged all the time and unless someone is trying to forge a Michelangelo or a Vasari, no one is prosecuted and that will not change."

"Well, maybe, but what will change is it will no longer be in Follamento."

Lorenzo said, "We have taken care of that."

Angelo now seemed to have regained some of his spunk. "You should think very carefully before you change my role in Follamento."

"I will explain the full story with Olmsted's leadership and the appropriate authorities in Italy. I doubt whether anyone would want you continue in your current role."

Angelo left without saying goodbye, but we both knew that his days were numbered as far as Olmsted and Follamento were concerned.

After he left the office, Lorenzo's affect changed as abruptly as Angelo's had earlier, and almost all of his bluster disappeared, but he didn't apologize for my imprisonment. "I made some mistakes. I am planning to retire. I am angry at myself for picking the wrong side in this fight."

I said, in a classic role reversal, "If you had come to me with the problem earlier, there may have been a less explosive way to address it."

"Angelo made it out to be him or Olmsted and I mistakenly backed him. My most glaring mistake was involving Guzman and Quintero, and then there was no turning back. The involvement of Charles Mannford with Guzman and Quintero made me think that this was okay but I should have known better. Guzman and Quintero promised that their allies in the prison would look out for you. Plus everything took longer than we thought with the move."

Little did Lorenzo know that Guzman and Quintero's so-called allies had their own agenda.

After a few moments, Lorenzo became less agitated. "Olmsted is creating a great experience that Roberto would be proud of, and with the art forgery business no longer an issue, there should be no more surprises. There are soft spots in the budget that were occasionally filled by the forgery business but Olmsted can adjust financially without it."

Lorenzo was serious about his desire to retire, and asked, "Can I have six months to move my law office to San Giovanni D'Asso, and can I keep my apartment in Follamento for a while? If you agree I can share additional details."

"Six months is workable if you immediately make the San Giovanni D'Asso office your working office. If you do that, I will ask for up to a year on the apartment. Any office or apartment accommodation depends on your full cooperation including your replacement on the two person committee." It was clear he was a broken man. "How much did Roberto actually know?"

"He knew a lot and a little. Angelo was a thorn in Roberto's side ever since he was a teenager. I was always getting him out of trouble, sometimes at considerable expense. Angelo lived a very privileged life and was constantly rebelling against that privilege. He still believes that with a little more time, he could have changed the will." Lorenzo paused and then said, "The gift to Olmsted was in every way driven by Roberto's desire to remove Angelo from playing a key role in Follamento's future, and he never would have changed his mind. I had been reporting on the growth of the forgery business to Roberto continuously until about five years ago when he said that he did not want to know any more. That was when he began to talk to me about how to insure Follamento's future without Angelo. I couldn't envision what a post-Roberto Follamento would look like and Angelo convinced me that the forgery business could continue without Olmsted's knowledge.

"What you may not know is that Charles had a long-term relationship with Guzman and Quintero. It seemed as though Guzman had something on Charles because he agreed not to try to get you out. Guzman also said that Charles did not want his connection with the firm known to Olmsted and that is why he did not sign the Follamento papers on his visit to Panama."

"Do you think Charles knew about the forgery business?"

"In fact, Jose Guzman told me that until Charles' visit to Panama, he did not know about the forgery business. I was surprised and I am not sure if I believe him."

Lorenzo was so smooth that I almost felt sorry for him but I kept reminding myself that he was a main driver of my ordeal. We parted cordially and I checked my phone. There was a text message from Cathy that Charles had resigned as board chair.

That night, Franny and I had a wonderful dinner at Il Leccio in San Angelo en Colle and for the first time in a long time I felt at ease. Only for a few minutes did she chastise me for trying to do it all myself. "Would Olmsted have been worse off if you enlisted some help and the gift was stalled?"

I have to admit, probably not.

"I worry that these ten weeks permanently changed you."

Just as I was about to go to bed on my final night in Follamento, my cell phone rang with a "private caller." I answered and the caller said, "This is Carlos, and I work with Uncle Eduardo. I want to talk with you about your role in New York."

I hung up and blocked the number.